Old Films, Young Eyes

Old Films, Young Eyes
A Teenage Take on Hollywood's Golden Age

SIMONE O. ELIAS

Foreword by Eliana Singer

McFarland & Company, Inc., Publishers
Jefferson, North Carolina

LIBRARY OF CONGRESS CATALOGUING-IN-PUBLICATION DATA

Names: Elias, Simone O., 2009– author. | Singer, Eliana, writer of foreword.
Title: Old films, young eyes : a teenage take on Hollywood's golden age / Simone O. Elias ; foreword by Eliana Singer.
Description: Jefferson, North Carolina : McFarland & Company, Inc., Publishers, 2024. | Includes index.
Identifiers: LCCN 2024041472 | ISBN 9781476696591 (paperback : acid free paper) ∞
 ISBN 9781476654973 (ebook)
Subjects: LCSH: Motion pictures—United States—History—20th century. | Motion pictures—Influence. | Motion picture audiences. | LCGFT: Film criticism.
Classification: LCC PN1993.5.U6 E334 2024 | DDC 791.430973—dc23/eng/20240912
LC record available at https://lccn.loc.gov/2024041472

BRITISH LIBRARY CATALOGUING DATA ARE AVAILABLE

ISBN (print) 978-1-4766-9659-1
ISBN (ebook) 978-1-4766-5497-3

© 2024 Simone O. Elias. All rights reserved

No part of this book may be reproduced or transmitted in any form or by any means, electronic or mechanical, including photocopying or recording, or by any information storage and retrieval system, without permission in writing from the publisher.

Front cover photograph of 1930 movie theater audience by Daniel Atelier (Helsinki City Museum)

Printed in the United States of America

McFarland & Company, Inc., Publishers
 Box 611, Jefferson, North Carolina 28640
 www.mcfarlandpub.com

Acknowledgments

Thank you so much to Lazarre, for being the sunshine of my life. I love you so much. You are everything to me. My mom, for guiding me and supporting my goals and dreams every step of the way. For dealing with me no matter the mood. I would never have been able to do anything if it weren't for you. My dad, for reading, editing, and helping me with the final manuscript, you are a stable guiding light in my life, and you support and love me no matter what. I love you!

Thank you to Lara Gabrielle: this book wouldn't exist if it weren't for you. Thank you for being a great mentor to me. Thank you to Amelia Arms for being my best friend and the person I can tell everything to, as well as for teaching me more about classic movies, especially Barbara Stanwyck. Thank you to Eliana Singer for teaching me about classic movies and letting me write this book while you do the podcast. I love you!

Thank you to my Grandpère, Robert Kraft, for being my creative support system and for sharing your thoughts on the manuscript. You're the funniest person I know. Thank you to Marilyn Elias, my grandmother, for doing a final edit of the book, always supporting my projects and listening to me.

Great thanks to McFarland for being a supportive and flexible publisher to work with—Siena Ritter was a helpful guide through my first experience with the publishing world. Thank you to Sophia Lyons at McFarland for answering all of my questions throughout this process.

Thank you to Michael Schulman, Katie Gee Salisbury, Dana Stevens, Lea Stans, Lindsay Lynch, Andrew Saladino, and Scott Eyman for doing email and phone interviews that advanced my knowledge and were included in the book.

Table of Contents

Acknowledgments — v
Foreword by Eliana Singer — 1
Preface — 5

How Classic Films Are Reflected in Today's Pop Culture — 9

Beach Party! What This Quintessential Sub Genre Says About 1960s Culture — 18

Guess Who's Coming to Dinner? Interracial Relationships and Ethnic Biases in Classic Hollywood — 27

What's So Bad About Feeling Good? The '60s Movie That Predicted the Pandemic — 31

New Hollywood: How Two Movies Inspired a Whole New Generation of Filmmakers — 36

The Effect of TV on the Movies — 43

The Jews Run Hollywood? — 46

What Musicals Say About 1950s Subculture — 54

The 1950s Housewife — 60

The 1940s Working Girl — 68

"No law says you've got to be happy": The Pessimism of Film Noir and Why the "Genre" No Longer Exists — 77

The Snake Pit: Depictions of Mental Illness in Classic Hollywood — 83

Table of Contents

The Romantic Comedy and How Modern Rom-Com Tropes All Draw Inspiration from One Movie	89
A Tour of the Old Hollywood Studio System	102
Should Ladies Behave? Pre-Code Women Say No	113
A Cultural History of the "It Girl"	124
Anna May Wong: Typecasting and Asians in Hollywood	133
Looking at Old Hollywood Through the Lens of the "Me Too" Movement	140
Why Were There "No Female Directors" in Old Hollywood? The Secret History of Women During Hollywood's Inception	148
A Public Service Announcement on Colorized Films	156
Epilogue	161
My Favorite Films	167
Where Do You Go from Here?	169
Chapter Notes	171
Index	179

"To move forward, you must look back."
—Proverb

Foreword
by Eliana Singer

I had never imagined that a single movie could have such a profound impact on my life. It was amidst the pandemic that my family's addiction to Netflix's cheesy rom-coms reached its peak. Despite the prevailing trend, my mother harbored a desire to steer me away from contemporary Hollywood clichés and urged me to delve into the realms of classic cinema.

Initially resistant to the idea, I did not want to explore films of past eras, influenced by the misconception that "old" movies were outdated and lacked the technological prowess of today's CGI-infused productions. However, my mother's requests eventually wore me down, and we decided to watch a movie. Reluctantly settling onto our black leather couch, I prepared myself for a potentially dull and overly experimental experience. Little did I know that the film in question, the classic screwball comedy *It Happened One Night* from 1934, would not only captivate me but also begin a significant shift in my perspective.

The enduring impact of this initial encounter with a classic film turned out to be one of the greatest gifts I've ever received. Reflecting on what drew me to *It Happened One Night*, I often find myself contemplating how a teenager in the 21st century could connect with narratives from the 1930s, almost a century removed from my own time. This curiosity marks the beginning of a personal exploration, unraveling the factors that forged a meaningful connection between me and a cinematic gem from the past.

The primary reason that the initial movie ignited my curiosity and sparked my enduring love for classic films was its ability to provide a profound escape from my reality. Throughout the pandemic, I experienced a significant creative slump and was detached from society. I felt disconnected from my friends, as well as from my true self, overshadowed by the façade I presented to others. Chained to my small desk and to a computer that endlessly played voices over Zoom, I longed for a break from the monotony.

Classic films, unlike their contemporary counterparts, provided me with a gateway to an entirely different world. Everything, from the intricately designed sets to the actors, seemed detached from the familiar trappings of the modern era. The visual aesthetics and thematic elements allowed me to transcend my reality. Yet, the question persists: Why do we find resonance in classic films despite their divergence from our present-day existence? I believe it's because, despite the disparities, we connect through universal human emotions. The thrill of adventure, the allure of romance, or the struggles of a character—these are experiences that bridge the gap.

Classic films, created to entertain audiences, were never meant to be dull, a fact that some teenagers fail to grasp. The enduring appeal is in our ability to still comprehend and empathize with the narratives woven into these films. Whether it's the suspenseful moments, the romantic entanglements, or the characters' adversities, classic films tap into shared human experiences, offering an escape that transcends the boundaries of time and societal changes.

Another significant reason for my connection to classic films and my desire to encourage teenagers to watch them is the historical values that films impart to their audience. You might question whether films are a suitable medium for learning history. Still, the moving image proves to be the most universal and accessible way to convey historical narratives in unconventional ways. While studying global and American history in school, I encountered challenges in visualizing and empathizing with the individuals behind pivotal historical moments that felt distant in time. Textbooks presented chronological fact after fact, leaving my classmates and me struggling to step into the shoes of those from the past and truly envision the people behind historical events.

Classic films could transport me to these core events in world history, such as the Civil War, the Great Depression, World War I, and World War II. Rather than overwhelming me with the complexity of these events, film aided me in envisioning the human experiences behind them. Classic films offer a unique perspective as many filmmakers lived through these pivotal historical wars, providing a different lens than modern-day filmmakers. By highlighting the emotional impact and human experiences rather than just the facts of historical events, classic films foster empathy and sympathy for people from the past. Furthermore, these films shed light on the dark sides of our world,

Foreword

addressing issues like sexism, homophobia, and racism. While discrimination may be depicted on screen, some creatives challenge societal norms, combat discrimination and educate against it. We must consistently acknowledge the presence of racism in movies as a means of learning from the past and evolving our behavior for the future. Recognizing the past is crucial, as we strive to avoid normalizing and accepting discriminatory actions.

It's evident that classic films often feature predominantly white casts and crews. Exploring why this was deemed acceptable as the mainstream narrative can shed light on issues that go beyond entertainment. Classic films not only humanize historical events but also provide insights into people's daily lives, showcasing cultural slang, technology, and clothing trends. We can witness a vintage way of living, observing how people navigated a world without digital technology, experiencing the authenticity of landline telephones, record players, and telegrams. The fashions of the 1940s, influenced by the onset of war and the need for women to join the workforce, or Dior's new look popularized

Simone (right) with Eliana Singer (left) and Eliana's twin sister Gemma in 2011 (author's collection).

Foreword

in the 1950s, offers a glimpse into the cultural shifts of those times. Film emerges as a central medium that not only teaches about historical events but also serves as a conduit for learning about new fashion trends, slang, and the evolving culture of the time.

Upon viewing my first classic film, I embarked on a cinematic journey, eagerly consuming as many films as I could find. It had been approximately two years since my initial discovery of classic cinema, and I was eager to channel the knowledge and insights gleaned from countless films, documentaries, and books into a creative endeavor. Determined to bring the world of classic films to a wider audience, I reached out to my family friend, Simone Elias, to share my passion.

In our conversation, Simone, an experienced and inspired podcaster, whose shows include *Street Spies* and *Travel Through the Parks*, generously shared her insights and tips on podcasting.

Intrigued by the idea, I decided to venture into the realm of podcasts as a means to introduce classic films to teenagers. Simone not only gave me valuable lessons on the importance of effective marketing to amplify our message but also guided me on how to captivate and involve an audience through the art of scriptwriting. Over several months dedicated to crafting every aspect of our podcast, Simone evolved into a classic film expert, cultivating a genuine passion for cinematic treasures.

Simone's dedication and thorough research on the subject are vividly evident in this exceptional book. Here, at the age of 15, she delves into every compelling reason for teenagers to explore classic films, unraveling myriad lessons and discoveries awaiting those who embrace them. Simone's zest for the American past and her feminist sensibility shine through. Most teenagers form their film preferences during adolescence, and genuine enthusiasm for classic film is a rarity in today's age, especially among young people. This book strives to reignite excitement around these hidden gems, presenting them not merely as relics of the past but as timeless works of art. The stars and films showcased in this book are not confined to their eras but resonate across time, beckoning a new generation to appreciate and enjoy their enduring brilliance.

Eliana Singer, a 17-year-old high school student based in New York City, is the founder and host of Teenage Golden Age, *a podcast where she interviews bestselling authors and documentary directors. She has interned at the Museum of the Moving Image and has taken film studies classes at both Brown University and Columbia University.*

Preface

My name is Simone Elias, and I'm a writer of everything you can possibly think of: songs, books, movies, TV pilots. I'm 15 years old, and I'm obsessed with movies.

In 2022, my family friend Eliana and I collaborated on a podcast about classic films called *Teenage Golden Age*. At the time, I knew almost nothing about classic films besides the fact that I had watched *Mary Poppins* a couple of times and thoroughly enjoyed it. Yet it seems strangely predestined that this opportunity came into my life at that time because my great-great grandfather's brother was a screenwriter in classic Hollywood. Back then, I didn't even know about that family connection.

Eliana and I teamed up and we brainstormed on a Google document and created an Instagram account, as Gen Z-ers do. We started our work in January, and the podcast came out in August, going through several revisions. We decided we wanted the podcast to take the perspective of the new generation, since there were plenty of classic film podcasts by older people already. There was a point in time when I was posting classic film clips at least six times a day to gain new followers. "Hey, Mom, do you think 50 followers is a lot? If you gather them up in a room, it's a lot of people!" It wasn't.

My classic film experience started with *Funny Face*, the 1957 musical starring Audrey Hepburn and Fred Astaire. I was completely hooked by the opening dance number, "Think Pink," and Audrey Hepburn's grace and elegance, but I skeptical about the age difference between the two stars, and the movie also had no plot. "I guess old movies don't have plots," I thought to myself. I was so wrong.

I remember watching *Sabrina*, a movie about a love triangle between Audrey Hepburn, William Holden, and Humphrey Bogart, in STEM class while everyone else was coding. "Are you watching something?" the girl next to me asked. I switched tabs. "No, I'm not." I truly

Preface

got hooked on the films when I watched *Roman Holiday*, a classic love story with humor and tragedy, and *Charade*, a thrilling ride of a mystery that sucks you in from the very beginning.

Next up were the musicals *Singin' in the Rain* and *Gentlemen Prefer Blondes*, among many other classics that people usually start with. I now call these "gateway" movies. I kept the list of films on a document and Eliana and I would boast about how many we had. "I've got 15 already!" I'd say over the phone. "Well, I have 200!" she'd say back.

It took several minutes, if not half an hour, for me to get into any particular film, and it still does. But I've developed that skill of patient watching.

When people ask me why I watch old movies, I like to talk about how pieces of beautiful art in art museums never lose their timelessness and relevance. If you walked into an art museum, would you say that Monet's water lilies are outdated? Would you say the same about Raphael's or Leonardo da Vinci's masterpieces? No, because they're a symbol of what life used to be like. Even if paintings of old civilizations and the way people used to dress are not the same as today, we still recognize how beautiful they are. I don't see anything different with movies. Movies are art, and the great pieces of art never truly age, just like paintings.

Teenagers never get credit for how hard it is to grow up in the modern world. I'm not excusing our behavior, but it can be hard to be us sometimes. As many of you know, teenagers' attention spans aren't long. And so if you've made it this far into the book, I applaud you. The adults around me tend to guilt me sometimes about being on screens or social media, so Dad, next time you say that you never went to bed late when you were a teenager, think about if you had a phone, okay? You would probably look at baseball cards on eBay if you were a teenager today. It's hard to live as a kid with the addictiveness of technology. Classic films help me go back to a time when a lot of aspects of being a kid were (a little bit) easier—before social media, and before technology was involved in every waking second of what we do.

To this day, I still struggle with loading up a classic film and staying through it. That's why I tend to veer toward comedies and musicals—because they are more entertaining. I also love Pre-Codes (see "Should Ladies Behave? Pre-Code Women Say No") because they are short and incredibly modern: they keep your attention. If you try hard enough, you will find something you're obsessed with in the classic film world, which is so fun. It's like when you find a favorite singer or actress and then you get totally hooked for months, except with this, it's your own little secret (unless Taylor Swift writes a song about your favorite actress). More on that later.

What makes classic movies so perfect for teenagers right now? First, it's important to realize what teenagers want these days in movies. UC Berkeley's Greater Good Science Center did a study on this. They found that teenagers want stories about people with lives unlike their own. This fits in perfectly with classic movies, which foster a connection with the very different ways people lived in the past.[1] Second, the survey showed that teens nowadays want uplifting and hopeful stories about characters defeating the odds. This type of arc is extremely common in old Hollywood, and it appears in pretty much every famous film: *Casablanca*, *It's a Wonderful Life*, *The African Queen*, *To Kill a Mockingbird*, and *Cool Hand Luke*. There's an old movie niche for every kind of teen.

I have learned more about the Roaring Twenties, the Great Depression, World War II, and the Civil Rights movement from classic movies than I learned from any history class I've ever taken. Instead of passively reading textbooks in classes, I've learned to observe how society and culture used to be by watching it.

You'll notice that this book has very clear feminist undertones, and that's because, while the topic is incredibly interesting and important to me, portrayals of women are one of the things that has changed in the years since the Golden Age ended—and so I wrote many chapters about how they have changed over the decades in film.

I now have a community of teens who love classic film to share it with me, and with you. If you're on Instagram already, go and follow us at @teenagegoldenage and @teenagegoldenagebook. It's incredible to have a group of people who love what you love—or you will soon after you read these pages.

Over the years, I've found films that have made me cry, dance, laugh, and get emotional in every way on that list of emotions you (hopefully) learned in your kindergarten social-emotional curriculum. I've also learned that my teenage perspective provides more value to the world than most people think. The teenage perspective in general is a powerful voice during dark times, and it's been that way for more than a century: from the Roaring Twenties to the Civil Rights movement, up until right now.

I bring my teenage vantage point to the chapters that follow, which explore the facets of film during its early period of development from the late 1920s to the 1960s. Although I've watched films from all

Preface

decades, it's the early decades that I write about because they are the least recognized by the younger generations—you *know* I love 2000s rom-coms. But everyone knows about *Legally Blonde.* Nobody knows about *Kitty Foyle.*

So if you stick with it, I'm ready to show you some masterpieces that will change your life. Are you ready?

This is *Old Films, Young Eyes.*

P.S. *Casablanca* and a couple of other incredibly famous classic films are not featured in this book. There are countless essays, books and websites devoted to the movies I left out. I wanted to give the gems that are hidden from the general public a voice. I've left a ton of books and essays for you to read in "Where Do You Go from Here?" if you're curious about the movies I didn't address.

How Classic Films Are Reflected in Today's Pop Culture

Naturally, we should start at the beginning. But how about starting now? You might be wondering if classic films are even relevant anymore or saying under your breath, "They're not even important. Why do I have to know about them? Why did my grandma buy me this book?" This chapter answers those questions, starting with what young people like me know these days.

This chapter details modern music, fashion, movies, characters, and all kinds of other things that can be drawn directly back to the Golden Age of Hollywood—proving its modern relevance.

On May 19, 1962, three months before her highly publicized death, Marilyn Monroe gave a seductive rendition of "Happy Birthday" to then-president John F. Kennedy at Madison Square Garden. Monroe wore a shimmery skin-tight dress, not an unusual style for her as the world's most famous sex symbol. The dress was designed by Bob Mackie. The performance remains one of American history's most legendary moments.

As a symbolic dress, the public demands the preservation of it. Kim Kardashian wanted to wear this dress to the Met Gala, one of the most prestigious events for celebrities and fashion. At the Met Gala, there are themes each year that designers for these celebrities follow to create more buzz around the event. In 2022, the theme for the Met Gala was "In America: The History of Fashion."[1]

Kardashian, eager to wear a piece of American history, reportedly lost 16 pounds in three weeks to attempt to fit into the dress, which had been tailored to fit Monroe. However, she still didn't lose enough weight to fit into it, and it had to be slightly altered.

As Kim stepped onto the carpet, cameras flashed and paparazzi uploaded the images to online sources, immediately igniting an online outrage, especially on Twitter. After five minutes, Kim changed into a

Marilyn Monroe sings "Happy Birthday" to JFK in May 1962 (Cecil Stoughton, White House Photographs. John F. Kennedy Presidential Library and Museum, Boston. Wikimedia Commons).

replica of the dress, attempting to not cause any further damage to it. Bob Mackie, the original designer of the dress, even stated: "I thought it was a big mistake ... [Monroe] was a goddess. A crazy goddess, but a goddess. She was just fabulous. Nobody photographs like that. And it was done for her. It was designed for her. Nobody else should be seen in that dress."[2]

Further outrage grew, with even more experts on classic film weighing in on the controversy. Alicia Malone from Turner Classic Movies told *Entertainment Weekly*: "There are all the issues with the actual preservation of the dress and things like oxygen can affect a dress. Usually, these outfits are kept very much in controlled environments. So, it was quite alarming that she was able to wear it. I wish she wore a replica instead of the real thing."[3] Dr. Kate Strasdin, a senior lecturer in cultural studies at Falmouth University, stated: "You can't even handle a dress like that without damaging it in some way, let alone wear it, so it was inevitable that there was going to be significant damage just by even wearing it on the red carpet.... There will have been oils in her skin, there will have been all of that chemical reaction with silk that is fragile."[4]

Marilyn Monroe is one of the only remaining classic film actresses that young people today still know by name. Her face lingers in every corner of the world. You can't go out without seeing "Marilyn Monroe Eyeshadow" in a CVS or Andy Warhol's experimental art of Monroe's face which everyone has seen at least once.

The influence of classic Hollywood on culture goes further than just the icons and familiar faces. The Golden Age has been referenced an uncountable number of times. One of my favorite references happens in *Sleeper*, when Woody Allen's character mimics the classic "mirror scene" in *Duck Soup*, the Marx Brothers film, clearly showing the ancestral line of Jewish humor from Groucho Marx to Woody Allen.

La La Land, a musical film starring Emma Stone and Ryan Gosling, was praised for emulating classic Hollywood–style musicals. I remember sitting with Sam Wasson, author of *Hollywood, the Oral History*, for an interview, and he said something about how *La La Land* will never beat Fred and Ginger. You can't capture lightning in a bottle twice.

Even though the past fades further into obscurity as time goes by (*Casablanca*, anyone?), so many of old Hollywood's stories linger in today's pop culture. The Golden Age of film, by my reckoning, ended in the 1960s. By the late 1970s people had already started reflecting on the Golden Age of Hollywood. This mostly began with the abundance of actor and actress biographies and autobiographies in the 1970s and with compilation films like *That's Entertainment!*

The reflection of past decades also seeped into modern 1980s pop culture. Madonna became a huge pop star in the early 1980s, coinciding with the rise of a completely new medium for visuals: MTV, or Music Television. Madonna had always been inspired by Hollywood icons, especially Marilyn Monroe. In 1984, Madonna asked her team if she could recreate Monroe's *Gentlemen Prefer Blondes* dance number, "Diamonds Are a Girl's Best Friend," in her video for "Material Girl."

In a 1987 interview with *The New York Daily News*, Madonna shared: "Well, my favorite scene in all of Monroe's movies is when she does that dance sequence for *Diamonds Are a Girl's Best Friend*. And when it came time to do the video for the song ["Material Girl"], I said, I can just redo that whole scene and it will be perfect. ... Marilyn was made into something not human in a way, and I can relate to that. Her sexuality was something everyone was obsessed with and that I can relate to. And there were certain things about her vulnerability that I'm curious about and attracted to."[5]

The video was shot in early 1985 and broadcast on MTV shortly after. It, too, became incredibly well known in a meta way, since it was reusing an already classic image. In the video, Madonna is showered with gifts and expensive items from men, but she ultimately chooses the man who pretends to be poor (he's a rich producer) and brings her hand-picked flowers. The song, however, has a different message: "the boy with the cold hard cash is always Mister Right."

Madonna regrets recording this song because she was pegged for decades as a "material girl" when the song was a satire. Of this, Madonna said: "I can't completely disdain the song and the video, because they certainly were important to my career. But talk about the media hanging on a phrase and misinterpreting the damn thing as well. I didn't write that song, you know, and the video was about how the girl rejected diamonds and money. But God forbid irony should be understood. So when I'm ninety, I'll still be the Material Girl."[6]

The influence of classic Hollywood on Madonna does not stop with this one example. In the bridge of her 1990 hit "Vogue," she namedrops not one but 16 classic icons: Greta Garbo, Marilyn Monroe, Marlene Dietrich, Joe DiMaggio, Marlon Brando, Jimmy Dean, Grace Kelly, Jean Harlow, Gene Kelly, Fred Astaire, Ginger Rogers, Rita Hayworth, Lauren Bacall, Katharine Hepburn, Lana Turner and Bette Davis.

How Classic Films Are Reflected in Today's Pop Culture

Whenever my mom does this song at karaoke, she gives me the mic for the bridge, because she doesn't know most of the actors' names....

Remakes of Hollywood classics reflect their continuing relevance. More than five years ago, Lady Gaga, another current star who (sometimes) emulates classic Hollywood, starred in the highly acclaimed third remake of the classic tragedy *A Star Is Born*. The first one, made in 1937, starred Janet Gaynor and Fredric March and was legendary for more than one reason: it was made in Technicolor, one of the earliest big commercial films be done in this way, even before *The Wizard of Oz*.

A Star Is Born is one of the earliest films that is still remembered today that deals with the dark sides of Hollywood, and it demonstrates the fact that a film about Hollywood (so meta!) could be highly successful.[7] The story in all three remakes is the same. A rising female star and a fading male star fall in love, but the man's story has a tragic ending. This storyline shows the juxtaposition of the darkness and loneliness of fame with the happy parts: performing, getting to do what you love, and getting paid a lot for it.

The first remake of *A Star Is Born*, starring Judy Garland and James Mason, came less than 20 years after the first film. It was one of Garland's last comebacks, and a huge box office success. The next remake, made in the 1970s, starred Barbra Streisand (a famous actress since she starred in *Funny Girl* on Broadway) and was a musical version of the film. Finally there was the 2018 version, which made a lot of changes to the story to depict current Hollywood, and it starred Bradley Cooper and Lady Gaga. Their duet of the original film's song "Shallow" was a major hit and won an Oscar.

Many, many songs by popular artists today come from classic Hollywood films. "Over the Rainbow" is one good example. A ukulele cover of this song by Israel Kamakawiwo'ole was a big hit, decades after the song's release in the 1939 film *The Wizard of Oz*, validating the song and the film's timelessness. I could list many more, but here are a few: "My Favorite Things," a famous song from *The Sound of Music*, was interpolated in Ariana Grande's number one hit "7 Rings" in 2019. "The Way You Look Tonight" from *Swing Time*, a classic Astaire and Rogers film, is a jazz standard that everyone from Frank Sinatra to Tony Bennett to "Mouse Rat," a fake band from the TV show *Parks and Recreation*, has covered. Added up, these covers have hundreds of millions of streams on Spotify. "Que Sera, Sera," a song from the Hitchcock film *The Man Who Knew Too Much*, starring Doris Day and Jimmy Stewart, was remixed and featured in a film trailer.

Old Films, Young Eyes

I remember sitting with my old friends watching the trailer, and I heard the song and was happy with myself for recognizing it. I thought of telling my friends it was in a 1950s movie, but it would've been weird. I know that if younger people knew all the references to classic Hollywood in popular culture, they might be a little more interested, but my friends at the time weren't.

Even the pronunciation "potato, potahto, tomato, tomahto" was invented in the song "Let's Call the Whole Thing Off" from 1937's *Shall We Dance*.

Watching old movies can take some getting used to. With the classics, whether it's a song or movie, the simplicity can be both timeless and boring at the same time. It's usually slightly more timeless than boring, but it can be the opposite depending on whether the movie was good or bad. Today's films and songs are much more produced, with CGI, colors, realistic animation, and the like that make things exciting for the listeners and viewers that MGM did not have in the 1940s and 1950s heyday of musical filmmaking.

Going back to the start with Monroe's "Happy Birthday," let's talk about Lana Del Rey, who calls upon this infamous performance in her 2012 music video for "National Anthem." The video shows Del Rey as both Marilyn Monroe and Jackie Kennedy, and this isn't even the beginning of her classic Hollywood references. Del Rey's video "Doin' Time" was inspired by *Attack of the 50-Foot Woman*, a B-movie from 1958.

Lana Del Rey came into the spotlight in the early 2010s for her distinct indie/jazz/indescribable genre that was the antithesis of the thumping dance floor EDM songs of the time. She's been incredibly popular with a huge niche fan base since then. Her style of music and lyricism is so directly tied to American life in the 1950s and 1960s it would be impossible to name all of the references she uses, from the way she dresses to her persona. Even her stage name was taken from a classic film star (Lana Turner). That someone so vintage-inspired could be so popular today goes to show that old Hollywood is still relevant. And even her producer Jack Antonoff covered a song from a classic movie, "Almost Like Being in Love" from *Brigadoon*.

Fashion styles from old Hollywood are ubiquitous today, even the relatively unknown ones. For example, the arrow and heart dress that Ginger Rogers wore in the film *Carefree* from 1938 became well known. The black dress features a heart on the left side and arrows piercing it. A similar dress was featured in the 1940s Schiaparelli collections, then brought back for the fall 2014 collection of the same brand. Madonna then wore the dress as one of her countless classic film references.

While Rogers isn't commonly considered a fashion icon, we can look back and see that she was. In 2010, the Met Gala theme was "American Woman: Fashioning a National Identity." Taylor Swift wore a dress from the Ralph Lauren 2005 Ready-to-Wear collection, which is almost exactly like Ginger Rogers' gown in *The Gay Divorcee* (yep, that's the title). Fashion writer Sarah Chapelle called the gown "deliciously old Hollywood."[8] I have never agreed more.

Swift's music catalog, videos, and red carpet looks often recall old Hollywood. Her video for the song "Wildest Dreams" depicts Swift as an old Hollywood starlet filming a movie in Africa. Many say the video seems to be inspired by Elizabeth Taylor.

Swift also recently released a song called "Clara Bow" on her album *The Tortured Poets Department*. The song directly references the classic era star Clara Bow, and Swift makes a point about the cyclical nature of fame with her comparisons between Bow, Stevie Nicks, and herself.

Back to old Hollywood style, one of the biggest fashion moments of all time was Audrey Hepburn's little black dress (LBD) from *Breakfast at Tiffany's*. The sequence has been recreated so many times, it would be hard to count them all. The most recent small reference I can think of is *Vogue Australia*'s article about how "in 2023, Old Hollywood glamor is well and truly back."[9] (Arguably, not as well. Wink, wink....) The article talks about how many are emulating the LBD silhouette lately including Kendall Jenner (ugh). "In Paris, she wore a full look from The Row's spring 2023 collection, donning a scoop-necked low dress with a cinched waist and a floor-skimming hemline. The accessories made it very *Breakfast at Tiffany's*: the looped black silk scarf, jauntily thrown over her shoulder, the opaque black oval shades, the retro-inflected court shoes."[10] I don't quite understand buying vintage-looking clothing from supremely expensive brands like The Row when you could get actual vintage clothing. But that's just me!

Natalie Portman did a shoot for *Harper's Bazaar* in 2006 where she modeled a little black dress and pearls in reference to Audrey Hepburn. Lindsay Lohan also recreated the scene at the beginning of 2004's *Confessions of a Teenage Drama Queen*. Ariana Grande posed in a similar dress for Givenchy's fall 2019 campaign. If you look online, there are thousands of women posing in their little black dresses and pearls, exactly like Hepburn.

Unlike Ginger Rogers, Hepburn is widely recognized as the style icon she was. Hepburn also pioneered the black jumpsuit in her legendary press photos for *Sabrina*. This jumpsuit started the designer Givenchy and the starlet's lifelong partnership (Givenchy also designed the LBD), and I'll talk about this more in an upcoming chapter ("A Tour of the Old Hollywood Studio System"). The black jumpsuit with black flats continues to be in style today, with many women sporting the look casually or for red carpets and fancy events.

Lauren Bacall and Katharine Hepburn were both influential in making the women's suit a trend: Hepburn leaned toward more masculine suits, while Bacall wore more feminine suits—with skirts tailored to perfection. The resurgence of shoulder pads in the 1980s was in part inspired by these looks from the 1940s. When women went to work in the 1940s during World War II (head to "The 1940s Working Girl" for more on that), they wore a lot of work suits and shoulder pads. Nowadays, the 1980s-does-1940s look is coming back.[11]

Even slang these days references old Hollywood. In the mid–2010s, people started referring to "gaslighting," which is when a manipulative person makes their victim think they're the crazy one. This term came from the 1944 Ingrid Bergman film noir *Gaslight*.

One of the highest-grossing movies of the last 10 years is *Barbie*, which has so many similarities with old Hollywood: the colors, the costume design, and even the characters, which are of course inspired by the Barbie doll's conception in the 1950s. The director of the film, Greta Gerwig, listed the films that inspired the cinematography: *Umbrellas of Cherbourg, Singin' in the Rain, The Wizard of Oz, Red Shoes, Playtime, An American in Paris,* and countless other classics.[12] The colors are so much brighter than films nowadays, which harkens back to the initial days of Technicolor. The costume design in the film is also over the top, created to entertain and distract, just like the costumes in 1930s films. Even the idea of the "dumb blonde" who learns a lesson was first used in old Hollywood with Jean Harlow and then Judy Holliday in films like *It Should Happen to You* and *Born Yesterday* and mimicked in films like *Legally Blonde*.

There's another part of old Hollywood in every movie today, but you will only notice this if you've watched a good load of classic films. Stock characters have existed since the beginning of storytelling. In addition to the dumb blonde, you have the evil witch, the mad scientist, the hero who saves the day, the wise old man, and the mean girl.

Like old Hollywood, today's cinema overuses character types. And since actors most commonly play the same sort of character in every one of their films, we think of the actor instead of a character. There are many exceptions, but think about many of the most famous actors in today's day and age and whether most of their characters fall under the same archetype. Most of them do.

It's quite fun thinking of the modern counterparts of these characters. Tom Hanks is the modern Jimmy Stewart, for example—the common man who displays heroic tendencies. Gwyneth Paltrow is the modern Grace Kelly—an uptight blonde heiress with charm and wit. George Clooney is basically Cary Grant—from the face, to the characters, to the career trajectory (Clooney became famous for crime movies with romance elements, like Grant, and he turned to thrillers later in his career). Harrison Ford is Humphrey Bogart.

Technically speaking, since these actors were some of the first to play these commonly used tropes on screen, they represent that character—which means that, since these character stereotypes are in every film, classic movies are present in almost every modern film. While there are exceptions to the rule, you can always find a connection to classic Hollywood films today—which answers the question you asked at the beginning of the chapter: Why do I even need to know about these films?

They're present in every aspect of storytelling, so if you're even somewhat interested in storytelling and film, or culture at large, it's crucial to understand these early films. My discussion of film starts with the end of the classic Hollywood era, the 1960s, and then goes back in time. However, the book is not presented in a linear way—instead, it's a collection of the most intriguing stories (and my opinions!) to get you started with old Hollywood.

Beach Party!
What This Quintessential Sub Genre Says About 1960s Culture

There are three phases to every cultural phenomenon: experimentation, elaboration, and embellishment.[1] Experimentation is the first phase, when everything is open and ready to be explored. Elaboration is usually the most prolific phase: people have explored enough to know what works but not too much to keep redoing things over and over again. Embellishment is the least important. It's when most things have already been done, but the art form still goes on, trying to replicate itself. Most phenomena are now in the embellishment phase—there are countless examples for every possible pop cultural expression.

Film has been around for well over a century now, and it has been through all of these cycles. At this point, all things that can be done with film have already been done in a slightly different way. It's the same with music. We're having problems with music copyright lawsuits now because there are only so many chord structures you can use in a song that sound good to the human ear. This isn't bad. It's my opinion that we need to accept that.

So what does this have to do with the 1960s, the decade of film I'm starting with in this book? The 1960s are the prime example of the elaboration phase. Films had existed for a long time, but there was still quite a lot to be explored, and more boundaries had to be pushed to get to that new undiscovered territory.

Even simple things like a film set on a beach had not been explored yet in the 1960s. One of the first films to explore a beach and surfer lifestyle was the 1959 film *Gidget*. *Gidget* was originally adapted from a novel by Frederick Kohner in 1957. He was a Czechoslovakian Jew who worked in the German film industry as a screenwriter until 1933, when he moved to Hollywood after the Nazis started removing Jewish credits from films.

Beach Party!

My great-grandfather, who was a painter and scientist, had almost the same story and also left Germany in 1935 because of Nazi rule.[2] I thought Kohner's story was interesting because of how brave he was to continue creating under such strict rules. Kohner and his wife, Franzie, decided to raise their two daughters near the beach. Meanwhile, he worked incredibly hard as a screenwriter for Columbia Pictures.

Surfing became a youth movement in the 1950s, and Kohner was fascinated by his daughter Kathy who persisted with her interest in a primarily male-dominated sport. He conceived the idea for a book and Kathy fed him details about the surfing world. He decided to name the book *Gidget* after Kathy's nickname—the somewhat unpleasant contraction of "girl" and "midget."

Soon after the book's publication, Kohner sold the film rights to Columbia Pictures for $50,000, even giving $2,500 of it to his daughter.[3] The film was made and was a huge success in the American youth audience and earned $1.5 million at the box office.

In my opinion, *Gidget* was the precursor to the second wave of feminism in the 1960s. It was just provocative enough to raise a few eyebrows but not too out of reach to be a box office hit, making it the perfect movie to push the boundaries on what women could achieve. In *Gidget*, a teenage girl named Francie is not interested in hanging out with her boy-crazy female friends. She meets a gang of surfer boys who don't treat her very well (debatable), but she realizes she loves surfing when a boy called Jeffrey "saves" her as she's drowning. The film pushes boundaries on women in surfing, and the inner life of the teenage girl—and I'd say it's pretty accurate.

The boys call her a "crazy tomboy" just because she has an interest in surfing and doesn't have the typical voluptuous figure of the 1950s. Gidget questions whether she's a normal girl and if anything interesting will ever happen to her—still things we teenage girls worry about today. The film also pushes the boundaries on having goals in life, with one surfer talking about jobs: "I tried that once, but there were too many rules," he says.

Gidget was teenage life but on a beach—not commonly done before. Usually, depictions of teenagers were in harsh environments like the New York street scene (e.g., *West Side Story*).[4]

Another interesting factoid about *Gidget* is that it's one of the only early films I've seen that showcases a crop top. I know what you're thinking: *Why is that relevant?* I personally don't like them, but I see them everywhere. And no, you won't get this commentary anywhere else but from a 15-year-old. When I saw Sandra Dee (Gidget) wearing one, I laughed in recognition. The movie was also filmed at Leo Carrillo State Park, a place I've been while visiting my grandparents!

Gidget's impact on culture went further than just the success of the film series (three *Gidget* films were made) and even the brief-run TV show that featured Sally Field. *Gidget* propelled surfing and beach culture into the public imagination, setting the scene for future party films of the 1960s. What I love about *Gidget* is that it has themes that aren't shallow. While a ton of men think Gidget is stupid (for example, in the movie's reviews), most of the things Gidget struggles with, like sexism, questioning who you are, and fitting in, are far from superficial for teens. This reminds me of the reception of *Barbie*, where some men called it frivolous and man-hating, when far more films reflect a hidden assumption that men rule over women. All in all, the things that some men think are frivolous are a reflection of what they don't understand or what they don't have to deal with.

The story of the beach party genre starts with American International Pictures, a motion picture company releasing films from 1955 through 1980. After that, it joined with Orion, which was then acquired by MGM, which is now owned by Amazon MGM. The studio prioritized movie ideas that would appeal to a wide teen audience. AIP also had an interesting practice of choosing a title and poster for a film before even writing the script.

I talked to Andrew Saladino, who created the YouTube channel *Royal Ocean Film Society*, and he said of AIP: "The practice of devising the title and poster before writing the script and producing the film was, as odd as it sounds, a standard practice for American International Pictures, the company that produced the beach party films and a number of other teenage-centric films in the 1950s and 60s."

Saladino recommended I check out Samuel Arkoff's autobiography, since he was the producer and co-founder of AIP. Arkoff wrote about his AIP co-founder, Jim Nicholson, relating how Jim would bring catchy titles into the office that had no script or even any notes about possible plots. Yet they were so good (think: *I Was a Teenage Werewolf, The Amazing Colossal Man, It Conquered the World, Reform School Girl, Diary of a High School Bride*) that the execs would draw up the poster artwork and make ad copy right away before even hiring a writer.

"The majors thought we were crazy," wrote Arkoff, " working 'back-assward' because we had the title, the artwork, and the catch lines finished before we ever gave approval to have a screenplay written.

But we reasoned, 'Why make the picture if the public isn't likely to buy it?'"[5]

In Italy in the summer of 1962, AIP's Sam Arkoff and Jim Nicholson were watching films to purchase for release in the United States. They stumbled upon a film about a man falling in love at a beach resort. They didn't like the movie but loved the setting on the beach. Nicholson pulled *Beach Party* out of his sleeve, and it seemed like a good title, so they tested it and hired a screenwriter, according to Saladino.

Beach Party differed from *Gidget* in that it removed all moral lessons, parental involvement, and anything that wasn't completely perfect and ideal. AIP added more young people with fewer clothes and catered to the trends of the early 1960s. Saladino also said: "These weren't films *about* teenagers, they were films *sold to* teenagers."

The perfect people for these roles were Annette Funicello and Frankie Avalon, who would become the hallmark couple of the movie that probably gets played on the Hallmark Channel every week.

Funicello was a Disney star who was featured in the 1950s on *The Mickey Mouse Club*, which would later be remade in the 1990s using future stars such as Britney Spears, Christina Aguilera, Ryan Gosling, and Justin Timberlake. Annette was set to star in the film, and she was paired with Avalon, a teen idol and singer, to create an irresistible couple for a 1960s teen audience.

The film emphasized "eye candy,"[6] which would help bring viewers in. After the most stringent days of the Hays Code subsided in the late 1950s, women were allowed to show their navels on film. At beach parties, girls and guys in swimsuits were running around, not very far from nudity. Although they were supposedly about surfing, these movies were not faithful to what a surfing lifestyle was.[7] Surfing wasn't all romance and almost-naked wholesome young people. It initially attracted more rugged drop-out types who were into the craft of modifying the surf boards and achieving more and more athletic feats on the waves, rather than cavorting on the sand. The beach party movies romanticized the sport, and they also drew upon the relatively new phenomenon of people flocking to beaches during vacations. Odd to us now, but beaches weren't always a place of leisure; it was only in the late 1800s that Americans didn't find them scary. Oceanside spots were associated with shipwrecks, pirates, and natural disasters, and it was only after air quality got so bad with the late Industrial Revolution that the upper classes needed to escape to get fresh air. But back to the 20th century, and the premiere of the film that would really get people slathering on the sunscreen.

Frankie Avalon and Annette Funicello filming *Beach Blanket Bingo* in 1965 (Wikimedia Commons).

Beach Party!

"When the picture opened ... the theater was flooded with kids. In many cases, house records were set, and new AIP gross records were also secured. All of a sudden, theaters began clamoring for prints of *Beach Party*. A new cycle had begun."[8] *Variety* described the film as "a bouncy bit of lightweight fluff," and this time, I agree. An aside: when they say "prints," they mean copies of the movie, because back then you had to actually have the physical film (made up of thousands of individual still shots) to be able to screen a film. Today, most cinemas project digital files that come on a hard disk or stream through a satellite.

Saladino called *Beach Party* "teen escapism taken to an overwhelmingly ridiculous level," which may have been exactly what teen culture needed at the time.

I am a strong believer that comedy is best mixed with real-life situations, and that's why I'm not a huge fan of stand-up or some 1950s TV shows because they just don't feel authentic.

Beach Party was the mold in which all the other beach party films were made.[9] It was an easy equation that could be done in slightly different ways every time to create a box office smash. There are lovers and haters of the beach party genre; for the shameless fun, or the stupidity and ineptitude—it's mostly a love or hate thing, like coffee or blankets that double as pajamas. Saladino states, in his video essay "The Beach Party Genre": "You put together a comedy filled with popular music, romance, a celebrity cameo, and you center it all around a marketable trend." In this case, that was surfing and beach life.

Speaking of the celebrity cameo, there were several: Buster Keaton, Stevie Wonder, Mickey Rooney, Nancy Sinatra, James Brown, Leslie Gore, and even the Supremes. This wasn't the first time and it wasn't the last time that a studio would capitalize on a trend only to completely overdo it and make it a cliché. My research has made one thing clear: when something gets popular, studio execs get dollar signs for eyes.

A primary example of this would be *Twilight*. After the film's success, studios exploited young adult fantasy films like *The Hunger Games*, *Divergent*, and many other films I have never watched. Another example would be the female-centric rom-coms of the 2000s. I love most of them, but there came a time when the same tropes repeated over and over again made me cringe. The good ones include *Legally Blonde*, *Bridget Jones*, and many other films. The bad ones are plentiful, like *Love Wrecked*, which was so clearly a cash grab.

This same thing happened with the beach party trend. The studios cashed in on it so quickly in such a short amount of time, only about five years. These films include *Surf Party, Beach Blanket Bingo, Muscle Beach Party, Wild on the Beach, The Girls on the Beach, How to Stuff a Wild Bikini, Ride with Surf, Bikini Beach*, and a million billion gazillion more. AIP started the trend, but most studios jumped in and made it their own. Paramount Studios released three rip-off films, *The Girls on the Beach, Beach Ball*, and *C'mon, Let's Live a Little*. Columbia did the *Gidget* films and *Ride the Wild Surf*, and Twentieth Century–Fox made *Surf Party* and *The Horror of Party Beach*, the latter widely seen as one of the worst films of all time. As expected, the market became highly oversaturated and the beach party film's popularity waned, but that wouldn't happen for several more years.

When AIP released *The Ghost in the Invisible Bikini*, they finally gave up on making beach party films for good. At that point, they moved into motorcycle gang films.[10]

The beach party film genre remains one of the oddest genres in Hollywood history, as it placed its value on one thing. "Look! These sexy young people are partying on a beach! If you watch the film, you can too!" The market was made by showing teenagers there was a better side to the teenage years, amid the social crises of the time. The seemingly endless Vietnam War, the Civil Rights movement, the second wave of feminism, and many other social problems—those were mostly ignored in films.

For example (aside from small celebrity cameos), these films were predominantly white, and it's extremely noticeable in these movies. The African Americans shown in the films are mostly performers—telling the audiences that the only reason people of color should be in movies is to be entertaining, not to showcase moral lessons, teach, learn or experience.

The films also barely had sex scenes or nudity, although they were promised. Instead, the films flaunted more skin than usually allowed in most movies at the time. This created a slightly misleading ploy to pull in viewers. If the studios made it all about sex, they could sell the films, even if they were basically the same thing copied and pasted over and over and over again. For example, the "beach party" poster states: "it's what happens when 10,000 kids meet on 5,000 beach blankets!"[11]

That was boundary-pushing but nothing like the films of the late '60s, *The Graduate* or *Bonnie & Clyde*, which dealt straight-on with violence, nudity, and sex. The beach party films do, however, somewhat reflect the undertone of sexual liberation of the 1960s. They were all about bodies and relationships, even if they were quite shallow regarding those topics. There's certainly an argument to be won here: if half of the film's plot is showcasing women in bikinis, is that liberating or is it objectification? I'd argue for both. Most of the movies are close-ups of women in swimsuits, but they seem to be having fun, so does that make it okay?

So even if the partial nudity seems minuscule compared to today's standards, it was a big deal, and in its time it was probably viewed as objectification to sell the movie. But by the girls who went to see it, it may have been seen as liberating. There's a fine line there.

Along with the sexual liberation undertones, the level of parental involvement in these films represents the youth rebellion of the 1960s. Before the 1960s, most generations did the same things their parents did. This probably accounts for why there are only a handful of generational names before the baby boomers (who were the teenagers and kids in the 1960s, essentially). The kids of the post-war era rose up and wanted to change things. And you can imagine that their parents weren't exactly happy about that. This is portrayed beautifully in *Hairspray*.

Part of why these films were successful was really because parents weren't involved in them to tell the kids that they shouldn't be running around on the beach "practically naked" all day with boyfriends and girlfriends. I can tell that was an appealing form of escapism for the kids then.

Now, here are the things I love about the real beach party films (not including *Gidget*, which doesn't count, because it was years before the superficial beach party trend started in 1963). The colors are phenomenal. The settings are beautiful. Teenage Stevie Wonder is amazing.

However, I don't think these films hold up. They do have a lot of modern relevance, considering that the entire genre was mocked in a Disney movie a little more than 10 years ago, with *Teen Beach Movie*. That film made fun of the 1960s' genre's very specific unrealistic aspects, like the fact that the characters can swim without getting their hair wet and spontaneously burst into song.

Gidget is worth watching, but most of the beach party films are pretty stupid. Here's a snippet of dialogue from *Beach Party* that is incredibly high on the cringe factor scale.

> **FRANKIE:** You know, the only thing I've studied this semester is you.
> **DOLORES:** Well, I hope you don't flunk!
> **FRANKIE:** Well, there's always summer school, you know!

It's so clearly manufactured that it becomes hard to watch. Despite this, these films are still significant, because they emphasize the point that I've been trying to make for a long time. Teens have been the center of American pop culture for decades now. We often don't realize the power we have as teens. We are the future. And that was what the studio system realized with this new sunny genre—they had to cater to what the young people wanted. And yet, adults still look down on teens and our media. Maybe it's because we're more powerful than they want to admit.

Guess Who's Coming to Dinner?
Interracial Relationships and Ethnic Biases in Classic Hollywood

Laws against interracial marriage have existed since the very beginning of the United States. There has long been a stigma about interracial relations in this country, because of many long-standing barriers between different cultures, segregation and racism. These attitudes included Hollywood, which has had a perennial issue with portraying any non-white cultures through a white lens.

In the early days of film in the 1920s, white stars would play so-called "ethnic" roles, in yellowface, an extremely hurtful and problematic side of the silent era. For example, Myrna Loy was typecast as an "oriental" woman in her many early roles, despite being a redhead from Montana. The studios thought her eyes were "almond-shaped" so they put her in many of these roles. The same thing happened with the portrayals of the African American community. Jim Crow laws were still in full effect, so the studios largely caved to the stereotypes in their movies, rather than face the consequences of not having their films played in the Southern United States.

Coating white actors' faces with dark makeup, or "blackface," was prominent in many alarming scenes in films, such as *The Jazz Singer*, *Swing Time*, and even in films from the 1940s such as *Babes on Broadway*. When I see these portrayals, they reinforce just how strong racism was at the time—I had never seen that on screen before. Most of the 1930s films that I watch have some African American actors who play incredibly dumb, mindless roles (as if they are not people!), reflecting the values of the time and teaching me what people thought about Black people. Seeing those portrayals was even more harrowing than reading a book like *Roll of Thunder, Hear My Cry*, because I saw it play out in real-time.

Old Films, Young Eyes

I have seen these biases play out on screen, and I've seen history change as I watch these films. An interesting film that sent shivers up my spine was *The City Without Jews*, an Austrian silent film from 1924, which essentially predicted the Holocaust in an uncanny manner: a government official thinks his country is ruled by Jews and passes a law forcing all Jews to emigrate by the end of the year. Sound familiar?

These films can teach us how history was and even how our own cultures were treated. I loved watching Gregory Peck stand up for the Jewish people in *Gentlemen's Agreement*; seeing Louise Beavers, an African American actress, depicted as a real person with real problems in *Imitation of Life*; and witnessing Audrey Hepburn and Shirley MacLaine battle with stigma around lesbianism (even if they hold that same stigma themselves) in *The Children's Hour*. Despite these films' clear biases and small issues with the portrayals, given the time period, it's illuminating to watch history play out in this way.

One particular film stood out to me that completely broke boundaries, or maybe instead of breaking boundaries, completely tore them to the ground: *Guess Who's Coming to Dinner* from 1967. My grandma says of this film: "I saw *Guess Who's Coming to Dinner* with [your grandpa], believe it or not, in the late '60s or early '70s, maybe. At the time, it was thought to be a breakthrough, a real revolutionary movie, because of a white woman and a black man falling in love, forming a healthy relationship, and getting married."

Only a few films about interracial dynamics had come out before *Guess Who's Coming to Dinner*, such as *One Potato, Two Potato* from 1964. These films were not as influential. Instead of making movies about racism, early Hollywood prioritized money and social status over rightfully portraying races.

For example, when Hattie McDaniel was nominated for an Oscar in 1940, she was going to be forced to sit outside of the segregated Ambassador Hotel where the ceremony was held, until David O. Selznick petitioned for her to be allowed to sit inside the auditorium, but *still* at a different table. McDaniel ended up winning the Oscar and made history for being the first African American actress ever to win. This didn't happen again until Sidney Poitier (the star of *Guess Who's Coming to Dinner*) won in 1963 for his film *Lilies of the Field*.

The story of how *Guess Who's Coming to Dinner* became one of the landmark films of the 1960s starts with one couple who loved each other yet still struggled to stay together—not because of their relationship, but because of the social norms of the time.

Guess Who's Coming to Dinner?

Richard Loving and Mildred Jeter fell in love in high school in the 1950s. Loving was a white man. Jeter was of African American and Native American ancestry, but she identified as Black in court testimonies. Mildred became pregnant in 1958, and the couple moved to Washington, D.C., to get married, hoping to avoid Virginia's anti-miscegenation laws.

In the early morning hours of a day in 1958, cops raided their house, hoping to find them having sex, but instead they found the Lovings peacefully sleeping in bed. When asked, Mildred pointed to their wedding certificate, which the police said was invalid in the state of Virginia. The Lovings had to go to jail, each for a year. After their conviction, they moved to Washington, D.C.—but were extremely disappointed by the fact that they couldn't travel outside of the district to see friends or family. Mildred wrote a letter to President John F. Kennedy, whose administration referred them to the ACLU, which went further with the case. As law goes, it took several years for anything to happen, but the Supreme Court decided on December 12, 1966, to allow the case for final review. In June, the Supreme Court unanimously decided in favor of the Lovings. Even though anti-miscegenation laws were unenforceable, several states kept them in action. But the decision had an undeniable effect, and interracial marriages continued to rise in the United States.

As this case was being decided, one of the most important movies ever made was being filmed. *Guess Who's Coming to Dinner* was written by William Rose and produced by Stanley Kramer. They both intended for the film to debunk racial stereotypes, which is the reason they made Sidney Poitier's character a "perfect" man to marry: a young, kind doctor with no real potential. This approach helped the public see the points they were trying to make instead of seeing the problems with Dr. John Prentice (Poitier). Ironically, Poitier wrote in his autobiography that he felt racially-tinged pressure from Katharine Hepburn and Spencer Tracy, who play the bride-to-be's parents, at their first meeting, not completely unlike the way they act in the film.[1] *Guess Who's Coming to Dinner* is about Joanna, a white woman, who meets John Prentice, a black man, on vacation, and after two weeks, they decide to get married (crazy times) and they only have one night to have dinner and tell their parents why they want to get married. But John has decided to marry Joanna only if her parents allow it. The movie follows the dinner with both sets of their parents trying to decide what to say to them.

During the filming of *Guess Who's Coming to Dinner, Loving v. Virginia* was decided, and the film was released only six months later.

Guess Who's Coming to Dinner was one of the very first films to depict interracial marriage positively, and it had a huge impact on the public's viewpoint on it. This film (in my opinion) was a reaction to the Lovings pleading innocent in their case and shifted the needle just enough for a cultural movement in the 1970s with Motown, disco, and the further rise of the Civil Rights movement.

One of the things that struck me as different about the film was how honest Joanna was about her and others' feelings. She never let anything awkward go unsaid, and that's what's so captivating about her character. The movie forces you to keep watching by continually referencing the dinner to come, making the viewer anticipate and anticipate until that moment finally comes—adding new challenges and guests as the day goes on.

While *Guess Who's Coming to Dinner* isn't a perfect film, I see it as an important cultural artifact. How else are we supposed to know how it actually was for interracial couples, other than to see it with our own eyes? There are not many films like this from the Golden Age, and I'm positive that this film will live on much further than intended—especially in today's political landscape.

What's So Bad About Feeling Good?

The '60s Movie That Predicted the Pandemic

I was only 10 years old when the Covid-19 pandemic shut down the entire world. I wasn't that scared, because it would be over in "three weeks," my school board said. Yet that turned into months. I put my efforts into writing essays and starting my first podcast. I even wrote an article all about what Zoom school was really like—my grandfather published it in his syndicated news column! Look it up: "Zoom Boom in the Classroom" by Simone O. Elias, to see how 10-year-old me coped with Zoom school.[1]

I'm honestly so glad that I was forced to be with my creativity during 2020. I wouldn't be who I am now without it. It angers me to see that Gen Z lost years of our social life and had experiences that left us paralyzed, and the effects are still felt now. I bet you thought those oh-so-recent feelings would never be articulated in a classic film, but guess what? You're wrong.

While I was trying to find movies to watch, I saw one called *What's So Bad About Feeling Good?* But when I read the description, I gasped. I watched the trailer and nearly exploded in shock. *What's So Bad About Feeling Good?* is a 1968 film about an exotic toucan who infects New York City with a virus that causes happiness. The virus quickly spreads and the citywide health initiative begins, with masking, plans for a possible vaccine, and even questioning if the virus was manufactured in China. I'm not kidding!

I watched 1960s actors using words like "quarantine" and wearing masks, things I had never heard of before March 2020. I was younger back then, but that just goes to show that those words and behaviors weren't mainstream for fourth graders, and probably not for a lot of other people—a huge difference from our post-pandemic era.

The movie begins by showing the audience just how mean-spirited the people of New York are. A woman trying to get on a bus falls, only for the rest of the people to ignore her. People angrily arguing on the street. A woman and a man hurling insults at each other. "What are ya, some kind of nut or something?" she says.

The scenes cannot be erased from the period: the artsy, bohemian culture of the 1970s is starting to creep in amidst these unpleasantries—men and women are smoking, meditating, and singing songs about peace. It's eerily similar to many 1970s movies with those same activities and tropes.

Suddenly, after five minutes of setting the scene, a toucan sits in the frame. "It was on a Greek freighter that had dropped anchor for quarantine inspection," the narrator says. The sailors on the boat act as if they are drunk, but it's just the virus that makes them happy. The premise of this movie hooks you by showcasing all of these drab people, including Mary Tyler Moore (hard to imagine as "drab," I know), who dress in gray and live off unemployment, and then they start acting insanely giddy because of the virus. George Peppard (the leading man) is suddenly mysteriously delighted. "Listen," he says.

"To the traffic?"

"No, the kids are laughing."

"'Cause they're not old enough to read the newspaper. You take a look at the front page and then try laughing. The world's a stinking, hopeless mess."

This sounded like something somebody would say about today's political atmosphere. If people thought that 60 years ago, that tells us two things: first, don't read the news, and second, there's usually more hope than we think.

When the mayor broadcast the message about the virus while donning a mask, I whispered under my breath, "Stop it!" It was a bit too close for comfort. In a later scene, the authority figures discuss why the virus is so bad: they don't care that it makes people feel good. They care that the economy isn't doing well because people aren't drinking or smoking anymore.

This movie was one of the cleverest films I'd seen in a while. It was a total flop commercially, but it deserves a revisit. I could even see it having a total comeback, with a remake that subtly mocks the Covid-19 response.

"I was floored by some of the parallels to now," Sean Cole of *This American Life* said in a 2020 episode of the popular podcast, "especially given that this movie came out in 1968, more than half a century ago. For instance, instead of a bat, the vector of this virus is a bird."

In the film, a man states, "It's a brand new virus, some kind of a mutation. We don't know how long it will take to identify it." Doesn't that sound eerily similar to what the public was told in early 2020?

The virus only starts with a couple of infected people, but it quickly takes over everything. Are you getting déjà vu? Let's play a game. Is this from the film or from an actual CDC regulation? "The commissioner of health recommends that you wear a surgical mask when you are out in public." Trick question. *Both!* That quote was from *What's So Bad About Feeling Good*, but it's also *exactly* what the CDC said at the beginning of the Covid-19 pandemic.

Right after this scene, the population of New York immediately masks up and the government starts to work on a vaccine. Uncanny!

The film pokes fun at this virus that causes happiness, which is of course a big difference when compared to Covid-19. The virus causes complete and total euphoria, with one man even echoing the title, saying, "What's so bad about feeling good?"

I think this film can teach us a lesson about how we can pretty much laugh at everything. I'm not saying we can laugh about mass death, but I think we can laugh about our reactions and fear post-pandemic and talk about how humor can be brought into almost everything. This reminds me of the *Saturday Night Live* sketch "Covid Dinner Discussion," which reflects how this topic, despite all of its controversies, can be incredibly funny. Kate McKinnon shares a story at a dinner table in this hilarious 2022 skit: "I went to a child's birthday party, careful, and they did gymnastics in masks, and then they went into another room and took off their masks to eat pizza, so did they really need the mask—" she stutters. "Oh no." The whole table chimes in. "Did any of us. Ever. Need. The Mask. Nooooooo!!!!!" She then asks: "We don't have to wash our hands anymore, do we?" "I never did," says John Mulaney.

Processing hard situations requires humor, part of the reason many comedians suffer from depression, and the most oppressed people often have comedy built into their culture.

It's important to address the most likely cause of this odd film, which was the impact of the Spanish flu of 1918. It was one of the deadliest pandemics in history—even some of my family who were alive in 1918 died of it. Many started wearing masks out on the streets.

The Spanish flu affected Hollywood in numerous ways, the most obvious being that it shut down theaters and delayed production schedules. Any huge event affects the culture around it—so perhaps the idea for *What's So Bad?* came from what happened during the Spanish flu.

Thinking that a pandemic on a global scale was a completely new thing, I found a book about a girl who lived through the Spanish flu in a bookstore when things were finally opening up again, and when I learned more about it, I was shocked to see pictures of people wearing masks and doing similar things we did back in 2020.

There was another underlying message trying to be sent to the public through this film. This film, like those in the beach party genre, hints at the need for carefree lifestyles and being happy, amidst Civil Rights protests, women's liberation, and Stonewall happening around the same time. However, it remains up in the air whether this film includes some kind of government-deployed message: there could either be something incredibly odd going on here, or it could be a straight-up coincidence. But let me lead you to this snippet of dialogue from *What's So Bad?* This is a conversation between two people working in the high ranks of the government, trying to figure out where the virus came from. The "You Know Who" in question are Communists.

> **JAY GARDNER MONROE:** Look at the facts. When people get the bug, they suddenly love the world. Now, if You Know Who was getting ready to act up again, what would be better than to give Americans a sense of security, a false sense of euphoria?
> **MAN:** Mr. Monroe, you're not suggesting this virus was artificially produced in a laboratory?
> **JAY GARDNER MONROE:** Yes, a virus produced—laboratory, yes.
> **MAN:** Medical impossibility. Just couldn't have happened.
> **JAY GARDNER MONROE:** Hah. That's what they said about the power failure here in New York in '65.
> **MAN:** And what about the Asian flu?
> **JAY GARDNER MONROE:** That came straight, believe you me, from Red China.

People didn't believe that Covid-19 could have been spread from a lab in Wuhan until the U.S. Department of Energy "concluded with 'low confidence' that an accidental laboratory leak in China most likely caused the coronavirus pandemic."[2]

Ultimately, the fate of our world isn't up to individual people like me or you. It's up to all of us to decide our feelings about what the last five years have been, where the virus came from, and what the future will look like. All I know is that there will be uncertainty. Especially the uncertainty I felt writing this chapter: I'll never know the true origins of how this film came about, uncannily depicting Covid-19 fifty years before it actually happened. I'll leave you with Sean Cole's words from that episode of *This American Life*: "watching the movie during this pandemic, I drew another, darker conclusion. Somehow, that wiggly weird jolt of recognition I got over and over again, what it felt like was, this is how it goes. When faced with a crisis like this, governments will minimize the severity of the danger. They'll value the wrong things. They'll focus on the economy over people's lives, and blame foreigners in an ugly, xenophobic way."[3]

Even if the filmmakers were trying to say something with this film, the message wasn't received because the film was a critical and commercial failure. At least it's an incredibly interesting case study, considering what's happening in our world.

New Hollywood
How Two Movies Inspired a Whole New Generation of Filmmakers

Culture never changes without new perspectives, whether they come from a new person speaking up or a new sub-culture being brought into the mainstream. In 1967, the studio system was rapidly losing money. The new generation wasn't particularly interested in the stories the old people in their big offices wanted to tell. The beach party was over. Audiences were interested in different perspectives. Before Hollywood could truly shift from old Hollywood to new Hollywood, two movies had to flip the script. They did this by putting new filmmaking techniques, structures, and ways of thinking into innovative films no one had ever seen before.

This chapter will not be discussing 1970s films; instead we're looking at the two films that made innovative 1970s filmmaking possible: *The Graduate* and *Bonnie & Clyde*.

Before the studio system was dismantled, there was (essentially) no such thing as "indie film." There were studio films made in Hollywood, and there were international films. To completely change the system, new filmmakers had to use the system to dismantle itself by making films accessible enough that the studio would cash in on them but not crazy enough to be total bombs. I know I'm talking about movies, but it does sound like I'm talking about a spy heist with all this use of "dismantle" and "bomb." Stick with me here.

I was completely enraptured when I first watched *Bonnie & Clyde*. It didn't seem different from any film I'd seen from after the 1960s. It moved super-fast, tackled a ton of different themes, and genre-mixed so much that it seemed like real life.

Unlike most Golden Age films, *Bonnie & Clyde* cannot be pigeonholed into any particular category. Think about it: it's an historical

Faye Dunaway and Warren Beatty as Bonnie and Clyde in 1967 (Warner Bros.–Seven Arts) (Wikimedia Commons).

film (set in the 1930s), it's a romance, it's a comedy (yes, I would argue that it is), it's a gangster film, it's a drama, and it's a tragedy. All at the same time. Something about the fullness of experience and true-to-life aspects of *Bonnie & Clyde* appealed to young audiences. They thought that life couldn't be labeled as a drama, a comedy, a romance, or a tragedy. It was a little bit of everything. And films that reflected that were exactly what Hollywood needed. *Bonnie & Clyde* was also revolutionary because of the attitude toward morals (more on that in a bit), the use of blood and violence on camera, and the use of sexual content, which, for the 1960s, meant kissing longer than three seconds.

If you haven't watched it, *Bonnie & Clyde* is about a couple (can you guess their names?) who rob banks and run away. They're outlaws, and they're on the run from law enforcement and anyone else who wants to enforce their rules on them. Even though the story was real—Bonnie and Clyde were a real couple from the 1930s—the tropes of the story were perfect for the '60s: whoever breaks the rules gets shot. Or, most simply, whoever breaks the rules gets punished.

Think about MLK. Think about Malcolm X. Think about anyone who truly challenged society's norms during that period. They were punished for it, correct? In some way or form, rebels always are. This is how society reacts to rule-breakers. They get crushed. It's wrong, but it's true.

This is still relevant today. If you want to change things, you're going to have to accept that people will push back. But that's the fun of it—same with *Bonnie & Clyde*. Would it be any fun if they could rob banks without being punished? Sure, in the beginning. But it would get boring! There's no challenge.

A lot of the time, people are scared to speak their truth for fear of being punished. But being punished is better than living in silence. And at least then you know you're truly changing things. If they'd never made *Bonnie & Clyde* for fear of people hating it, the movie industry would not have been the same. This relates to the theme of being a teenager. We're the only ones who can make the most change because we're primed to rebel and we're not afraid—or at least we're less afraid than the adults.

Unlike in many old Hollywood films, lessons and morals are irrelevant in *Bonnie & Clyde*. These two people are selfish and stupid, and yet you can't help but love both of them. Many older people were concerned: what would this morally experimental film say to the youth, especially in a time of crisis with the Vietnam war and social rebellion at the time? But it turned out to be great for the culture; pushing boundaries always is.

Bonnie & Clyde became a huge hit not just because it was a good film but because teenagers and young people at the time weren't looking for scolding or answers. They were looking for youthful energy. Teenagers are rebellious, cynical, and sarcastic—yet hopeful and determined to make their dreams come true. What happens to teenagers when they don't grow up? You get *Bonnie & Clyde*. And that's pretty awesome. If you can channel that into something other than robbing banks.

Bonnie & Clyde was a watershed moment that opened the door for the idiosyncratic, odd, and true-to-life 1970s films like *Taxi Driver*. Another movie that pushed the boundaries and allowed a completely new generation to break through into the film world is *The Graduate*.

The world of the titular character, Benjamin Braddock, is a depressing and listless reality. Do teenagers want films that say "everything's going to get better"? No way. We want to pretend we're super depressed and then go to a party. Or at least most of us do. In my opinion, that's why *The Graduate* hit so hard. Occasionally before it, film characters revealed that they didn't know what they wanted to do. But never in the history of film after the Hays Code (see "Should Ladies Behave? Pre-Code Women Say No" for explanation of this) had a character revealed they didn't know what they wanted and then gone off and had sex with an older woman and her daughter. Trust me, no Post-Code 1930s film is about that.

Benjamin, a college graduate, upon arrival back at his parents' house, questions what he actually would like to do. Some say the future is in plastic (and they were right), but others say differently. Benjamin eventually gets seduced by his parents' friend Mrs. Robinson, who is twice his age. Mrs. Robinson prohibits Benjamin from going on a date with Elaine, her daughter, who he eventually falls in love with in a 1960s suburban upper-class *Romeo and Juliet*.

In order to fully understand what made *The Graduate* such an influential film, you have to think about the cultural context and who the film was meant for. The Boomer generation, especially in the late 1960s, felt alienated from their parents who stood for different things. *The Graduate* arrived perfectly at the time that the new generation was entering and leaving college—so it struck a chord with them.

"The Sound of Silence," the film's first and last song, represents the existential dread the character of Benjamin feels throughout the film and his mindset. It disappears and reappears throughout his trajectory, and through the end, it is still with him, but somehow he has found his happiness with it. Throughout most of the movie, the song is in a minor key, and at the very end, it's in a major key.

When Benjamin first arrives back at his parents' house, he's anxious and depressed, upset and lonely. He's unsure about what he wants, and he doesn't fit in his parents' circles.

When Benjamin and Mrs. Robinson are in a hotel room toward the end of their relationship, he asks her why they never talk. He tries to get her to talk about anything at all—asks her questions about her past, about art, about Mr. Robinson. But she's closed off and keeps asking, "Why?" It seems that Mrs. Robinson forgot what a healthy relationship looks like after an unsuccessful marriage, and Benjamin hasn't had enough experience to want anything less: he wants to talk, and he wants to have a normal relationship.

This represents the difference between Mrs. Robinson and Benjamin: while they are both unhappy characters, Benjamin is unhappy because he doesn't know what he wants to do. Mrs. Robinson is unhappy because she has lived the life that she wanted to live when she was Benjamin's age and she's still not happy with it. In this sense, what draws them together isn't anything besides their circumstances—they're both in crisis.

When Benjamin finally finds something great with Elaine, he's different because of having had a secret relationship with her mother. He has adopted her mother's pessimistic view of relationships. Luckily, with time he realizes that view wasn't going to help him anyway, and he chases Elaine, driving all over California to win her back.

The remarkable part of *The Graduate*, aside from its topics, is the cinematography. Robert Surtees and Mike Nichols worked to create many evocative and vivid shots using close-up, focus, and many shots in the dark where all we see is half of a face or a wall.

What makes *The Graduate* even more innovative is the Simon & Garfunkel soundtrack. "Previously, traditional orchestral film scores were used simply to provide background music for onscreen action." So *The Graduate*'s heavy reliance on the folk-rock songs of the popular duo Simon & Garfunkel was unprecedented: "By the time the film was released, many of the major tunes were already well known," Kristin Doidge wrote in *The Atlantic* of the film's soundtrack.[1]

The Graduate was very important for Simon & Garfunkel and made their songs even more memorable by adding visuals to the already-famous tunes. Before MTV, songs did not have visuals unless the band was famous enough to create a music film, which rarely happened in cases other than the Beatles.

Nowadays, artists compose songs for films all the time—but that usually didn't happen in the Golden Age of film unless it was a musical.

New Hollywood

Other than that, there was usually a score that went along with the film. But as Doidge mentioned, that was usually seen as background music and ignored for the most part. This changed in the 1960s with *The Graduate*, but also six years earlier with the song "Moon River" in *Breakfast at Tiffany's*, which wasn't a musical. That song stands out to me because, like "The Sound of Silence," it represents what the film is as a sort of theme song.

For me, *The Graduate* is the last classic film. In 1968, the Hays Code was abolished when the industry officially decided to scrap it and instead use a ratings system (MPAA) which is still in place. Since *The Graduate* came out at the end of 1967, it still counts as a classic to me. But it's the very end of the classic Hollywood era. But what exactly was so special about *The Graduate* that made it one of the best movies of its generation, over any other 1960s film?

Firstly, the Baby Boomers strongly identified with it, but it was influential mainly because of how it addresses sex, affairs, and divorce without harsh judgment. If films before 1967 (back until 1934) discussed these themes, they had to include a strong moral message about how the story was told to advise the viewer *not* to have sex or affairs or get divorced. That older, more homogeneous strain of American culture still held. *The Graduate*'s Ben Braddock gets consequences for his actions, but he ultimately escapes them.

Because it was a massive hit, the movie influenced how sex was talked about in the movies. *The Graduate* was a low-budget film not meant to have a big impact—but when it did, it changed Hollywood by showing that a movie tackling these subjects could be successful. Remember, Hollywood usually does not want to take big risks. When those small risks are successful, executives finally realize that these seemingly out-of-bounds ideas may not become failures.

Another completely revolutionary aspect of *The Graduate* is the casting. "In casting the leading man—Benjamin Braddock, described in the book as tall and athletic—[the film] took its biggest risk. They passed over [Robert] Redford for an unheralded, height-challenged 29-year-old Dustin Hoffman," Alec Scott of *Smithsonian Magazine* wrote.[2] The casting of Hoffman adds to the character of Benjamin's insecurity and anxiousness, and while I didn't notice while I watched the film, Hoffman is actually only 5'5"!

Instead of casting a tall, more stereotypically attractive guy, the filmmakers chose the guy who completely inhabited the energy of the character, which can truly only be done on low-budget films, and that's the beauty of indie or low-budget movies. More risks can be taken.

The Graduate is a snapshot of a world both disappointing and angering—and equally happy and hopeful—which captures the exact views of teenagers.

Ultimately, what I take from the 1960s as a whole is that young people can reweave the entire fabric of culture. The confused yet empowered youth of the 1960s protested for their rights, created era-defining music, provided fashion inspiration for generations to come, and made movies that dismantled Hollywood as it was known. In the process, they changed the world.

Think about how different the 1950s were from the '70s. That's the impact of one single generation. Think about what the new generations could do to transform the world for the better. That's what I find so inspiring about the past: it shows us that we can do things we never thought imaginable. If our grandparents could do it, we can. But maybe we can be even better than them. After the changes experienced in the 1960s and '70s, Baby Boomers have been noted (as a whole—there are many exceptions) for being materialistic and selfish.[3] Every generation learns from the past, and we certainly will in many ways. Hopefully, our generation's landmark movies won't be about people who rob banks and ruin marriages. We'll see!

The Effect of TV on the Movies

The effect of TV on culture isn't about how broadcasting, cable and antennas work. TV is about the exploration of characters' lies. Take any sitcom, and the characters, whether the main or the minuscule, are trying to cover up something—trying to tell someone a crucial detail they're missing but not knowing how. My screenwriting teacher said that the key to great dialogue isn't what the characters are actually saying but what they *mean*. This is especially crucial for TV.

Television as a medium is completely different from the movies. First of all, it's short form. Most of the time, a standard episode is 22 minutes or less. Yet, the art form is all about telling a narrative over a longer arc than a movie, at least typically. Television also differs from movies (or at least it did back then) because of the structure of episodes. Normally, an episode has an A-plot, a B-plot, and, occasionally, a C-plot. These plots are usually about many characters—in fact, television is, at its core, about character *interactions*, whereas movies are about character *evolution*. Is there an evolution of Jerry Seinfeld over his nine seasons? No. Is there an evolution of Lucy over the seasons? Perhaps slightly, but it's more about what she does with the people around her than it is about what she does with herself, her values, or *her life*.

Over the last 20 years amid the streaming era, movies and television have essentially merged into one art form. But they used to be distinct. The TV shows I am talking about are not series on Netflix that have clear character development and basically act as an eight-hour movie. I'm talking about the standard 22-minute sitcom here.

Before TV came along, radio, plays, going out to movie theaters, and reading were the standard forms of entertainment. This is a key element to why television was so revolutionary. Before TV, people had to dress up, drive somewhere, and pay to go see a film. And if they didn't like the film, they couldn't change the channel. They had to stay through it or leave.

This is where convenience comes in. Most American inventions that have changed day-to-day life revolve around convenience. *How can we make life easier and cheaper for consumers, until they have to do practically nothing?*

I think this convenient approach that American culture takes is fundamentally wrong. I don't believe that convenience equals happiness in a lot of cases, but I still love TV. Self-driving cars are a different story.

There was a movie boom in 1946 after World War II ended—most Americans went to the movies that year, but the attendance rates steadily dropped off as the '50s came along. New parents decided to spend more money on their families, new appliances, and schools instead of movies.[1] With this trend already setting films back, TV came along at the perfect moment to set the studios up for a complete failure. By the time the 1960s arrived, more than half of all American homes had television sets. The only question was, "How far would Hollywood go to keep its esteemed, high-profile position in American culture?"

The only logical next step to get consumers back into movie theaters was to capitalize on what television did not have: a wide screen or color (yet). It also didn't have loads of inappropriate content or 3D vision. So the studios went all-in on everything that TV didn't have.

Widescreen films became the norm, with pretty much all of the famous '50s movies you love being in this format. Most films from that decade, especially musicals, were in bright, beautiful color to draw viewers in. But this doesn't even scratch the surface of what Hollywood tried to do—they used new technologies like 3D and even Smell-O-Vision, a technology where an odor would be released in the movie theater as the movie played. Seriously! That happened.

The content in the movies changed ever so slightly to pull more people in. And more specifically, these changes were aimed at men. The industry took advantage of the fact that more provocative scenes could not be aired on TV and included more of this sauce in movies. "One of the things that Hollywood tried to do to set movies apart was to experiment with some more provocative material that would not be appropriate to air on television," said YouTuber Mina Le in a video about Marilyn Monroe's impact. This is partially why Monroe was so popular—because her movies meant more provocative scenes, and people couldn't see those on TV.

An example of this is the infamous subway grate scene in *The Seven Year Itch*, where Marilyn Monroe is standing on a subway grate in a white dress and the hot air from under it sweeps up her dress, revealing her legs. While extremely risqué for the time, it can't even compare to Lady Gaga's 2023 Oscars butt dress or Janet Jackson's Nipplegate at Super Bowl XXXVIII in 2004.

Moving on, TV affected movies in more ways than it may appear. Even the storylines of movies reflected the new change. For instance, *Singin' in the Rain*, a classic musical about Hollywood's change from silent to sound film, was especially relevant in the '50s, because the silent/sound and movie/TV changes seem to replicate each other.

The TV boom can also be compared to when photography was invented. Painting suffered as a result, and it had to offer something photography couldn't—for example, Kandinsky-style abstract art. At least with painting, there aren't people who say that the art form died, like they did with movies. Some people go as far as to say that "TV killed good film." This wasn't the first and it wouldn't be the last time that one industry pushed out another. After all, "video killed the radio star."

Despite everything the film industry did to push back TV, it still grew, and eventually the mediums grew together in the modern era. But these new inventions did lure viewers in enough to keep the film industry alive. And thank God it did because we wouldn't have *Ferris Bueller* (or *Bonnie & Clyde*)!

The Jews Run Hollywood?

On March 20, 1952, my great grand uncle, screenwriter and playwright Hy Kraft, testified in front of the House Un–American Activities Committee for allegedly being a communist in the entertainment industry, in spite of no proof. He was Jewish, just like me. Despite the lack of evidence, he was blacklisted and could not work in Hollywood anymore. He was sneaky and instead decided to work under the pseudonym Harold Kent.

Unfortunately, many Black and Jewish actors, screenwriters, directors, and musicians were blacklisted and barred from working in the entertainment industry in the mid–20th century. Usually, it was because of information that they had been part of the communist party, which was very often false. This was called the Hollywood blacklist.

The Hollywood blacklist, one of the most well-known aspects of the 1950s "Red Scare," badly affected many in the entertainment industry for several decades until the system was finally dismantled. The Red Scare is representative of the government and Hollywood's treatment of Jews, then and now. Jews make up only 0.2 percent of the global population, yet approximately 20 percent or more of Hollywood talent agents, managers, and screenwriters are Jewish.[1]

"I've been to Hollywood," Dave Chappelle mentioned in his controversial 2022 *Saturday Night Live* monologue. "It's a lot of Jews. Like, a lot." In response, many Jewish writers wrote think pieces about why so many Jews work in Hollywood, and most of them settled on one thing: For most Jews, it may not have been their first choice to work in the industry, but it was one of the only places where they didn't encounter harsh discrimination. Note that when I'm talking about Jews in Hollywood, it's mostly Ashkenazi Jews, although there were some Sephardic Jews involved also. (Ashkenazi Jews come from Eastern Europe, France and Germany, and Sephardic Jews come from the Middle East, Spain, Portugal, and Africa.)

AMERICANS.....
DON'T PATRONIZE REDS!!!!

---•---

YOU CAN DRIVE THE REDS OUT OF TELEVISION, RADIO AND HOLLYWOOD.....

THIS TRACT WILL TELL YOU HOW.

WHY WE MUST DRIVE THEM OUT:

1) The REDS have made our Screen, Radio and TV Moscow's most effective Fifth Column in America . . . 2) The REDS of Hollywood and Broadway have always been the chief financial support of Communist propaganda in America . . . 3) OUR OWN FILMS, made by RED Producers, Directors, Writers and STARS, are being used by Moscow in ASIA, Africa, the Balkans and throughout Europe to create hatred of America . . . 4) RIGHT NOW films are being made to craftily glorify MARXISM, UNESCO and ONE-WORLDISM . . . **and via your TV Set they are being piped into your Living Room—and are poisoning the minds of your children under your very eyes ! ! !**

So REMEMBER — If you patronize a Film made by RED Producers, Writers, Stars and STUDIOS you are aiding and abetting COMMUNISM .. . . every time you permit REDS to come into your Living Room VIA YOUR TV SET you are helping MOSCOW and the INTERNATIONALISTS to destroy America ! ! !

Anti-communist propaganda from the McCarthyism era in the 1950s (Wikimedia Commons).

"The Jewish moguls and film professionals who played a seminal role in the development of the industry rose to heights of prominence at a time when most Jews in America were excluded from leadership in all other businesses due to antisemitic quotas across industries, private clubs, hotels and universities. These barriers did not exist for the Jewish studio founders in the emerging film industry at the time, in part because the industry was considered by some as disreputable," Jonathan Greenblatt wrote in *The Hollywood Reporter*.

Hollywood was one of the only growing industries in which Jewish families could make money in the early days of immigration. Many couldn't work in the established journalism industry if they liked writing because they would be turned down due to anti–Semitism, especially in the 1910s. By contrast, "there were no social barriers in a business as new and faintly disreputable as the movies were in the early years of this century," Neal Gabler wrote in his book *An Empire of Their Own*, the book about Jews in Hollywood. As he mentioned, Hollywood was a completely new industry, and so it wasn't established enough to turn away most people. Plus, since Jews ran production studios, it was easier for other Jews to get hired.

Once your family is working in an industry, it makes it easier for the new generations to break in using their connections, and this is part of why we still see so many Jews in Hollywood. But why is this a problem?! Nobody publicizes damaging conspiracies about white men wanting to rule the world because they take up most political positions.

Commenting on Chappelle's remark, American University professor Pamela Nadell told *The Times of Israel*: "Whenever the Jews enter into any kind of position where they might influence people who are not Jewish, then all of a sudden it's seen as some kind of conspiracy."[2] Chappelle would go on to poke fun at this phenomenon too in his famous monologue, which put his comments in ambiguous territory—is he really anti–Semitic? "If they're black, then it's a gang. If they're Italian, it's the mob. But if they're Jewish, it's a coincidence and you should never speak about it," he told the crowd.

This isn't the first time that Jews have been haunted by conspiracies in Hollywood. This happened with the Red Scare, and it also happened in the 1930s. At that time, Joseph Breen (who ran the Hays production office) blamed Jews for "sneaking sex, violence, and moral depravity in the movies."[3]

Frankly, this seems ridiculous to me. Anyone who knows Jewish people knows that we have one of the strictest moral codes. Let me ask

The Jews Run Hollywood?

Joseph this: Have you ever met a Jewish grandmother? She's like "let me ask you if you're getting married and having kids soon, let me guilt you for not doing it, and then let me make you soup." And the men are essentially the same way, except they read their newspapers instead of making soup.

Misbehaving is generally not accepted in Jewish culture, and although most of us love humor, it's mainly because we make fun of our parents and the crazy rules we have to follow with it. This is partially from personal experience, but I also went to a Jewish day school for many years, and I understand a lot of the family culture. Just put on Gertrude Berg's "How to Be a Jewish Mother" and you'll understand.

Breen advised Hollywood producers not to mention Nazis or Jews in films, and they abided. He said: "There is a strong pro–German and anti–Semitic feeling in this country ... and while those who are likely to approve of an anti–Hitler picture may think well of such an enterprise, they should keep in mind that millions of Americans might think otherwise."[4] It seems that Jewish writers and directors were not at all interested in stirring up any trouble politically. In fact, in one of the first Jew-centered movies, *Gentleman's Agreement* (more on that later), very few Jewish people participated.[5] There were a couple of Jewish writers, but writing is the job least involved on the set, so those writers were likely not there for the filming.

Golden Age Hollywood's best directors were Jewish, and yet most of them never said anything about that in their films (Billy Wilder, Herman Mankiewicz, Ernst Lubitsch, George Cukor). While promoting his film *The Fabelmans*, Steven Spielberg talked about being Jewish in Hollywood: "Being Jewish in America is not the same as being Jewish in Hollywood. Being Jewish in Hollywood is like wanting to be in the popular circle and immediately being accepted as I have been in that circle, by a lot of diversity but also by a lot of people who are Jewish."[6]

So it makes sense why, especially in the Golden Age of Hollywood, there were so many Jews involved. If there are going to be many people working with you at your job who are part of your ethnic group, you're going to feel more comfortable—especially back in the 1940s, when an evil dictator was leading the quickest and deadliest genocide in history on your kind.

At that time, my ancestors were fleeing Europe and Hitler in Nazi Germany. And 40 years before, the other side of my family was fleeing Russian pogroms. If the people similar to my ancestors who survived these near-death traumas were lucky enough to make it to the United

States and find a job, they'd probably feel more comfortable with people of their own ethnicity. Can you blame them? Nearly every group that has immigrated to America has found a home within a particular industry: Germans came to farm the Midwest; Italians arrived and filled the ranks of law enforcement; Mexicans formed the labor force for Western farms; Chinese came to mine gold and build railroads. Yes, many of these groups also encountered xenophobia and discrimination, but this just proves that most new immigrants stay together for opportunities and protection.

Back in the 1910s, it wasn't much different than today in terms of Jews in the industry. Before movie-making centered on Southern California, New York was the place to be for Broadway and the early film industry, but as movies moved to Hollywood, Jews moved there to work behind the camera as directors, writers, producers, and costume designers and on camera as actors, dancers, singers, and more.

The men who founded Hollywood were mostly Jews: Louis B. Mayer, as much as I despise him (you'll hear about this in "A Tour of the Old Hollywood Studio System" and "Looking at Old Hollywood Through the Lens of the 'Me Too' Movement"), was a Jew, as was Adolph Zukor, founder of Paramount Pictures. Hungarian Jew William Fox founded the Fox Film Corporation. Even the Warner brothers were Jewish! So you'd think, since there were so many of them, that there would be films about Jews.

Nope!

There is only one 1930s film about Jews, *The House of Rothschild*, produced by Darryl Zanuck, the lapsed Nebraska Methodist who made *Gentleman's Agreement*. Other than that, I assume that the writers didn't want to bring up anti–Semitism in a time of confusion and distress. Or perhaps there were other forces at work stifling Jewish stories.

One movie that stands out to me among all the others is Charlie Chaplin's *The Great Dictator* from 1940. In the movie, Chaplin parodies Adolf Hitler and renames him Adenoid Hynkel. He wears the thick mustache that both Chaplin and Hitler are famous for, and he essentially plays Hitler, ordering a "purge of the Jews" and for many to be sent to concentration camps. However, *The Great Dictator* was made long before the public knew just how appalling the treatment of Jews was at that time. Chaplin said he "would not have made the film" if he had known how Hitler was actually killing millions of innocent people and not just discriminating and hurting them. This information did not become public until years and years later. However, *The Great Dictator* still serves and holds up (for the most part) as a call for peace during a horrendously painful time for many people. In his famous final monologue, Chaplin wrote:

> In the name of democracy—let us use that [inner] power—let us all unite. Let us fight for a new world—a decent world that will give men a chance to work—that will give youth a future and old age security. By the promise of these things, brutes have risen to power. But they lie! They do not fulfill that promise. They never will!
>
> Dictators free themselves but they enslave the people! Now let us fight to fulfill that promise! Let us fight to free the world—to do away with national barriers—to do away with greed, hate, and intolerance. Let us fight for a world of reason, a world where science and progress will lead to all men's happiness. Soldiers! In the name of democracy, let us all unite!

Movies like *The Great Dictator* make you realize how little we have changed over 85 years. We still have war, we still have fighting, and we still have hate. It's very depressing, and it makes me sad considering the current situation with Gaza and Israel.

Most Holocaust survivors living in America during the 1950s did everything possible to avoid their past. In the book that psychologist (and my grandfather!) Robert Kraft wrote, titled *Memory Perceived: Recalling the Holocaust*, a survivor named Alan Z recalls his life in 1950s America: "I tried not to live with it [the Holocaust] all the time. Live a normal life with my wife. And this way we could build a family which was normal."[7] This attitude was extremely common. Even my great-grandparents named their kids Thomas and Peter (two names used in most cultures) so they wouldn't always be bullied for being the children of Jewish immigrants but also just in case Nazism arose in America.

The movies largely reflected this attitude of ignoring the Holocaust, too. After the war ended in 1945, it seems that Hollywood was not quick to make any films about the Holocaust until the mid–1950s. As with anything, there were outliers. *The Diary of Anne Frank* was made into a film in 1959, and then *The Pawnbroker*, about a man dealing with memories of the Holocaust while in America, came out in 1964. Other than that, barely any movies were made about the Holocaust until 1993's *Schindler's List*.

You might be asking yourself how this chapter connects to the theme of teenagers in this book: this is evident with Anne Frank. She changed the way people viewed the Holocaust, and she changed many, many people's attitudes toward Jews, simply by sharing her truth (or her dad sharing it for her). And that was largely because she was young, and therefore her opinions were new and fresh. Anne Frank taught the world that we all have the power to change minds through our truth. When we all share our experiences, we humanize ourselves and everyone else.

In the late 1940s after the war, two films about anti–Semitism caught the public's attention. There was *Gentleman's Agreement*, the story of a gentile journalist pretending to be Jewish for six months for the sake of an op-ed, and there was *Crossfire*, a claustrophobic noir about an anti–Semitic soldier who murders a Jewish war veteran. The latter was a B movie and didn't get too much attention at the time, but *Gentleman's Agreement* was a blockbuster, even winning Best Picture at the Academy Awards.

Gentleman's Agreement is an odd film to watch nowadays: it takes itself way too seriously, yet it makes some important points, while also being ... weird and problematic? In the film, Phil Green, played by Gregory Peck, is a journalist who's given a newspaper assignment to write about anti–Semitism. He searches for an angle and comes up with the idea to pretend to be Jewish and write about it. He begins to experience discrimination himself and also through his friend Dave's experiences. His new romantic relationship is complicated by the endeavor.

I was fascinated by the premise when I first watched the movie about two years ago, but I'm still hung up on the moral aspects of it. I don't think you should pretend to be someone you aren't for the sake of anything, but in this case, it's a novel experiment, I guess? The movie points out all the different ways that anti–Semitism affected Jews in the 1940s, but it doesn't seem as relevant now because Jews can do those things (e.g., get a hotel room). *Gentleman's Agreement* is, however, ahead of its time, just not *that* ahead of its time.

One part that is progressive even today is Phil's realization about his Jewish secretary, that she herself is anti–Semitic. Today, we still don't realize that people of any race can be racist, including against themselves. Phil's secretary Elaine is a possible example of a self-hating Jew.

There started to be more Jewish characters in movies in the late 1950s with *Marjorie Morningstar*, *The Ten Commandments*, and *Anne Frank*, although there were still very few. In the 1960s, Barbra Streisand's *Funny Girl* brought a new vision of Jewish women to the screen. The book *Talking Back: Images of Jewish Women in American Popular Culture* by Joyce Antler describes just how important this representation was. "Streisand is able to portray a character that is obviously Jewish, and in this role, she creates a space for the intelligent Jewish woman to be depicted. In this role, the Jewish woman was presented as smart, comedic, beautiful, and talented."[8] During the 1950s and 1960s, Jewish women were stereotyped as being dependent on men, but *Funny Girl* defied that. Technically, *Funny Girl* is (sort of) a Golden Age movie, but like *The Graduate*, it was released at the very end of the era, so it's debatable. But its relevance to today isn't. *Funny Girl* recently had a revival on Broadway, showcasing its timeless musical numbers, characters and storyline.

In the 1970s, Jewish performers, directors, writers, and comedians started embracing their Jewishness, with 80 percent of comedians at the time being Jewish![9] Still today, many very popular comedians are Jewish: Sarah Silverman, Amy Schumer, Jerry Seinfeld, to name just a few.

Woody Allen's films had Jewish humor at center stage while the mainstream appeal of *Fiddler on the Roof* and *The Frisco Kid* proved Jews' newfound relevance. The reason for this mainstream acceptance was the Civil Rights movement. While not commonly associated with Jews, Civil Rights did affect the way that all marginalized ethnic groups were treated, including Jewish people.

On September 30, 2021, the Academy Museum opened with exhibits and artifacts from *Citizen Kane*, *Casablanca*, and *The Wizard of Oz*. Major museum donors Cheryl and Haim Saban protested the museum's complete omission of the original Jewish founders of Hollywood.[10] "Why would the museum organizers, with $484 million and more than 300,000 square feet, decide to tell the story of the motion picture industry and neglect to mention the people who created it?" Rob Eshman wrote in an opinion piece in *The Forward* titled "Why Did the Academy Leave the Jews Out of Its Museum, Anyway?"

After many pointed this out, the Academy Museum started planning a new permanent exhibit, "Hollywoodland: Jewish Founders and the Making of a Movie Capital," which opened in May 2024. Many old Hollywood fans still don't know that Hollywood was essentially founded by Jews, and hopefully, the exhibit showcases just how important people like the Warner brothers and Louis B. Mayer were to Hollywood's golden age.

The entangled story of Jews and Hollywood is still going on, and as more time goes by, it becomes evident that you can't have one without the other. Next year in … Hollywood?

What Musicals Say About 1950s Subculture

Most people have seen a 1950s musical, whether it was *Singin' in the Rain, An American in Paris, Funny Face,* or *Guys and Dolls.* The musical genre exploded over the course of the decade, and these films are widely remembered today. But what many can't see is that every single one of these movie musicals says something about 1950s subculture—and oftentimes, the films are saying something very important that's relevant today. I won't be talking about many of the classic 1950s musicals: *Gentlemen Prefer Blondes, Guys and Dolls, Singin' in the Rain, Gigi, Pal Joey, A Star Is Born, Funny Face.* These are all extremely influential movies and I highly suggest you watch them on a plane sometime. This chapter will focus on the weird movies people don't remember as much and what they say about 1950s culture. There's real value in the movies that everyone forgets, which shows the real truth about the decade.

I'm not paying as much attention to classics people know today—of course, we'll talk about some of them, but I'm a believer that "classics" are only "classics" in hindsight.

Jayne Mansfield's publicity photograph from *Kiss Them for Me* in 1957 (20th Century–Fox) (Wikimedia Commons).

When these movies came out, they may have been huge! They're just not remembered by history for whatever reason.

History seems to have not remembered Jayne Mansfield, the Marilyn Monroe copycat of the late 1950s. Mansfield became a *Playboy* model after being rejected by studios because her boobs were too big.[1] I find that odd, considering that she became famous for them later on. Even today, there's a hilariously meme-able photo of Sophia Loren and Jayne Mansfield that circulates on Instagram. Please look it up!

Anyway—the reason I speak of Mansfield is not because of *that*. It's because she starred in the 1956 box office hit *The Girl Can't Help It*.

The movie is about Marty Murdock, who employs agent Tom Miller to make his girlfriend Jerri (Mansfield) a singing sensation. However, she can't sing a note. The plot reminds me of *Singin' in the Rain*, which also has a blonde who can't sing. I guess it was some kind of trend in the 1950s.

The Girl Can't Help It is a satire of rock and roll culture, and the entertainment magazine *Collider's* Kelcie Mattson even says that the Beatles wouldn't exist without this movie. "For 1950s audiences, *The Girl Can't Help It* was a literal cultural reset. Since full-length concert movies didn't exist and Elvis Presley had just one film credit under his belt, this otherwise mediocre comedy was the only way rock and roll fans could see their idols in the flesh," she wrote.[2]

While that alone was super influential in the meteoric rise of the Beatles eight years later, apparently John Lennon and Paul McCartney were also heavily inspired by seeing other artists in the film like Little Richard and Fats Domino. The group even opened for Little Richard in 1962, and he mentored them. *The Girl Can't Help It* inspired Lennon to start his own group, The Quarrymen, which evolved into the Beatles years later. So technically, this movie directly led to the formation of the most important band ever.

The movie also inspired other musical legends—it came out a year before Elvis's "Jailhouse Rock," which contains many similarities to "Rock Around the Rockpile," a musical number in *The Girl Can't Help It*. "Rockpile" seems to channel Elvis's style of dancing and singing, which had only recently become popular.

The Girl Can't Help It shows that Black artists were the backbone of rock and roll, even in a time when they were pigeonholed into R&B. While *The Girl* makes fun of the rock and roll movement, it also celebrates it at the same time. The movie was only supposed to be a vehicle for Jayne Mansfield that had a subplot about rock and roll—but

Old Films, Young Eyes

the result, according to music biographer Philip Norman, is the "most potent" exhibition of rock ever captured on film.[3]

Artists like Elvis and Johnny Cash spearheaded the rockabilly and the rock and roll revolution. The origins of this genre of music came from R&B and soul music, which white singers copied to make their careers. This wasn't just any normal musical phenomenon—it brought together teenagers of all races who rebelled against their parents. We talked about this in "How Classic Films Are Reflected in Today's Pop Culture Beach Party!" The musicals of the 1950s were very much classic or show tune–based until the late 1950s when they started to become rock and roll to capitalize on the huge cultural movement. This was largely started by *The Girl Can't Help It* but also with *Love Me Tender* and *Rock Around the Clock* the same year.

I won't go into what the 1960s movement entailed, because we already discussed that—but *The Girl Can't Help It* was a huge part of bringing rock into mainstream culture, which led to more social change. So even if Jayne Mansfield's character is a total bimbo, at least she (sort of) inspired change? Maybe.

This movie satirizes the music industry in a way that still holds up today. The way *The Girl* depicts the music industry as a mechanized factory of artificial talent is relevant today in a world of Reddit discourse about whether certain stars are "industry plants" (people who claim to be self-made but have tons of support from corporate partners). As much as the music industry then and now tries to commercialize and manufacture music, it will always be the best when it comes organically from people who want to do what they do because they love it.

Athena is another film that hints at themes of the 1950s. *Athena* is about Adam Shaw, a lawyer, who meets Athena Mulvain. She tells him that according to numerology, they'd be perfect together. Adam is already married, though. He gets to know her health-crazed family who owns a health food store and is eventually won over.

The portrayal of the Mulvain store is funny to me. The sisters all have Greek goddess names: Athena, Aphrodite, etc. There's also a strange fixation on sassafras. To me, this movie is such a clear satire of the health food industry—and the wellness industry in general, way before Gwyneth Paltrow's goop and the Peloton craze. The Mulvain family is anti-drugs, anti-alcohol, anti-sheepskins in the house, pretty much anti-anything you can think of. The movie, while mostly about relationships, situates the running of the health food store as an interesting background plot, where regular customers come into a very zany scene.

What Musicals Say About 1950s Subculture

This sets up people who are skeptical of the health fads against the people who back them. I'm not going to lie—the health food store is not too different from today. All you would need to make it seem modern is some acai powder, turmeric pills, and gua sha stones on a shelf or something.

Athena's grandfather shows Adam all of the men he's training to become body builders. He makes them meditate, lift weights, and perform other exercises to train for the Mr. Universe contest. The Mulvain family believes in astrology and numerology, and they routinely predict things by asking people when they were born. I really do not like astrology—it's not real.

Athena is relevant today because most of the practices of the Mulvain family still hold up. For example, they are vegetarian and they eat bean burgers instead of beef. This movie came out decades before burgers made out of plant-based materials were actually widespread. Adam thinks the way they eat is unheard of, and, naturally, he starts smoking.

"If Mr. Shaw wants to commit suicide, that's his choice. I only prefer that you don't do it in my house," Grandpa Mulvain says about smoking. This attitude was also new, because it would be confirmed only in the following years that smoking causes lung cancer.

When Adam gets mad, the grandpa says: "That comes from eating too much meat. If people only ate more sensible foods like nuts and berries, they'd behave more like plants and flowers and more like animals!" Athena's grandpa needs to be goop's advertiser.

Vegetarianism was not very popular in the United States until the early 1970s, so I was surprised that in the 1950s, of all decades, there would be a film that showcases that lifestyle, especially since the 1950s lifestyle was all about the new processed foods and TV dinners. I wonder what the intention behind this film's focus on different diets and lifestyles was about.

This film's musical numbers are largely forgettable, but its two female stars are some of my favorite musical stars ever: Jane Powell and Debbie Reynolds. Reynolds most famously starred in *Singin' in the Rain* two years before *Athena*, and she performed in many great musicals over the decades. Powell was one of the best dancers of the studio era and romped around with Fred Astaire in the 1940s. *Athena*'s musical numbers make the movie more entertaining, especially the ones set in the health food store.

Overall, this film isn't my favorite, but I think the most interesting part is the portrayal of "insane" healthy people and their habits in the 1950s, especially in a time when these attitudes weren't yet mainstream.

Another sardonically 1950s musical is *It's Always Fair Weather*, one of the few truly satirical musicals of its time. It could be the only musical that is truly depressing at times. It tackles the story of three former World War II soldiers, Ted, Doug, and Angie, who, in front of a doubting bartender in October 1945, agree that they will meet back up at the same place in October 1955. They end the night with a total binge, trotting on garbage can lids and pledging eternal friendship as they eye their future prospects and imagine their coming success, drunk to excess.

When those 10 years pass, the three men convene at the bar and realize they have not achieved what they wanted—one's an ad man getting divorced, one runs a diner, and the other is just a gambler (he wanted to be a senator). They don't get along very well, and none are content with their lives. So much for their youthful dreams! The movie deals with the depressing aftermath of World War II, marriage, friendship, and, of course, TV. The most telling plotline of the film that foreshadows today's image-obsessed social media landscape is when two television executives (one is the alluring Cyd Charisse) overhear them and scheme to do a story on their reunion. After many hijinks and darts lobbed at advertising and TV, which has purportedly killed the true art of theater, one of the former soldiers admits on air that all he's gotten from the reunion with his pals is the understanding that he's just become ... a loser. While its bleak themes may have hurt it box office–wise, in modern times we can look back at *It's Always Fair Weather* as a reflection of the darker parts of the 1950s.

While we commonly regard scenes of rebellious kids dancing around to rock and roll as the cultural touchstone of the 1950s and 1960s, this was also a time of hardship for many parents and older people, especially considering that the 1950s were just a short time from one of the most grueling and destructive wars in history. Despite the fact that we now have a "trauma-informed" culture, we rarely reflect on the PTSD much of the population had back in the '50s, do we?

It's always odd talking about Gene Kelly (the star of *It's Always Fair Weather*) because for some reason Millennial and Gen X women are *obsessed* with this "guy next door." My former principal at my old school used to talk to me about classic movies: "My favorite old movie star? Oh, I just love Gene Kelly. I mean, I love him. I actually do. I've seen every one of his movies and ahhh [she looks up at the ceiling lovingly]. What of his have you seen?"

And then I would just reply *"Singin' in the Rain"*—which ended the conversation.

What Musicals Say About 1950s Subculture

I find it so funny that multiple women I've met have been obsessed with him. I think he's an amazing dancer, but I find it rather random!

The satire most aligned with the time was *It's Always Fair Weather*'s scathing critique of television. TV is depicted as something shallow, foolish, and stupid in the film. I guess this reflects the attitudes at the time—people publicly proclaimed that TV was inane and cited its negative influence on young people, but they secretly watched *I Love Lucy* every Monday night, eagerly waiting for the next one to air. TV was the ultimate guilty pleasure.

Aside from the satire, *It's Always Fair Weather* is just a great musical. Cyd Charisse is an incredible dancer, as usual, and the dance numbers are incredibly innovative, especially "Baby, You Knock Me Out," which takes place in a boxing ring. And Cyd Charisse is wearing heels while dancing better than anyone alive ever could.

They don't make musical numbers like that anymore. I adore the other decades in musicals (especially the '30s and '40s ones), but I find that the 1950s have the most potent satirical themes. Throughout the entire decade, the musical made fun of every single aspect of the subculture, whether it was fitness obsession, comic books, the music industry, or depressing former soldiers (OK, I admit that's out of place). Ultimately, the music (and musicals) of a time period can be picked apart and analyzed for details about what people did, loved, hated, and felt in any given time. If TikTok songs and dances are like today's "musicals," what will future audiences take from them in 60 years? Maybe that teenagers loved chicken wings, hot dogs and baloney? Or more likely that we swore a lot.

What I can learn from obscure 1950s musicals is that movies of any given time perfectly articulate what it was like living in that time: people's mannerisms, the way they talked, the way they danced, and the way they lived. This is exactly why, as John Sullivan in the 1941 Preston Sturges film *Sullivan's Travels* said, "film is the greatest educational medium the world has ever known." And this is why it's so interesting to study film: because film imitates life, and life has changed so much. To quote another famous musical, *It's a Whole New World*!

The 1950s Housewife

She's good at cooking. She respects her husband, probably too much. She is happy with her life yet aspires to something more. But only for her husband, and only for her children. *Not* for herself.

The typical 1950s housewife stereotype depicts an obedient servant with no aspirations, goals, or hopes besides those for others. This is how domestic life ran in the 1950s. A lot of women enjoyed having babies and cooking and cleaning—but a lot of women felt stuck in an abusive or unhealthy relationship or felt they were slaves to their husbands and kids, got bored, and longed for careers.

The thing about being a housewife is that the mothers and wives who were in this position had no financial independence—they couldn't leave their relationships easily because their husbands were the breadwinners. In my opinion, true freedom and equality for women means financial independence. But it also means that women get to do what they want to do, and that doesn't just include a career. It can include a family, a husband, and even a 1950s-style life. *As long as that's what she wants.* If that woman is truly happy doing what she is doing, then what is the real problem?

What was really driving those seemingly happy, smiley women in glamorous dresses and heels while in the kitchen? In this chapter, I'll highlight the role of the housewife in 1950s pop culture, the backlash, and the effect in generations after.

She was born out of the war's end, which led to the baby boom and the food surplus, and was depicted in many movies. Most movies from the 1950s, actually. And her creation stemmed from the war. As I'll talk about in depth when we travel back to the 1940s, the Second World War was an incredibly desperate time for the United States, so desperate, in fact, that women started working. You may be familiar with Rosie the Riveter, the character from a 1940s government-issued poster, which is now a ubiquitous feminist image (more on that in the next chapter).

The 1950s Housewife

After the war ended and the men came home, women were expected to go back to their usual position as the caretakers of the household, because the men made the money.

Since everything needed to live a stable, normal life was taken away from most people during World War II, after the war ended, there was a need for material and cultural items. For complicated economic reasons, there was a surplus—for example, food, which we'll talk about in "A Cultural History of the 'It Girl.'" But in this case, the surplus also meant babies. Men came back from the war and wanted kids, and the women obeyed. Obedience—I will do what you want, because you hold my fate in your hands. That was the reality that unhappy housewives had to face. And yet in '50s cinema, these women were depicted as "happy housewife heroines," like Betty Friedan wrote in her 1963 book *The Feminine Mystique*. Friedan encapsulates the housewife life perfectly in her book, which is a work of genius. Each suburban wife struggles with it alone. As she made the beds, shopped for groceries, matched slipcover material, ate peanut butter sandwiches with her children, chauffeured Cub Scouts and Brownies, lay beside her husband at night—she was afraid to ask even of herself the silent question: "Is this all?" And the "Is this all?" is what makes the housewife such a well-known figure. She's subtly unhappy and not rageful, but she longs for true meaning and fulfillment.

And the 1950s was the childhood setting for those kids that came out of the baby boom. For the most part, the mothers were obliged to stay home and care for these children for the entire decade.

Naturally, a lot of women wanted careers, but the only acceptable ones were caretaker of children (nanny or babysitter), teacher, nurse, secretary, and, occasionally, actress. Many famous actresses' families were not happy with their career decision. One example that comes to mind is Claudette Colbert, whose family shut her out after she decided to work on Broadway.

The one performer I can think of who was pigeonholed into the 1950s housewife role for most of her movie career is Doris Day. Day's image in the early 1950s was that of a "girl next door." While the audience might view Day as one of them, a counterpart, they viewed Marilyn Monroe as apart from them. Monroe was the 1950s version of a "slut" and lots of people didn't like what she meant for women. So let's define the difference between these two female figures who elicited opposite responses.

Day emits a subtle cynicism in all of her characters that reminds

me of how Ginger Rogers acts in the beginning of nearly all of the Astaire and Rogers films. Take *Swing Time*, for example. Ginger completely rejects Fred, and even though he is over the moon to do anything for her, she just wants him to go away. Let's compare this to Day in *Teacher's Pet*. The character played by Clark Gable chases Day and lies to her just to get her to even tolerate him. Day is open-minded but at the same time doesn't take things too seriously, and she plainly hates him. If this movie had Monroe in the lead role, instead of those attitudes, she most likely would have affected an attitude of flirtation. It's that subtle detail of completely going along with everything men want that made Monroe's reputation and gave Day the opposite one.

Day, however, actually hated her image and her whole movie career was plagued by who people thought she was. Sound similar to anyone? Monroe, maybe? So despite the differences, they both ended up unhappy with what they came to represent.

Another film—of the many—that displays Day as a housewife is *Please Don't Eat the Daisies*. Lawrence MacKay, a drama professor, leaves his job to become a theater critic. His new fame causes trouble with his three sons and wife Kate. Kate becomes increasingly jealous of frivolous Broadway star Deborah Vaughn, a woman Lawrence has been seeing.

The way this film uses Kate's jealousy toward other women and her husband creates even more of a narrative of Day being just the girl next door. This brings us closer to Kate's struggles and helps us to feel like she's reaching for something she doesn't have, just like us, just like everyone.

Day's character Kate has four boys in this movie, which I would just hate to have. Can you imagine the stress? And along with that, she has to handle her husband who is achieving success for the first time, and I can only imagine how jealous she is with her husband out enjoying parties and plays while she has to stay home caring for the rowdy children. Day never seems to rebel in any way. She just handles what is put in front of her graciously, making her the perfect example of how women were supposed to act in the 1950s.

In contrast, the happy side to this era was *I Love Lucy*, which was a huge television sitcom. The show was the top television program in the United States for four straight years and is widely known as the most popular television show of the 1950s and beyond.

Opposite: **The poster for *Please Don't Eat the Daisies*, Doris Day's film from 1960 (MGM) (Wikimedia Commons).**

Lucille Ball plays Lucy Ricardo, an off-the-wall, quirky housewife whose husband, Ricky, is a bandleader. They live next to their best friends, another couple, Fred and Ethel Mertz. *I Love Lucy* makes staying at home all day seem fun because of the antics Lucy gets into with her best friend. I'd like to highlight a specific episode of the TV show where Lucy switches places with Ricky and works while he stays home.

"Job Switching" was the first episode of the second season of *I Love Lucy*, and it aired on September 14, 1952. At the beginning of the episode, Ricky says, "Having a job is a lot more difficult than lying around the house all day long." Saying that obviously leads to some questioning and grumbling, which leads to the women and the men switching jobs. The men stay at home cooking and cleaning, and the women attempt to get jobs. "Do you think this man can really get jobs for us? We don't know how to do anything!" Ethel and Lucy ask each other in the unemployment office. Lucy's makeup is cakey, she has fake eyelashes on, and

(From left) Desi Arnaz, Lucille Ball, Vivian Vance, and William Frawley in *I Love Lucy*, which ran from 1951 through 1957 (CBS Television) (Wikimedia Commons).

her lips are accentuated in their usual bow shape. She and Ethel are making faces at the employment guy, who gives them a job at a chocolate factory.

After a day of switching jobs and pretending they made food they ordered in, Ricky and Fred pull out chocolates to apologize to their wives and admit that housework is harder than they thought. I got the feeling that men and women have their different roles for a reason; they're good at them. I didn't particularly like that idea, because it made it seem like men are horrible cooks and that all women are good at is cooking and cleaning. If you watch this episode, it'll help you gain an understanding of the overwhelming social constructs of the time that had to be followed. But at least Lucy was pointing them out with her comedy.

The Mindy Project, Mindy Kaling's Fox sitcom from the 2010s, had a very similar episode to the Lucy one. In a season 4 episode, Mindy is sick of trying to be the perfect stay-at-home mom for her boy Leo, and so she switches jobs with her husband Danny—she goes to work and he stays at home. And while he initially excels at it, he is revealed to have used his mom for help. This parallel to *I Love Lucy* shows the housewife's perpetual relevance.

The 1950s housewife is just as present outside of 1950s media as it is in the decade itself. Even three commercially successful recent projects centered on her: the hit TV series *The Marvelous Mrs. Maisel*, the controversial film *Don't Worry Darling*, and the series *Lessons in Chemistry*, based on the best-selling book.

Don't Worry Darling is about Jack and Alice, a couple in the 1950s who live in a community called Victory. It's an experimental town that makes men work on a secret project. Alice and the other women seem to lead perfect lives, with their husbands working as they stay at home. When the cracks begin to form in their idyllic lives, Alice questions what Victory really is—and what those men are actually doing.

While a film about female oppression in the 1950s sounded like a good idea initially, the movie couldn't even stay true to the actual time period. In one scene, Alice is shown wearing only a man's button-down shirt outside her house, and another woman is shown bathing poolside topless—two things that *never* would've happened in a 1950s film ... or in the 1950s.

A better portrayal of the '50s housewife came a couple years prior with *The Marvelous Mrs. Maisel*. As a Jewish woman from New York, Miriam Maisel is expected to go to college, meet a "nice Jewish boy," get married and have children. I enjoyed watching this, because it was exactly what my great-grandmother and my female Jewish relatives went through at the time.

This series starts similarly to *Don't Worry Darling*—in the beginning, Miriam (Midge) has everything she's ever wanted, until the cracks start to form and her husband Joel leaves her for another woman. Instead of dealing with it "normally," she decides to become a stand-up comedian.

The pilot begins with Midge's toast at her own wedding, and she talks about how her "ultimate dream was to meet a man. A perfect man." She also discusses how she starved herself for three weeks to fit into her wedding dress. Everything about the pilot is incredibly 1950s, down to a reference to Katharine Hepburn in the first scene.

Mrs. Maisel is a surprisingly accurate depiction of what being a housewife in the 1950s may have truly looked like: from the fashions to the cooking, cleaning, cheating husbands, and dreams of a career. One scene I found incredibly interesting was the scene when Midge and Joel go to sleep, and she's in her makeup. Once Joel falls asleep, she puts on a mask and curlers and goes to bed. Then, 10 minutes before he wakes up in the morning, she gets up and does her makeup, undoes her curlers, gets back in bed, and pretends she never did anything. To me, this represents the narrative back then and still today that women have to look perfect all the time. Just like with *Don't Worry Darling*, there's a glossy shine to her life: the pastel perfect kitchens, perfect hair, no repeated outfits. And yet underneath, there's way more going on than what appears.

I much prefer watching comedy TV shows in my free time, but I enjoyed the new lens on the 1950s that the show provides, and I look forward to watching more of it.

I remember walking into a bookstore early last year and picking up the book *Lessons in Chemistry*. I thought that the premise (of a woman in the 1950s who starts a cooking show) was intriguing and was excited to see how it played out. The book is about Elizabeth Zott, a chemist in a department filled with sexist men. Disappointed by her current career, Zott turns to an unlikely pastime: hosting her own cooking show on television.

I thought that the book's portrayal of a woman in a male-dominated profession felt extremely relatable today—and when I found out it was being made into a television series for Apple TV, I was excited. The television series feels an equal amount genius as it does clichéd—there are a lot of forced lines, as when Dr. Calvin Evans tells Elizabeth, "To assume that [you were a secretary] was wrong and buffoonish." I thought that was a bit odd. The problem with depicting a bygone era you didn't experience is that you cannot possibly get everything right, because you haven't experienced it firsthand. And that's the only real problem I find with these new 1950s stories: they feel a bit removed from what the actual era looked like and more of a caricature of popular media around that time reflected through today's lens. I don't blame anyone for that, though. *Lessons in Chemistry* was thoroughly enjoyable and I recommend it. But once again ... '50s movies are better at helping you understand the time period.

All of these examples reflect the struggle of women to define the terms of their own happiness. But what the 1950s housewife truly symbolizes is oppression in its purest form: when society was so repressed that you could do nothing else in your life other than cook, clean, and care for children, even when you had dreams you wanted to achieve. When I see these women, I not only feel sorry for them, but I also hope they know how much better things are today (albeit not perfect). I hope all restrained and used women who were forced into things they did not want to do know that, today, we acknowledge them for what they did—because it was just as important as what their husbands did.

No matter how stressful, lonely and unfulfilling some of these women's lives were, they did it for us—so that we can do what we want to do, right now.

The 1940s Working Girl

She's standing, flexing her arm. She's got a blue work suit on and a red polka-dotted bandana wrapped across her head. "We Can Do It!" she's saying on the poster, talking to the women of the United States.

Rosie the Riveter stands for women's empowerment in a time when it wasn't socially acceptable. The famous wartime poster was released as propaganda, trying to get women into the workforce during World War II. The image was created in 1942, at the height of the war. When global conflict happens, countries need to utilize their entire workforce to defeat their enemies— "We Can Do It!" refers to women being able to join the workforce during the war.

Surprisingly, Rosie the Riveter didn't become a feminist image until the 1980s. The poster disappeared for four decades after being used briefly in the 1940s—so it seems it only became the symbol it is today with time. However, *Rosie the Riveter* was a film from 1944, so the name was already known.

Naturally, this new age of working women in the war was reflected in film, because even though it isn't widely accepted, film is essentially propaganda, and it can help us see what was frowned upon, what was good, and what was expected of women at any point in time.

Rosie the Riveter is a cheaper remake of *The More the Merrier*, a film released the previous year, 1943. *The More the Merrier* is about a working woman, Connie, who rents her apartment out, as it's her "patriotic duty" because of the housing shortage during the war. Connie thinks she will get a female roommate, but instead, she gets two male roommates. Connie is engaged, but she becomes interested in one of her roommates, Joel McCrea's character. This movie is considered one of the best comedies of the 1940s, and it's far superior to *Rosie the Riveter.*

When Mr. Benjamin Dingle storms into her apartment without asking and decides to live there, he also invades her personally. "Why

The 1940s Working Girl

The "Rosie the Riveter" poster from the World War II era (War Production Board. Wikimedia Commons).

aren't you married?" he asks her before bed. They're both in their striped pajamas, but they look very different because Dingle (I keep saying that because, what a last name!). He has a huge pot belly, and Connie's clothes are perfectly tailored.

"Maybe I don't want to get married," she says. A shocking revelation for her time.

"Well, maybe you do," Benjamin says. Connie is confused and annoyed.

Then he starts yelling metaphorically about "manning the torpedoes" and getting a husband, so she shuts him out and tells him it's none of his business.

"These days, everybody's business is everybody's business. War brings people together, you know," he says. She shuts the door. This scene showcases just how much power Benjamin has over Connie, even though he's in *her* house. He can intrude in her room, ask her personal questions and be incredibly rude, and he doesn't feel bad at all.

Unlike some other 1940s movies, the time period cannot be separated from *The More the Merrier*. The situation simply wouldn't work—the movie heavily refers to the war.

The housing crisis in World War II was a serious issue, and yet this movie still manages to spin it in a funny way. You know it's a good movie when it makes fun of real problems and still manages to make you laugh.

Connie and her friends all carpool together to work at 7:32 a.m. (she's very precise). While this scene is brief, it showcases how women during the war supported each other in their new careers and endeavors.

The fashion in *The More the Merrier* also reflects the war. In one scene, Jean Arthur (Connie) wears a crop top, a fashion created in the 1930s and 1940s due to the fabric shortage. This was particularly popular in the 1940s when fabric was low in stock. Stockings and tights were also at an all-time low, and to create the appearance of tights, women would draw a line down their calves with a pen to look like seams on stockings.

The typical 1940s working girl lives with her friends in an apartment in New York, pulling together every cent to go dancing or go to a movie. As I talked about in the last chapter, this was a response to the war, but I think it was also because women were fed up with having to stay at home and care for their husbands. They saw the war as an opportunity to pitch in for their country at a convenient time.

The reason *The More the Merrier* isn't my favorite 1940s working girl film is because every one of the characters is pretty unlikable to me, starting with the two men who think they can just live in Connie's house. I also don't see anything I haven't seen before in Connie. She's kind of a neat freak and that's all there is to her. What this film does well is display a comical approach to the events of the early 1940s in America. I can definitely see why people love this movie.

The 1940s Working Girl

In 2023, I went to see *His Girl Friday* in the theater, which was a great experience. The film centers on Hildy Johnson and her ex-husband Walter Burns, who both work as reporters. Burns tries to lure her away from a suburban, domestic (boring) life with a stable (boring) husband by pulling her into the case of a convicted murderer to make them fall in love again. It was so fun to watch in a theater because of the audience's reactions to the snappy dialogue. I felt like I was right there in that wood-paneled newspaper office with Hildy and Walter. And the boring fiancé, too. We can't forget about the boring fiancé.

The dialogue in this film is so fast that the screenplay is probably 300 pages long. The film depicts the hardships for women of choosing career over family, especially during a war, showing how women *could* be good at jobs that they weren't stereotypically proficient at. It shows how sometimes, women truly want a career, for reasons other than filling in during a war or trying to meet a husband. It can be so rewarding!

My great-grandmother Lillian was a working girl in the 1940s and then became a 1950s housewife—like many women at the time—so I have some interesting stories about her life. Grandma Lil worked with the government during the Roosevelt and Truman administrations, but then got married to my great-grandpa Al after three weeks of dating and quit her job to be a mother (to my grandpa!). So I can't say I'm disappointed.

The 1940s city girl life is depicted masterfully in *Kitty Foyle*, one of my favorite films. It was originally subtitled *The Natural History of a Woman*, which is very fitting. It's a complete time capsule of work, life, and love in the 1940s for women. It can be a bit sappy at times but in an ironic way, at least to me. Kitty (Ginger Rogers) works and lives with her friends and dreams of a better life. She represents the unsure woman. She doesn't know what she wants, but she goes on. An example of her ambivalence is the love triangle in this film: Kitty must choose between marrying a poor doctor or running away with her long-lost love to South America. This is representative of the 1940s working girl. She doesn't know when the war will end, and she doesn't know who she'll end up with, where she'll live, or what she'll end up doing. With all this uncertainty, she has to be practical most of the time. But she has fun anyway. In these working girl films, despite their emotional weight, I love the scenes of these women with their friends. Seeing female friendship in classic films is one of my favorite aspects of watching them—usually, these films feature a woman and a man or two men in a business setting. Seeing non-romantic and non-working relationships play out on screen feels unexpected and interesting.

Ginger Rogers on the cover of *Life* magazine for her movie *Kitty Foyle* in 1940 (Wikimedia Commons).

Another one of my favorite films featuring the prototypical 1940s working girl is *My Sister Eileen*, which is about two sisters who move to New York to achieve their dreams. One, Ruth (played by Rosalind Russell), wants to be a journalist, and the other, Eileen (Janet Blair), wants to be an actress.

The film is mostly physical comedy jokes, but it also has important dialogues about working women. When I first watched this, I noticed a lot of deep metaphors that relate to how hard it was for women to have careers in the '40s. In one of the first scenes, the Sherwood sisters are trying to open a storage locker they rented and are really struggling. A guy comes over and opens it as if it was the easiest thing in the world. This is a precursor to the entire film, with a big part of the movie always being that women needed men and, to some extent, still do to succeed professionally. This is one of the first times this film uses symbolism to subtly make a point.

There's another big moment later in the film where a newspaperman takes Ruth out to dinner. The only reason Ruth goes out with him is that she knows she needs his support as the owner of the magazine to succeed—even if he talks her ear off and doesn't even let her answer the questions he asks. This moment in the film shows how women had to and still have to put up with whatever men give them so as not to be labeled as controlling, mean, or even unattractive, a sentiment that was given huge attention in the famous "cognitive dissonance" speech that America Ferrera's character gives in *Barbie*.

There are small moments that underscore this idea of women in the workplace. In one scene, Ruth is at a job interview, and her heels keep coming off. There's a closeup of her grappling to keep them on while looking composed—which I thought was such a good way to describe the struggles of working as a woman.

There's a theory that when the world is in crisis, the height of women's heels goes up. This is evidenced by the heel height increasing in the 1930s, when the stock market crashed, and heel heights going up with the popularity of the platform shoe in the 1970s corresponding with the Vietnam War.[1] So there's a very real chance that working women in the 1940s were adjusting to higher heels than before, especially with the platform heel being invented in the late 1930s and rising to popularity in the 1940s with actresses like Carmen Miranda wearing them.

One more of my favorite 1940s working girl films is *Woman of the Year* starring Katharine Hepburn and Spencer Tracy. This movie was the first that starred the two, and they went on to make nine films together including one we already talked about, *Guess Who's Coming to Dinner*.

Woman of the Year is about Tess Harding, a journalist with progressive ideas, and Sam Craig, a man with conservative beliefs. When they begin to date, gender roles go out the window in an interesting battle of the sexes.

I watched *Woman of the Year* with my sister on a tiny TV in my living room one afternoon. My sister is obsessed with Katharine Hepburn, and a couple of years ago, we watched most of her films together. *Adam's Rib* was incredible, *Alice Adams* was great, and *Bringing Up Baby* was our favorite.

Katharine Hepburn is the quintessential 1940s working girl. When I think of the 1940s, I think of her. I know it's not like that for everyone—most people think of war and disaster when they think of the '40s, but I think she's somewhat representative of that time. Instead of sitting there for men to look at like Rita Hayworth did, she wore pants and she advocated for women's rights.

Hepburn was very different, and her career suffered in the late

1930s because of that. She was even labeled "box office poison" after several flops. At the lowest point of her career, she decided to return to Broadway, and Philip Barry wrote her a play called *The Philadelphia Story*. The play ran for more than 400 performances. When the play was finished with its run, Hepburn aimed to create a movie that would abolish her status as "box office poison" and so she purchased the film rights to the play. She sold the rights to MGM and had the power to decide the screenwriter, director and cast. When I think of someone who is still relevant today, I think Katharine Hepburn is the #1 choice. Her feminist principles, beliefs and mannerisms may have been impolite at the time, but today, they hold up.

About *Woman of the Year*: the movie is comedy gold, but it also came in the middle of the war (1942) when it was generally acceptable for women to be working. And as a result, it's the perfect 1940s working girl film. There are suits, there is Katharine Hepburn, there's Spencer Tracy, and there's lots of inappropriate indoor smoking. What's not to love?

What makes *Woman of the Year* a perfect romantic comedy? It has opposite romantic leads in terms of personality and political beliefs—a plot technique that was very common in screwball comedies. In most popular romantic comedies, there's some kind of rift between the two protagonists that keeps them apart. Otherwise, what's interesting about it? Hepburn's character Tess Harding is incredibly smart and hard-working. In one early scene, she starts speaking a million different languages, and Sam just sits there. You can see in his eyes: *I only know English...!!!*

Tess asks Sam on dates, receives awards (Woman of the Year), and gives him gifts: a reversal of the sexes. With every small thing that Tess does, the roles reverse a little more, tipping Sam further and further in the wrong direction.

The Hepburn films are not typical 1940s working girl films. In most of these movies, the working girl isn't opposed to traditional roles; she's just trying to work because of the war. That's what makes Katharine Hepburn stand out among others: she was willing to push back.

In my opinion, the best of Hepburn and Tracy's movies is *Adam's Rib*, another film with Hepburn in a working role. *Adam's Rib* is about Adam, a prosecution lawyer, and Amanda, a defense attorney. They get assigned to the same case where a woman shoots her cheating husband. The couple's trial causes rifts in their household, with each side not giving up to prove their point.

The 1940s Working Girl

Katharine Hepburn in 1942's *Woman of the Year* (MGM) (Wikimedia Commons).

The title is biblical—in some versions, it says that God created Eve out of Adam's rib. But in later versions, it says that the two were created equal. *Adam's Rib* is a showdown between the sexes: who came first? Or in other words, who wears the pants in your family?

When I first watched the film, it seemed unusual that Amanda, instead of being a housewife, is a defense lawyer. Especially since *Adam's Rib* is from 1949, four years after the war ended. The fact that she's still working and not "tending to the household" is revolutionary. It may be the fact that they don't have children together, but even *that* wouldn't justify a woman working in the late '40s.

The court case seems a bit odd today because the double standards Hepburn tells the jury about (a man can cheat and a woman can't) don't exist now. Today it's more about how cheating is wrong for both sides. Judy Holliday (one of my favorite actresses) has an incredible performance in this movie. Following *Adam's Rib*, she got cast in *Born Yesterday*, for which she won a Best Actress Oscar in 1951.

There are so many other 1940s working girl movies I could talk

Katharine Hepburn and Spencer Tracy in 1949's *Adam's Rib* (MGM) (Wikimedia Commons).

about, but while writing this chapter, I asked myself one question: What is the importance of this era of women today? Why do we still talk about them? Aside from the fashion and the seminal images of the 1940s working girl, it comes down to a thirst for freedom that lies inside of everyone, even seemingly happy women whose only goals were to become mothers before the war.

The working girl gives me, as a teenager, endless inspiration. She has everlasting importance (like in modern shows such as *Sex and the City* or *Girls*) because she represents more than just one of us. No matter what a woman wants to do, there will be obstacles along the way, and when that image of Rosie the Riveter looks up at me, flexing strong arms and all, telling me that I can do it, I can't help but listen to her.

"No law says you've got to be happy"

The Pessimism of Film Noir and Why the "Genre" No Longer Exists

As Mary Astor tells an upset Van Heflin in 1949's *Act of Violence*, "Relax. No law says you've got to be happy." This encapsulates the entire genre of film noir in one (two) sentences.

When I think of film noir, I think of shadowy gunshots, stressed men with gas stains on their suits, femme fatales with blonde wigs that don't look good on them, depression, and pessimism. Not my favorite things. But the genre still has an inexplicable allure to it—especially nowadays when these types of films fizzled out a long time ago. In this chapter, I'll be discussing my favorite film noirs, the melancholy approach these films take, and why the genre no longer exists in the same form in the current film landscape.

Film noir was a genre created in retrospect; even today, students and teachers of the genre don't agree on what qualifies as film noir. Some say that the look makes the noir genre, the shadows, darkness, and urban settings, but ultimately, it's a philosophy more than anything else: a pessimistic quality about the unpredictability of situations and fate.

One of my favorite noir films is *Dark Passage*, the 1947 Bogart and Bacall movie about Vincent, an innocent man accused of killing his wife, who escapes jail and stays with a woman, Irene, who finds him on the side of the road. The movie is one of my favorites for two reasons: it has beautiful shots of San Francisco, the city I grew up in, and it has *the* Lauren Bacall. Obviously!

Film critic Bosley Crowther described Bacall in the movie as "a sharp-eyed, knows-what-she-wants girl," which I think completely describes her in this movie. She's more caring than she is in the other

Lauren Bacall and Humphrey Bogart in *Dark Passage* publicity photograph from 1947 (Warner Bros.) (Wikimedia Commons).

noir films with Bogart, and it really suits her. You can tell the character of Irene is much closer to Bacall's actual personality.

Dark Passage uses the subjective camera technique, where a scene or a shot in a movie is from the character's perspective. The first scenes in the movie are shot as if the viewer is Vincent, and the subjective camera is used so that the crew didn't have to hire a different actor or change Bogart's face for the scenes that happen before he gets plastic surgery to hide his recognizable "criminal" face.

This technique was used previously in *Dr. Jekyll and Mr. Hyde* from 1931, *Lady in the Lake*, some brief scenes in *The Graduate* and 1927's *Napoleon*, among many other films.

What makes *Dark Passage* a noir film (besides the name)? To me, it has more to do with the time the film was made than any specific plots in the movie. The late 1940s were still a dark time, because the world had to recover from extremely traumatic events. *Dark Passage*'s lighting is shadowy and dramatic, and it's obviously in black and white, which accentuates contrast. The plot—like most noir films—is about crime and murder with a hint of romance. Most define it as a crime genre with cynical characters, many flashbacks, shadow lighting, and existentialist philosophies.

With a genre that emerges and disappears so fast, it's interesting to examine why these movies came to be. Following the Great Depression and World War II, many were not optimistic about the future, due to the horrifying 15 or more years behind them (from the stock crash in 1929 to the war's end in 1945). Out of people's attitudes came films with this approach. It was either that people wanted to escape into a Technicolor Judy Garland musical dreamland for two hours, or they wanted to watch a hard-boiled, cynical movie about how we're all doomed and everybody's going to get murdered. Pretty rough, huh? If women went to the musicals and men went to the noirs, we could be looking at a post-war gender gap in terms of entertainment preferences.

Crime novels were increasingly popular in the 1930s, and many wanted to make these novels into films a couple of years later in the 1940s. This was another reason why film noir was so popular during that decade—the creators had excellent source material.[1]

Film scholars argue about whether film noir is truly its own genre or whether it was too specific, and so it only qualifies as a style of filmmaking. Noir was influenced by German expressionism, a way of painting, poetry, and, eventually, film that presents the world from a subjective perspective, often tinting it and distorting it to evoke certain ideas or moods. As opposed to a realistic, portrait-style type of art, German Expressionists used vivid colors, distorted reality, and artistic form to express feelings of discomfort around the state of the world.

I know this is complicated, but think about the depressed and negative narrators of many noir films. Is this how the world actually was? Probably not. It's simply their perspective. With the rise of Hitler in Germany, many German artists moved to the United States, and this could be why film noir is influenced by German expressionism.

I have a close connection to this period, because my great-grandfather Hans Elias[2] was a German Jewish painter and doctor who emigrated from Germany in the late 1930s to the United States with my great-grandmother due to the Nazi reign in Germany.

Germany was not the only foreign influence on film noir—Italy also inspired many noirs. Italian neo-realism is a film style that centers on lower-class people and stories, many quasi-documentary or influenced by real life. The films were gritty and real, often without "professional" actors, and shot in real low-class neighborhoods vs. on sets like in Hollywood. New genres and styles often emerge from a mixture of cultures, as we talked about in "New Hollywood: How Two Movies Inspired a Whole New Generation of Filmmakers." Noir was a mixture of Italian, German, and American styles. It seems that some people were happy with the new depressing genre, and others hated it. By 1947, many realized Hollywood's new turn. "Whoever went to the movies with any regularity during 1946 was caught amid Hollywood's profound postwar affection for morbid drama. From January through December, deep shadows, clutching hands, exploding revolvers, sadistic villains and heroines tormented with deeply rooted diseases of the mind flashed across the screen in a panting display of psychoneurosis, unsublimated sex, and murder most foul,"[3] Donald Marshman wrote in *LIFE* in August 1947. Seems like Donald wasn't a fan.

Just as *Gidget* and the beach party genre essentially invented marketing toward teens, noir re-invented the word and classification of what a teenager is. An anonymous blogger on classicfilmnoir.com wrote: "The shift which film noir brought to the moral landscape of America in the 1940s comprises of so many complexities brought up through the cracks, suggested a richer, wilder and more dangerous life ahead for the world. Film noir even birthed the teenager by discussing generational stress, often by attaching it to murder."[4]

This is evident in the 1948 noir *They Live by Night*, a story which is "psychologically bound to emergent teenage culture."[5] The film centers on an unfair prison sentence where an innocent young man gets mixed up with criminals. *They Live by Night* has been compared to *Rebel Without a Cause*, another film that was crucial to the early days of teen culture. *Rebel* is arguably a noir itself.

A thesis on teen noir by Anja Tucker in 2008 explained how in recent years (mostly late 1990s, 2000s) there have been more noir tropes in teen films (*L.A. Confidential, Veronica Mars, Heathers, Brick*, etc.). While I don't fully agree, I do think that noir is present in current films

"No law says you've got to be happy"

in some ways. There are always going to be depressing films about murder because, apparently, some people like that. Not me.

I'd like to talk about one of the "best" noir films, *Double Indemnity*. The movie is about an insurance salesman named Walter Neff (Fred MacMurray) who gets pulled into a murderous plan when he falls for Phyllis Dietrichson (Barbara Stanwyck), who is intent on killing her husband played by Tom Powers and living off his accidental death claim. Meanwhile, Mr. Dietrichson's daughter learns more and more about the truth by looking into the case.

Billy Wilder directed *Double Indemnity*, the third film he made (outside of writing films) after the Ginger Rogers' comedy *The Major and the Minor* and the war thriller *Five Graves to Cairo*. With Wilder's work, most of his characters exist in some sort of gray area of morality: you can't quite tell if they're good or bad from the beginning, but you watch them anyway. This is the case with *Double Indemnity*. The cruelty of the plotline is outstanding, but that's what makes you keep watching.

Barbara Stanwyck plays the role of Phyllis perfectly, luring Walter into her web of lies and seduction. This type of character that Stanwyck

Fred MacMurray and Barbara Stanwyck appear in *Double Indemnity* from 1944 (Paramount Pictures) (Wikimedia Commons).

plays is called a femme fatale, a woman who uses her attractiveness to harm men. *Double Indemnity* helped launch this trend. It takes a lot of acting talent to play a character playing another character, which Stanwyck does brilliantly. The dialogue and script aren't like real life:; they're poetry.

When Walter first sees Phyllis, she's in a robe standing at the top of a staircase. This first scene symbolizes the power dynamic between the two: Phyllis is so far above Walter, and she can control him with every word she says. Every single shot is so perfectly mapped out: how does each shot symbolize something in the story, and how does it move the story forward?

Noir is my least favorite genre, so I can't say I thoroughly enjoyed *Double Indemnity*, especially since I saw it in a theater at 9:00 a.m. right after I woke up at the TCM Classic Film Festival (I hate going to movies in the morning). I can't deny that it's a great script and that it has an undeniably genius cast and director. But dark murder just isn't my cup of tea.

I'm pretty sure most of my generation isn't familiar with the noir genre, because it died out. But why? Some believe it never ended but evolved away from the dated noir style. I'd argue differently. There are essentially no films in the last 10 years with femme fatales and cynical detectives anymore unless they're set in the 1940s or 1930s. I want to see film noir again, but I'm sure that Hollywood would do it wrong. I agree with the theory that film noir ended in 1958 with the Orson Welles film *Touch of Evil*. There are some exceptions as with everything, but it's nowhere near as prevalent as it was back then.

Yet I think film noir is still relevant today. As people respond to the looming crises we face today, many adopt a cynical, pessimistic outlook. I predict that film noir will become more relevant. In the end, culture moves in waves. There's nothing new under the sun, and the good and bad of each era of Hollywood and culture will inevitably cycle back into fashion.

I also admire how noir films were involved in birthing the word and concept of a teenager. The negative parts of these movies appeal to me as a teenager: a bunch of people killing others out of spite and being super angsty, depressed, mad, and emotional. But what we can learn from their decline is that, eventually, we get sick of negativity. It always passes in the end. Noir has never been my favorite because of this darkness, but as I grow up more and more, I learn that noirs have their place and importance, especially in the film world.

The Snake Pit

*Depictions of Mental Illness
in Classic Hollywood*

Virginia Cunningham sits on a bench outside next to her friend. She doesn't know where she is. She is led back inside and forced to stand in a line with other women. Once inside, she thinks she may be in jail.

"That's it! A prison! Let me go! Let me go!"
The psychiatrist corners her.
"Who do you think I am?"
"The warden of this prison," she says.
"Is there any reason why you should be in prison?" he says back.
"Why, yes. I'm writing a novel about prisons and I've come here to study conditions and take notes."

Virginia is a schizophrenia patient at a crowded mental hospital. She's forgotten who she is. She occasionally remembers certain things but struggles to retain many crucial aspects of her core identity and memories.

Part of the reason I wanted to talk about *The Snake Pit* is because I have struggled with mental illness for as long as I can remember. I had pretty severe OCD (it's been treated, not severe anymore) and I also live with a mood disorder. A couple of years ago, it got so bad that I had to go to a mental hospital. I spent two weeks there, and it was a traumatic and life-altering experience, seeing how everyone struggles just like me—it also taught me not to judge people as harshly as I used to, because you never know what they're going through. I was interviewed about this in *Psychology Today* last year, if you're interested.[1]

I don't have experience personally with Virginia's disorder, schizophrenia, so I can't confirm that *The Snake Pit* is an accurate depiction of it. I can confirm that the movie surprisingly doesn't get much of the mental hospital experience wrong. "I'd be really sorry to leave those poor girls," Virginia says at the beginning of the movie. Connecting and making friends is a big part of any stay in mental institutions. Since you're in such close contact with the other patients, you tend to bond over the shared horrific experience. Patients often have to share a room, creating even more intimacy.

The scenes where Virginia's husband Robert visits her do remind me of my time in the hospital. When people visit you and bring treats, they taste better than anything else because the food in mental hospitals is horrendous. Imagine school lunches but for every meal, days and days nonstop.

There's something about the way this movie captures the jail-like, intense setting of a mental hospital that feels so accurate. Olivia de Havilland and the creators of this movie did a lot of research on mental hospitals, and instead of filming the movie in a studio, they did it in a real facility in southern California.

I also can confirm that the movie depicts recovery surprisingly well. It takes a long time to return to mental stability, but it's not as hard as you initially think it is. And once you realize the root of your problem—with a diagnosis or finding out the thing that really scares you—you're already a step ahead. The movie handles this perfectly. Virginia realizes that her problems originate from not feeling loved by her mother when her father died and passing that trauma from her father's death on to the men she dates. Not everyone's original issue can be traced back like this—sometimes it might just be genetics.

"You may never know why everything happened, but now you do know how and when it started and that does matter," Virginia's psychiatrist tells her. He turns off the light in the room. "If you wanted to turn on the light, you couldn't, because you didn't know where the switch was." He turns the light back on. "Now you do. You may never know why turning the switch makes the light go on, but you don't have to. As long as you know where it is, you may never have to be afraid of being in the dark again. And that I'm sure you'll be able to do very soon." Dr. Kik, Virginia's psychiatrist, is a guiding light in this movie as Virginia recovers. He's the only good part about the hospital.

The hopelessness Virginia feels is the most realistic thing about *The Snake Pit*. Virginia is comforted by the idea that she "just had a mental breakdown" and won't be the way she is forever. When her husband asks her if she wants to leave, she says, "Anybody would want to leave *this place*."

Another realistic element of this movie is the different people

The Snake Pit

Virginia meets. There are many cruel nurses and patients and there are just as many kind ones. It isn't completely one way and it isn't completely another. It's somewhere in the middle. And that's how life is.

The Snake Pit is not without flaws—Virginia's ultimate "cure" is going back and living with her husband, which some find to be anti-feminist, but I think that her husband Robert is a truly caring guy and that they deserve each other. It's not like the cure for mental illness was motherhood! Had this movie been remade, I would've loved to have seen more of the patients' relationships with each other and more of the psychotherapy scenes.

This movie prompted transformation in U.S. mental institutions. The studio Fox reported that because of lawmakers and others seeing the film, up to 26 states passed legislation reforming treatment at mental hospitals.[2] This proves the power of stories and portrayals on real-life issues—movies can affect politics!

I still don't understand why mental institutions are as hostile and uncaring as they are. There are some positive aspects (some nurses are nice, you make friends) but the worst part is that you have almost no control over what happens to you. A nurse can wake you up at 6 a.m. and put a needle in your arm without asking you … that's just what happens. They can strap you down if you don't behave. They can give you a shot of the antipsychotic Haldol that makes you sleep for days without asking you or your parents. That's the scary part about it—and this movie perfectly encapsulates that feeling in less than two hours. The doctors and nurses give Virginia a shot as treatment. They talk about her trauma as she cries and keep asking her more and more questions. They even have something that looks like snakes that they put in a bathtub and they put people in it because they wrongly assume that "things that would drive a normal person crazy can make a crazy person normal." The snake pit is briefly shown in an imagined sequence, but it's really more of a metaphor than anything else. The pit represents mental institutions: overcrowded, uncontrollable, and wildly uncomfortable for any sane person.

Some of the doctors in *The Snake Pit* even try to get unhealthy patients discharged because they "have too many." This shows very clearly what the intentions of mental hospital workers are: let's get the job done as quickly and easily (for us) as we can. *We don't care if somebody is suffering. We don't care if somebody wants to die. We care that we get what we want.*

Sadly, this hasn't changed. There's nothing worse psychologically than feeling alone and actually being alone. Nobody in authority seems to care when you're at the ward. The nurses act like they've seen it all before—shocking events are just part of a regular day. Why can't they make people care a little bit more? I never thought that an old movie could talk about things that I think about every day, but *The Snake Pit* did that. And I know that not a lot of people have had the same experiences as me, but that doesn't matter, because the whole reason (to me) that films exist is to show us a different side to life and to make us feel less alone.

The Snake Pit is based on a semi-autobiographical novel by Mary Jane Ward, who had spent time in a mental hospital to treat her schizophrenia. It's amusing that her name is "Ward." This kind of verbal coincidence is quite common—there's even a term for it. When your name connects to your job coincidentally, it's known as an aptonym. Go look that up. You'll enjoy a 10-minute Wikipedia rabbit hole.

Mary Jane Ward wasn't the first woman to write about her experiences in a mental hospital. Nellie Bly was the first to attempt this in her book *Ten Days in a Madhouse* from 1887. Bly disguised herself as mentally ill and went undercover at Blackwell's Island asylum in New York City to document the terrible conditions there. This is believed to be one of the first exposés of a psychiatric facility.

Before the partial normalization of mental illness (especially among women), patients were severely mistreated. In Victorian England, all mental illness in women (sometimes not even illness, just odd behavior), from "swooning" to overdramatic emotions, to epilepsy and bipolar disorder, was all classified as one disorder: "hysteria." Women were sent to asylums where the only treatment for "hysteria" was being inappropriately touched by nurses operating massage machines in the pelvic area. Many believed this could "cure" all types of mental illnesses in women, and these authorities were mostly men, of course.[3] *The Snake Pit* shows the tail end of this insanity. Some treatments portrayed in the film are evidence-based and others are completely made up. Luckily, these days, most, if not all, treatments are backed by rigorous experimental studies. This also doesn't stop mistreatment from happening.

Film historian Dorian Bowen wrote about mental illness in classic films: "It is important to remember that early films were a reflection of a society that still lacked the diagnostic insight, vocabulary, and empathy to convey mental illness as more than a series of erratic behaviors or evidence of moral failing. And yet this is exactly why, with the benefit of hindsight, it is particularly compelling to uncover performances that stand out as authentic now."[4]

The Snake Pit

Depictions of mental illness grew in popularity over the 20th century as psychiatric drugs, therapy, and other treatments became more and more normalized. After World War II, and as the Hays Code diminished in importance, many directors and writers became bolder in their story choices about the topic.

Mental health as a topic was extremely rare in films from the 1930s. Either somebody was completely mad or they were normal. Most portrayals of mental illness were similar to *Dr. Jekyll and Mr. Hyde*, which showed actors descending into madness, screaming—you know, people who really seem "insane." The reality is that these characters (or caricatures!) didn't help the public view of mental illness with more compassion or understanding. Truthfully, most people with mental illness appear completely normal from the outside. And it's hard for outside observers to realize the presence or understand the severity of someone's psychological issues. I have experienced this myself. I feel like people distance themselves from me when they know that I have to contend with mental health issues that can be severe. Many have negative preconceived notions about mental health issues, even those who also have psychological diagnoses. It carries a stigma.

The real depictions of mental illness in film started in the 1940s, right before modern psychiatric drugs were discovered in the 1950s. As shown in *The Snake Pit*, there were treatments such as electric shock therapy, psychotherapy, and some outlandish treatments that never work. But then lithium came along as the first successful medication to treat bipolar disorder in 1948, and chlorpromazine was available to treat bipolar disorder and psychosis by the 1950s. Soon, the first antidepressants would be developed at the end of the 1950s, setting the stage for a revolution in the development of psychiatric medications over the next several decades, many of which would be featured in cinema.

There were films before *The Snake Pit* that gave realistic depictions of mental illness. Billy Wilder's 1945 film *The Lost Weekend*—about alcohol addiction—was one of the first classic films to delve further into the addict's experience and the devastating impact it has on their family and friends. *The Seventh Veil*, from 1945, also tackles addiction. The film deals with a woman who hires a hypnotist after attempting suicide. As much as we like to ignore it, suicide has had a huge impact on Hollywood. Many stars, directors, and screenwriters committed suicide, and it wasn't addressed enough in film until much later.

In the 1950s, two films tackled dissociative identity disorder, formerly known as multiple personality disorder: *Lizzie* and *The Three*

Faces of Eve, both from 1957. *The Three Faces of Eve* is about a psychiatrist who treats a woman, Eve, who has three personalities, which was based on a true story. *Lizzie* follows a similar storyline.

One of the experiences that consistently gives me hope for teenagers liking classic movies was when I was in the mental hospital in 2022. We would get to watch a movie every night, and some nights it would be up to me to choose for some people who wanted to watch one. I chose *Vertigo* one night, *Charade* another night, and the next, *Stormy Weather* (which Hy Kraft wrote!). It amazed me that after I left to go to sleep, the remaining patients finished the movies and loved them.

Film portrayals of mental illness in the classic era reflect my experiences. No matter how much you feel that you're alone, you're not completely. And I'm also sure that movies can help you feel less alone. It helps even more that people had the same problems as us 80 years ago. It even helped me and others when we were actually in a ward. (Imagine that famous *Us Weekly* feature remade: "People from Old Movies! They're Just Like Us!") I love thinking about how nothing truly changes.

The Romantic Comedy and How Modern Rom-Com Tropes All Draw Inspiration from One Movie

Romantic comedy seems to affect every single genre of film and television made today, and to me, it's still the most popular type of movie or television plot there is. Think about it: most of the 2000s movies my generation has grown up on have been rom-coms: *Mean Girls, Legally Blonde, Easy A, She's the Man,* and more modern movies and television shows like *To All the Boys* or *The Summer I Turned Pretty*. Even superhero films often have romantic comedy storylines.

While I enjoy some of these movies, I usually prefer the older films. One gift that watching old movies and new movies has brought me is the ability to compare past and present with a high level of detail. I find that most new movies have subtle references to old ones, as I briefly talked about in the first chapter. In this chapter, however, I will prove to you that all seemingly "modern" rom-com tropes (the "meet cute," fake identity, best friends-to-lovers, enemies-to-lovers, contract relationship, etc.) have existed since the very beginning of the rom-com. Unfortunately, that's one thing that most historians can't agree on. But I have determined it, folks. Drumroll, please…. The most classic classic movie to ever exist, *It Happened One Night*, essentially invented the modern rom-com. Many argue that *Girl Shy* or *Sherlock Jr.*, two silents, were the first romantic comedies, but I argue that the modern rom-com's foundation is built upon dialogue, and without dialogue, it cannot truly be a modern romantic comedy. *It Happened One Night* is a 1934 movie starring Claudette Colbert and Clark Gable. The movie is about Ellie Andrews, a rich, spoiled heiress whose dad controls her romantic life and forces her to marry a man she doesn't like. Ellie runs away from

Clark Gable and Claudette Colbert in *It Happened One Night* (1934), the ultimate romantic comedy (Columbia Pictures) (Wikimedia Commons).

her father's yacht with no money or possessions. She then meets Peter Warne, a journalist who agrees to help her stay undercover in exchange for an exclusive story. But while they are on the road, their plans change when they start falling in love.

It Happened One Night was such a huge hit that there's a widely circulated rumor that when one scene featured Gable taking off his shirt, revealing no undershirt underneath, men's undershirt sales plummeted for months.[1] It's probably not true, but still. That's a huge hit movie if it did happen.

The movie was a phenomenon and swept all five categories at the Academy Awards. But as the ceremony began, Claudette Colbert was boarding a train. She assumed that she would not win, as she never had that much faith in the film. "What kind of reception can this kind of picture actually get?" she recalled thinking of the film in a speech while accepting the American Film Institute Life Achievement Award in 1982.[2]

She was proven wrong because, as the legend goes, studio executive Harry Cohn sent someone to fetch Ms. Colbert when she won the award for Best Actress. "Miss Colbert! Miss Colbert!"

The Romantic Comedy

"I won?"

They rushed her back to the awards at the Biltmore Hotel in Los Angeles. She was wearing her train outfit: a suit designed by Edith Head she was wearing no makeup. Shirley Temple handed her the award. I guess Gable and Colbert had never thought that *It Happened One Night* could be such a crowd-pleaser, because it was a completely new type of film.

So what made it revolutionary?

There are hundreds of tropes that *It Happened One Night* invented (or at least invented for Hollywood, since these were present in Broadway long before) that the current rom-com uses. We'll discuss this in depth later in the chapter.

It also invented the road-trip romance. Part of what made *It Happened One Night* such a good movie was that it constantly kept moving, not just because the script was so fast-paced, but also because the two characters were road-tripping. Road trip movies have exploded since *It Happened One Night*, and they're present in every decade of film: take the Audrey Hepburn late 1960s classic *Two for the Road*, the genius *Little Miss Sunshine* from the early 2000s, or the 1980s-tinged weirdo movie *National Lampoon's Vacation*.

The success *It Happened One Night* garnered wasn't that complicated. It all came down to a great script and amazing chemistry between leads, two things that still make a great rom-com today. It is only one of three movies to win all five major Academy Awards.

The way I usually gauge how much a movie holds up in the modern era is if modern movies and TV shows make references to it. With *It Happened One Night*, it was referenced in more than one! The characters watch *It Happened One Night* in both *Sex and the City 2* and *The Summer I Turned Pretty*. Double importance!

In the 1930s and 1940s, there was a special genre of rom-coms called "screwball comedies." Lara Gabrielle, film historian and author of *Captain of Her Soul: The Life of Marion Davies*, wrote that *The Patsy* was quite possibly the "first screwball comedy."

A screwball comedy is a satirical romantic comedy, often with a woman who challenges a man's masculinity by claiming higher economic status than him. Screwball comedies often include hilariously hyper, slap-sticky characters. A screwball in itself is defined as a crazy and eccentric person. Before the prominent genre, a screwball was known in baseball as a player or ball that moved unusually or unexpectedly.

"It's a genre that was born out of the evolving socio-economic and industrial changes that shaped studio era filmmaking," Olympia Kirakou, author of *Becoming Carole Lombard: Stardom, Comedy, and Legacy*, wrote. "Screwball is arguably the first 'Code era' genre, and those self-regulatory guidelines shaped how filmmakers represented love, relationships, and gender. Screwball is a world of fast-paced dialogue, eccentricity, madcap characters, and romance." Kiriakou is also the podcaster behind *The Screwball Story*.

The Patsy is a 1928 movie about two sisters: Jane and Patricia. Patricia is jealous that her sister has a successful boyfriend, so she schemes to charm him by imitating other silent film stars of the time and completely changing herself. It's a very modern romantic comedy storyline, and I could see it being remade.

According to Gabrielle, Marion Davies was the first screwball comedienne—but Davies doesn't get credited with that often because her career was fading when talkies became popular. Davies worked in Hollywood until 1937, the height of the screwball comedy. She may have made a more lasting impact on the genre if she hadn't retired.

The screwball comedy completely took off six years after *The Patsy*, in 1934. That was the year the Hays Code started to affect the production of movies and what kind of topics could be talked about. The screwball comedy is the direct result of the Hays Code because screenwriters couldn't talk about the same things they had talked about before (like alcohol, drugs, sex, and violence), so they had to change how they entertained the viewers and kept their attention.

American film critic Andrew Sarris described the screwball comedy as "a sex comedy without sex," which is an apt description. Writers and directors had to swerve around several topics, and to keep it interesting they made the storylines outlandish and the physical comedy *psychotically* slapstick at times. There are two main reasons for this: (1) the Depression forced the film industry to move into a state of purely entertaining, rather than questioning culture at large, and (2) the Hays Code, which I just mentioned. Elaborating on the first point, author Ted Sennett said in his book *Lunatics and Lovers*: "Not many films of the early thirties confronted the real problems of the depression head-on. For every film such as *I Am a Fugitive from a Chain Gang* or *Our Daily Bread*, there were dozens in which the numbing poverty and desolation were either handled glancingly or simply ignored."[3]

The result was the most hysterically comedic and over-the-top genre of the 1930s, whose primary purpose was to entertain, as most movies were in that decade. That's why these crazy set-ups were used: how else could they take viewers' attention and lure them back into the theater when the public had almost no money in their pockets? For the audience, it might have been a choice between eating dinner and seeing a movie, especially in the early to mid–1930s, so you can imagine how captivating these movies had to be.

This is the main reason why the 1930s is by far my favorite decade for romantic comedies. They're so over the top!

One of the key components of a screwball comedy is an unusual situation that leads to love. This could be a poor man with a rich woman (*My Man Godfrey*), a woman who needs help with a leopard (*Bringing Up Baby*), or a man in love with his fiancée's sister (*Holiday*). This genre is hard to define, but I think the weird situation set-up is the key. All screwball comedies have two characters from very different backgrounds that clash perfectly for eccentric humor and storylines.

Another key element of the screwball comedy is the third wheel, a love triangle (or a "love square" in *The Awful Truth*). This plays out in many screwball films: *Holiday*, *The Philadelphia Story*, *The Awful Truth*, *His Girl Friday*, *My Favorite Wife*, and *The Palm Beach Story*, to name just a few. You can see how many of the tropes from the screwball comedy have been carried into today's romantic comedies (unusual situations, love triangles).

This genre was so successful largely because it had women at the center. For every single screwball comedy (and every romantic comedy), there's a famous actress who makes the movie shine. And that's why the genre is still so popular: female actresses had great comedy chops, and their acting remains funny today. I can't name one screwball comedy without a leading lady who steals the show.

Aside from *The Patsy*, *Twentieth Century* with Carole Lombard and *It Happened One Night* with Claudette Colbert are some of the first real screwball comedies. These films are so classic that when you watch them, they may feel like nothing new. It's like eating vanilla ice cream and calling it bland, without understanding that you're enjoying an incredibly exotic flavoring. So though it may seem cliché now, *It Happened One Night* essentially invented the modern romantic comedy as we know it, and *Twentieth Century* launched Carole Lombard as the screwball queen of the 1930s. Her frantic energy and quippy lines in the film inspired many other films of the decade.

Claudette Colbert was a screwball comedienne and romantic comedy heroine in her own way: she was slow-paced and witty yet still laugh-out-loud funny. The adorable Colbert is such an underrated actress for today's audiences, but she was one of the biggest box office stars of the 1930s and 1940s. I remember I was reading a biography of Claudette Colbert in public a couple of years ago, when somebody asked me what I was reading. When I told them, they didn't know who Claudette Colbert was. But when I was reading a Jean Harlow biography the next week, they somehow knew who she was. It seems history has forgotten some of the best actresses, actors, and movies.

One part of screwball comedy that didn't remain as present in the decades following was the class and financial divide that the original screwball comedies implied. Take *It Happened One Night*. The film relies on the fact that Ellie is from a much higher economic class than Peter, her romantic interest. This also comes into play in most 1930s screwball films, most notably *My Man Godfrey*, a film about a rich socialite, Irene (played by Carole Lombard), who needs a "forgotten man" to win an upper-class scavenger hunt against her sister. She finds Godfrey (played by Bill Powell) and hires him as a servant for her family. They inevitably fall in love.

My Man Godfrey (according to many, including me) is the peak of screwball comedy. The funny set-up with romantic schemes, the rich woman/poor man, the family dynamics, and the slapstick energy mixed with witty dialogue make for a perfect screwball comedy, from beginning to end. When I first watched this, I watched a colorized version (see Chapter 15) and somehow it didn't take away much from the film. That is a sign of a good movie. I didn't get hooked on the film from the first 25 minutes, but after that, it was a breeze. The movie is quintessentially 1930s with its clash of the economic classes.

The Guardian did a feature on *My Man Godfrey* at the beginning of the pandemic, calling it "My Streaming Gem." They had some great insights on the movie: "It's a sly film that satirises and glamorizes in the same breath, where a hotel foyer full of high-society types is compared to a lunatic asylum."

It's such a classic rom-com trope to put two completely different people together and watch them fall in love. The screwball comedy 100 percent made that popular.

The result of the culture clash in *My Man Godfrey* is a real, true love between completely different people. Irene is a rich socialite, and Godfrey is a homeless man. The movie is an accurate reflection of life during the Depression when the class divide became so deeply engrained that movies couldn't help but satirize it.

I'd love to see more movies today about the wealth gap and how some people live like kings and queens while others live like beggars. It's like 17th-century England and the Great Depression all over again! I think that there are way too many movies that focus on the rich and the middle-class these days. We need more movies where everyone interacts, like *My Man Godfrey*! That's the beauty of the screwball comedy—people from totally different backgrounds and experiences can still love each other.

Another quintessential screwball movie is 1940's *My Favorite Wife*. Ellen, played by Irene Dunne, disappears at sea. Her husband Nick has children with her. Nick waits seven years before remarrying another woman, Bianca. He declares Ellen dead. Ellen reappears when Bianca and Nick are on their honeymoon—and tells Nick that she has been stranded on a desert island the entire time. Turns out Ellen has her own island companion—Stephen. Nick goes insane with jealousy and the slapstick comedy set-up begins.

What's so perfect about this set-up is the crazy and unrealistic idea that somebody could be declared legally dead and still be alive—it's something that fascinates all of us sometimes. If we never found that person's body, could they still be somewhere? *My Favorite Wife* utilizes this idea and turns it into an ingenious situation comedy set-up. Situation comedy usually begins with something the characters don't know, which in the case of this movie is that Ellen is still alive. Once the secret is uncovered, the characters must deal with the repercussions of the odd situation. Lies and repercussions happen to everyone, and very often in real-life situations. So what's the difference between that and a true situation comedy?

The difference lies in creating a set-up that would never happen in real life yet still feels realistic enough to suspend our belief. It's what makes screwball comedies and sitcoms so easy to watch and so interesting. Situations that could happen in real life are dramas. You can go and watch those in your real life. People watch comedy to see things that can only happen onscreen. For example, a wife and mother is declared legally dead after being stranded on a desert island for seven years. I can guarantee that would never happen in real life. It has never happened once. But could it? Well ... yes!

My Favorite Wife is one of my favorite classic screwball/romantic comedies. I could not put it down! I know it's a movie and not a book, but it's a good saying. Cary Grant is one of my favorite actors and he is hilarious in this movie. He's both sensible and completely insane and I love it. Irene Dunne is also funny, especially when she does her Southern accent.

Bringing it back to the modern day, there's a scene in *My Favorite Wife* that directly parallels *The Parent Trap* from 1998. Both films are about a couple who have children together and have been separated for a long time. In this scene, Nick is with his new wife Bianca in an elevator. As the elevator is closing, he jerks his head down and abruptly catches a glimpse of his old wife. This happens in *The Parent Trap* too, when the father of the two twins, Nick, coincidentally the same name, is staying at a hotel with his fiancée Meredith, and he sees his ex-wife Elizabeth as he gets on the elevator, and the same thing happens. Both movies also have a scene where someone falls into a pool fully clothed.

In their press interviews for *Ticket to Paradise*, the 2022 romantic comedy, George Clooney and Julia Roberts talked about *My Favorite Wife*. "In those movies, one of the great things that they always do is, whoever the 'bad guy' is supposed to be—so the new wife, it's so subtle how they make her a villain. Because [viewers] have to like her enough to think [Nick] would marry her, but you don't want to like her so much that you want them to stay together," Julia Roberts said.

Following *My Favorite Wife*, the romantic comedy continued to be a staple for decades to come. It barely evolved, keeping the same structures and dynamics, simply adding the different clothes and societal expectations of each decade. One big innovation came in the 1950s, when the "battle of the sexes" type of comedy became popular, a comedy that demonstrates the differences between the sexes in a comedic way.

In most of these films, the two romantic interests are pitted against each other because of work, circumstance, money, or any other obstacle that has to do with gender. The only problem with battle of the sexes films in the 1950s is that, usually, the man wins. For example, in *Adam's Rib*, while we don't like to admit it, Adam wins by getting Amanda back. While they try to say, "There is no difference," we all know there is.

I can't think of one classic battle of the sexes movie that has the woman "winning," if there even is a way to win. So for this reason, I'm not too into the genre. There are modern versions of battle of the sexes: *How to Lose a Guy in Ten Days*, *Mr. and Mrs. Smith*, and the actual movie *Battle of the Sexes*, a micro-biopic about Billie Jean King and Bobby Riggs' tennis match in 1973.

In the 1970s, experimental, "real" romantic comedies like *Annie Hall* became popular, and then in the 1980s, teen rom-coms made it big.

The Romantic Comedy

But not much ever changes with a funny love story: that's what I find interesting about the genre and also why audiences get sick of it so easily. Through all the years, there never was a more influential building block than the genius of *It Happened One Night*.

One of the most recent successful romantic comedies of the last few years is *Anyone but You*, which has a perfect example of the first trope I'm explaining—the "meet cute." A meet cute is when two people meet in an unusual, "cute" or funny way either in a movie or real life. The meet cute in *Anyone but You* was one of the best ones I've seen in a long time. In the modern yet classic rom-com's opening scene, the two romantic leads, Bea and Ben (very similar names) meet when Bea needs to use the bathroom at a coffee shop. The workers won't give her the key unless she buys something, but the line is huge. Ben, at the front of the line, sees her and pretends to be her husband so that she can order something and go to the bathroom. And that's how they meet.

Unlike real-life relationships, most romantic comedy characters meet in an odd way because it makes the relationship seem interesting and different, as opposed to when the characters meet at school or work or through friends.

The term "meet cute" has actually existed way longer than you think. Some say it originated from the play *Will Success Spoil Rock Hunter?* from the 1950s, when one character explains, "Dear boy, the *beginning* of a movie is childishly simple. The boy and girl meet. The only important thing to remember is that—in a movie—the boy and the girl must meet in some *cute* way. They cannot ... meet like normal people at, perhaps, a cocktail party or some other social function. No. It is terribly important that they meet cute."[4]

The meet cute trope was very popular with screwball comedies in the 1930s and 1940s, precisely because the romance always forms out of odd situations in screwball films.

The meet cute originated way before we actually had the term. The classic example of a "meet cute" people refer to the most is from the 1938 Claudette Colbert movie *Bluebeard's Eighth Wife*. Aside from the hilarious name, *Bluebeard's Eighth Wife* is a genius romantic comedy script from Billy Wilder. In this "meet cute," the two romantic leads meet when they are both shopping for pajamas. One is seeking a pajama bottom and the other a top. This type of meet cute is my favorite because it is so clever. You have to have some kind of weird situation with a clever hook or concept in order to make a romance seem new.

The other examples of meet cutes are kind of endless. There is one in *It Happened One Night*, when Ellie is forced to share a seat with Peter. You'll see that as I present you with these tropes, *It Happened One Night* will have every single one of them. Another great example is in *Bringing Up Baby* when the leads meet after Katharine Hepburn accidentally steals Cary Grant's car. *Roman Holiday* has a great one, too: Princess Audrey Hepburn escapes her palace and falls asleep on a bench, where a reporter slated to cover her press conference finds her and takes her back to his apartment to sleep it off.

A trope that is heavily used in romantic comedies today is forced proximity, or when two characters are forced to be with each other and fall in love. Modern movies with this trope include *What Happens in Vegas, Two Night Stand, The Proposal*, and lots of others I don't like. As I said, the rom-com doesn't really change over time, and so this trope appears in tons of classics, including one we already talked about: *The More the Merrier*. Jean Arthur's character is forced to live with Joel McCrea for a week because of the housing crisis, and they fall in love because they're in such close quarters. *It Happened One Night*, once again, uses this trope. Ellie and Peter are stuck together on a road trip, and they never would've fallen in love if they hadn't been forced to be with each other. From a technical standpoint, any movie with romance at work or school is "forced proximity," but I think of it more as a snowed-in thing or a stuck-in-a-closet type of thing. It has to be actual forced proximity, not just being in the same environment.

Another extremely common rom-com trope is the case of fake identity. This happens when a character hides who they are or lies about it and then the other romantic interest eventually finds out. This happened in that (*bad*) Netflix movie, *Sierra Burgess Is a Loser*. Please don't watch that movie. I watched it on my Kindle at 2 a.m. during the pandemic because I was bored out of my mind.

I do like this trope a lot, because no matter what the characters do, there's some source of conflict—you know, from the constant lying. For classic films with fake identity, *Thirty Day Princess* is a super-underrated early 1930s fun comedy. It also uses the split-screen technique, where one character appears on the screen twice. The movie is about a princess who gets the mumps after traveling to America, and her team finds a woman in America who looks exactly like her to pretend to be the princess. Cary Grant falls in love with the princess, but she's not who he thinks she is. This is a classic example of the fake identity or "catfish" trope in rom-coms.

The fake identity trope also occurs *big time* in *Some Like It Hot*,

The Romantic Comedy

where the two main guys pretend to be women to everybody, including one romantic lead, Marilyn Monroe's odd alcoholic character Sugar. There is also a fake identity case in Audrey Hepburn's 1964 movie, *Charade*.

The "enemies to lovers" and "best friends to lovers" tropes were just as prevalent in classic Hollywood. In *It Happened One Night*, Peter and Ellie start off as enemies, but slowly, after forced proximity, they start to like each other. Best friends to lovers was the only trope I could find that wasn't in *It Happened One Night*—but it was in the Claudette Colbert movie released just months after, *The Gilded Lily*. It's a classic love triangle where Claudette Colbert must choose between her best friend, Fred MacMurray, and her love interest, Ray Milland. *The Gilded Lily* is such a perfect rom-com, and the ending is so touching. I highly recommend it. The best friends to lovers trope has been used in so many movies and TV shows—*The Office, 13 Going on 30, Always Be My Maybe, Love Rosie, My Best Friend's Wedding* (obviously), and thousands more. It's probably the most common trope because it's such a natural construction.

Fred MacMurray and Claudette Colbert appear in *The Gilded Lily* in 1935 (Paramount Pictures) (Wikimedia Commons).

Another good one is "pretend relationship." This is where the two romantic leads pretend to be in a relationship to prove something to other people. The earliest example I could find of this happening was in Barbara Stanwyck's 1932 film, *The Purchase Price*. Here, Barbara Stanwyck plays Joan, the mail-order bride to a wheat farmer named Jim, played by George Brent. While Jim and Joan don't pretend to be together in front of anyone else like the other movies this trope occurs in, they still have to learn to like each other and pretend to be together for each other's sake. I'd say *The Purchase Price* also fits in with the forced proximity trope. These pre–1936 romantic comedies predicted the entire genre's lifespan!

Another trope appears in *It Happened One Night*, where we see the pretend relationship, when Peter and Ellie pretend to be a bickering married couple so she wouldn't get caught by the police and taken back to her father. It ends up bringing them closer together.

One of my favorite movies, *Shall We Dance*, the Astaire and Rogers musical from 1937, also uses this trope. The movie is about Peter Keene, a ballet dancer who becomes taken with Linda Keene, a tap-dancing sensation. They meet after Peter uses his connections to find her, but Linda is unimpressed, like in a usual Astaire and Rogers plot. But when a rumor starts circulating that the two are secretly married, they decide to marry and then divorce to stop the rumor. Like a classic pretend relationship movie, the two end up falling in love, and it's even better than all the other ones, because it's Ginger and Fred. They're my favorites.

These pretend relationship movies often involve marriage. Speaking of that, another occurrence of this trope that I could think of was 1940's *The Doctor Takes a Wife*, a Ray Milland and Loretta Young film about a writer and a neurologist who confirm rumors of their marriage because they can both gain different things from the union. It's a modest and predictable screwball show and it's pretty outdated and sexist, so I wouldn't recommend it, but it's an interesting use of the trope. I do like the movies where two people decide that they can gain something from being in a relationship. It's a fun predicament.

Another movie from 1940 that uses this trope is *Hired Wife*, a Rosalind Russell movie that lands on the idea that she's ugly ... which is annoying. The movie is another sexist, weird one, but it does tell us a little bit about marriage in the 1940s. A man asks his secretary to marry him as a loophole for an important finance deal he's making. When the deal ends, she refuses to divorce him, resulting in a perfect rom-com set-up. Rosalind Russell carries the entire movie, and with a useless, weird plot and misogynistic lines, it's not worth your time. But it's interesting to note because this set-up would not work today. Today, anybody can get a divorce without their spouse's consent. This was different in the 1940s. This basically did a gender swap remake in 2009's *The Proposal*, though, which wasn't much better than the original.

Today, this trope is much more common, happening in movies like Adam Sandler's *Just Go with It* and many others like *Picture Perfect, Pretty Woman, To All the Boys, She's All That, What Happens in Vegas,* and *Easy A.*

At the core, the romantic comedy is passionately loved and just as passionately hated because it inspires a hopeless romantic in all of us, someone who might believe that a perfect relationship and a perfect life are worth aspiring to, and maybe even possible.

That's why some people hate these movies so much, because they make you feel hopeful about your own life. And that's exactly why I think rom-coms are so relevant today: from *The Summer I Turned Pretty* to the *To All the Boys* film series to *Never Have I Ever, The Mindy Project*, and *Anyone but You*. We could all use a little bit of hope. That's the message behind these movies—they're trying to tell us a bunch of things, but that's the one that stays through all of them, even starting with *It Happened One Night*. We need to hope that good things will happen to us. Even when they don't.

A Tour of the Old Hollywood Studio System

The classic Hollywood studio system was a vast and complex machine of stars, secretaries, directors, musicians, cashiers, cooks, publicists, nutritionists, painters, furniture makers, executives, and thousands of other people in countless jobs. They were all interconnected, working for each other, and contributing to one (or more) of the five major studios: RKO, Paramount, Warner Brothers, MGM, and 20th Century–Fox. These people worked to put out almost 800 films every year: each film with its own stars, director, screenwriter, makeup artist, and costume designer.

It was important in my Golden Age film journey to learn about how these systems actually worked, and that's why this chapter exists—to show you the factory system behind your favorite stars, movies, and even your favorite makeup products.

I like to think of Hollywood as a vast ecosystem. The stars were at the top like apex predators, and every other job descended further and further down the food chain. I'm starting my tour of the old Hollywood studio system with the actors because when people think of classic Hollywood, they think of the stars. Marilyn Monroe seductively walking in her pink dress in *Niagara*, Cary Grant as a spastically screwball character in *The Awful Truth*. They think of Judy Garland singing about the boy next door in her prairie dress, or Audrey Hepburn and the effortless glamor of croissants and little black dresses. How were these seemingly flawless figures constructed? How did they start with insecure and unsure actors and end up with timelessly elegant forces of nature?

It all started with an actor or actress—either on a stage, in a magazine, or out on the streets. If these people were lucky, somebody would see a star quality in them—the "it" factor—and decide to bring them to the studio where they worked. I've written countless mini-biographies of stars for episodes of the podcast with my friend Eliana, and in most

A Tour of the Old Hollywood Studio System

cases, a career on the screen starts with a career on the stage. Actors and actresses such as Lucille Ball, Audrey Hepburn, Ginger Rogers, Fred Astaire, Katharine Hepburn, Judy Garland, Bette Davis, Cary Grant, Clark Gable, James Stewart, and Spencer Tracy all started on stage. Before them came the actors who started acting in plays, musicals, or vaudeville in the 1920s. This was the way that people were "discovered" most of the time.

Women could also be discovered as models. This happened with men but only rarely. A woman might start as a model, and somebody in the industry sees her in a magazine or an ad, and contacts her for a screen test (we'll get into what that means later). The most notable example is the one and only Marilyn Monroe. She started as a model and worked her way into the acting industry: she was actually working in an airplane factory during the war, and she was spotted by a photographer who took her picture and asked if she wanted to be a model. Lauren Bacall also went this route. She was discovered by Howard Hawks when she was on the cover of *Harper's Bazaar* in March 1943. Additionally, Grace Kelly started as a model and worked her way into getting cast in films and television. Very rarely, actors and actresses would be spotted on the street and asked if they would like to do a screen test. This happened most notably with Lana Turner, who was discovered while buying a Coca-Cola at a soda fountain.

Then the makeover would start. If MGM was interested, Louis B. Mayer would sit you down in a swivel chair across from his curved white desk surrounded with awards and photos of family and friends. He would ask you questions about your past experience and all sorts of questions he needed to know before signing you as an actor.[1]

If they picked you, they'd develop you into a star. They'd start with a screen test. An actor or actress would read a scene, and executives would judge it.[2] I would hate to undergo this process; it seems incredibly dehumanizing. Screen tests are an unexplored area of history. Many have disappeared, but not Audrey's. Audrey Hepburn did a screen test for *Roman Holiday* in 1953, and it's one of my favorite clips of her. You can find it on Google or YouTube. She exudes charm and elegance, as usual. But this is before she is made into a "star," so she seems more normal in the video. You can usually tell when a celebrity has been media trained by the way they hold themselves in public; young celebrities are more naive and normal-seeming, often not knowing what to say, swearing or saying things they shouldn't—like a normal human.

There is also the infamous Fred Astaire screen test story. Fred danced, acted, and sang for the camera and executives as they took notes, which read: "Can't act. Can't sing. Slightly bald. Can dance a little." This goes to show just how harshly the executives were scrutinizing the stars: if Fred Astaire can't dance, who can?

In her book *The Star Machine*, Jeanine Basinger details the exact steps taken to make a bankable star. Here they are, in my words.

First: they'd usually rename you. In the case of Rita Hayworth, her real name was Margarita Cansino. They took her nickname, "Rita," and used it because it was "appealing" to American audiences. The name would go along with the character that these stars would play in every film. "Jimmy Stewart" sounds like the everyday man. "Barbara Stanwyck" sounds seductive yet smart (the last name, not the first—at least to me). Her original name was Ruby Stevens. Judy Garland sounds like the everyday girl yet unusually charming and talented. Her original name was Frances Gumm. Lots of thought was given to these names.

After finding you a new name that you may not even like, they'd interpret your life story in an appealing way to a magazine, after interviewing you. Sometimes they'd even make it up completely, but most of the time, they didn't outright lie. Instead they completely exaggerated all stories they found to be interesting for a consumer to read.[3]

After that, they'd take all sorts of photos of you, in every setting. These were sent to magazines and press throughout your early career.[4] They even took photos of actors and actresses in their swimsuits. These were called "cheesecake photos."[5]

The part that was the most secretive was the "dates" or fake relationships they'd put new stars in with established stars. Cary Grant's career is at an all-time high? Set him up with a new star on a date, invite the press, and boom! The new star gets peak interest.

Sometimes the people who would be set up weren't even heterosexual: in fact, oftentimes gay actors were set up in lavender marriages and relationships to conceal their true identity to the public. This is the case with Rock Hudson, who even married a woman to keep the public from knowing his sexuality. That corner of Hollywood is often the shadiest and hardest to learn the truth about. I wonder about different classic Hollywood couples and if they were real or not. Looking at old drama and relationships is fun. Perhaps they set up an actor with a director to create more press around the film they made together. This ties into the characters and personas these actors assume in their movies, too. For example, Ginger Rogers played a lot of soldier wives when she was dating a soldier during World War II. That's probably not a coincidence.

A Tour of the Old Hollywood Studio System

This is not unlike today, where a celebrity's films or albums are tied to who they are dating or their persona. This is evident with Taylor Swift, especially, who ties her music and musical "eras" to her love interest at the time.

Before doing photo shoots, studios would request that actors change aspects of their bodies and faces. Lucille Ball had to get dental work done. Clark Gable's ears were taped back.[6] Cosmetic surgery has always been popular in Hollywood. Bebe Daniels and Valentino apparently had surgery very early, before it became common or even known. For the women, their noses were changed. For the men, their ears. I guess big ears were not appealing to the studios.

Rita Hayworth's story with this is even sadder than a usual old Hollywood makeover. She went through a painful treatment on her hairline to look "less Latin," her name was changed, she dyed her hair, she got completely new makeup and styling, and she was taught how to stand in a "sexy" way.[7]

Even Ingrid Bergman was told that her "hips were wrong for the job."[8] Even the most beautiful actresses in the world were told this kind of thing. Ingrid was also treated as if she was going to be "sold" to other studios, as if she was a cheap piece of plastic. I can't imagine the feeling these actresses had with all these male executives telling them what to change about their bodies to make them "marketable."

The star makeover is depicted perfectly in *A Star Is Born*, both 1937 and 1953, especially with the eyebrow scene, where they figure out how this female star's eyebrows should look and how her persona aligns with her physical look.

Everything could be fixed. If the executives at a studio liked the actor, they would do anything to get them into tip-top visual shape for fame. The system was made for this. Even personal problems could be fixed—they could buy off jealous husbands, wives, and siblings with money.[9]

The main difference between the star system now and then is that back then, stars were contracted to studios. In fact, it was very rare to "go independent" (which meant that you weren't contracted to a studio). Nowadays, actors are all "independent" and sign contracts for one movie with a studio and then do a different one with another.

After the makeover, the filming of movies would begin, and the stars would be in movie after movie for the rest of their career, learning scripts, going on location, repeating photo shoots, attending events, giving interviews, and providing endorsements. To me, it sounds grueling and horribly exhausting to be used in such a commercial way.

Speaking of makeovers, makeup was also a big part of the old Hollywood studio system and isn't often talked about in chapters like this. Makeup *created* an image for each star, differentiating them from the other stars of the time. In an email conversation, Lea Stans, creator of the blog *Silent-ology*, explained that in the 1900s, 1910s, and early 1920s you "tended to see heavier pancake makeup, eyeliner, eyebrow liner, and lipstick—some actors/actresses put it on heavier than others, some tried to look more natural. Silent comedians, of course, often went crazy with fake mustaches, exaggerated eyebrows, and the like. One thing you *won't* ever see is any rouge on the cheeks—since reds didn't register properly, it made you look disturbingly gaunt."

Makeup was an art form for movies. Specialists had to know the exact products and shades that would look great on screen. *Some Like It Hot*, the comedy from 1959, had some issues with makeup on screen. The film was set to be in color, but the makeup that Tony Curtis and Jack Lemmon had to wear (they were in drag) made them look "ghoulish" on screen.[10] The film had to be shot in black and white, which gives it a classy feel that sets it apart from other late 1950s films.

Most people don't think about makeup and how it affects how a film looks and feels. Would Charlie Chaplin be the same without the grease paint mustache? Would Monroe be the same without her glossy red lips? These images are burned into our minds because of how different each icon's style is.

You can't mention classic Hollywood makeup without Max Factor, the "Makeup Man." Factor is widely credited with popularizing (and inventing) some forms of modern cosmetics. Factor was a Polish Jewish immigrant who began his job selling cosmetics to early Hollywood studios. This makeup was primarily made for the camera, but it was also commercialized once the studios realized how much demand there was for it. Factor created the first commercially available foundation, Pan-Cake makeup. He had a highly famous clientele: Clara Bow, Joan Crawford, Bette Davis, and many others.

His makeup products left a huge mark on classic Hollywood makeup styles. Many Max Factor ads featuring famous actresses talk about how you can look like her if you "only buy Max Factor makeup." I don't love these ads, because it's not true that you can put on makeup and look like someone else, but it's important to showcase how marketing to women has always been: You're lacking X, buy Y, and you can be better.

Clothing is one area of marketing toward women that's a little more creative than the classic "make you feel bad" advertising. Clothes are a form of expression rather than an avenue to "better yourself" or make yourself look like someone else.

Costuming is an area of old Hollywood that I've always loved, especially seeing how dress can reflect characters' personalities and lifestyles. A lot of the time, costumes go over my head, and the thought that goes into them remains unappreciated. Costumes in films play a huge role in suggesting who the characters are, their progressions and changes as people, and who they feel most comfortable around.

To help you get to know how the costume world worked in old Hollywood, let's start with the beginning of Hollywood wardrobing, the 1920s. Wardrobes in the 1920s were less organized. Each film had a wardrobe man and woman who put out clothes needed every morning, kept track of what an actor wore when, and sometimes chose what would be worn from the stock wardrobe—a collection of everything a studio had bought for previous films.[11]

Most costumes were found in a gigantic wardrobe from each studio. A notable example of this system failing is the story of Monroe's orange dress. Marilyn Monroe wore a widely known orange dress in the movie *Gentlemen Prefer Blondes*. The dress was moved into 20th Century–Fox storage departments and was worn again in *The Girl Can't Help It* (the Beatles antecedent and the Jayne Mansfield flick), by Abbey Lincoln, an African American actress and vocalist. Lincoln even was featured on the cover of *Ebony* magazine wearing the dress. (I realize how odd that sentence sounds. Just imagine the other famous Lincoln in the orange dress.)

Lincoln said, in an interview from 1993, that she saw the gown as a symbol of objectification and an overly sexualized image and couldn't quite handle the backlash she received for

Simone at Edith Head's star on the Walk of Fame in early 2024 (author's collection).

re-wearing the dress. Right after wearing it, Lincoln burned it in an incinerator to be 100 percent sure she'd never have to wear it again.

A common costuming method was sketching and creating custom designs for characters. You can't talk about classic Hollywood wardrobing and sketching without mentioning Edith Head, who designed costumes for Hollywood from the 1930s to the 1980s. (I visited her star on the Walk of Fame.)

Edith Head was a daughter of Jewish parents, born in California (me too!). She went to Berkeley and Stanford for undergraduate and graduate school and then went to get work as a costume sketch artist at Paramount. Although she eventually became one of the most widely known costume designers, she was initially overshadowed by the designers Howard Greer and Travis Banton and struggled to gain respect among some of the stars, as some of them preferred her colleagues. This happened until Banton resigned in 1937 and Head could finally step into the spotlight. She started designing costumes constantly and became famous among the Hollywood community for her sarong dress for Dorothy Lamour in *The Hurricane* in 1937 and Ginger Rogers' red dress in *Lady in the Dark* from 1944.

Head became friends with many stars and became their go-to designer for films. This list included Ginger Rogers, Barbara Stanwyck, Jane Wyman, Rita Hayworth, Grace Kelly, Shirley MacLaine, and Elizabeth Taylor. Edith Head received the Academy Award for Best Costuming eight times, an unbroken record. Some of Head's most famous designs are Grace Kelly's wardrobe in *To Catch a Thief*, Audrey's wardrobe in *Roman Holiday* and the black bow dress in *Sabrina*, Bette Davis's wardrobe in *All About Eve*, and countless other well-known outfits.

Another seminal costume designer from old Hollywood still remains a high fashion brand today: Givenchy. Hubert de Givenchy met Audrey Hepburn when he was chosen to design costumes for *Sabrina*. Before meeting Hepburn, he only heard her last name and assumed he was designing for Katharine, the other famous Hepburn. Instead, the outcome was even better, because Givenchy and Hepburn (not Katharine) became lifelong friends and worked together for her costuming in several of her films, including *Sabrina*. Givenchy and Hepburn are credited as having the original designer and muse relationship, with Hepburn inspiring Givenchy with her clothing style and naturally elegant posture and figure from being a ballet dancer. Givenchy and Hepburn had a long working relationship from the 1950s to the 1990s and created some of the most recognized fashion moments in cinema history together.

A Tour of the Old Hollywood Studio System

The preservation of classic film costumes has not been prioritized, despite how important they are to cinema history. Debbie Reynolds was passionate about preserving classic Hollywood's costumes and spearheaded a project to save them for decades. She said to the *Las Vegas Sun* in 2011, "My lifetime dream has been to assemble and preserve the history of the Hollywood film industry. Hollywood has been an enormous part of my life, as I know it has been for countless fans all over the world."[12]

Reynolds began collecting costumes in 1970, after MGM was consolidated and bought out. She offered to buy all the costumes, but they were sold to an auctioneer. Unfortunately, after a long battle trying to make a museum out of her collection, the last of her collection was sold off in 2014. Reynolds told the *Hollywood Reporter* in 2014: "The stupidity and the lack of foresight to save our history. Oh yes, they gave them away if you came up and said that you have something you had to offer. It was no matter about the history."[13]

The history of a huge part of Hollywood, the screenwriters, is kept in the shadows most of the time. But last year, screenwriters' genius and work ethic were represented with the writers' strike.

On May 2, 2023, the Writers Guild of America went on strike. It was a complicated ordeal, with writers asking for two things they weren't getting from Hollywood studios under their contracts: financial compensation from streaming and a promise that AI would be built to help screenwriters, not to take their jobs away. Screenwriters are still undervalued, even as they make up the backbone of Hollywood. Without screenwriters, no movies would exist. To me, they're more important than directors due to their mark on the work that they make, which can't be erased or replaced with film editing or CGI.

Despite almost every American watching movies, most of them don't know how the system works or how the ideas start: with a screenwriter and a blank page. Movies are stories, and without writers, stories don't exist. It seems that most people subconsciously think movies come from the actors or directors or that they are improvised—at least when I have talked to some.

Here I will help you understand how stories were developed in the Golden Age of Hollywood: from the idea, to the rewrite, to the production. My first question had to be about how the stories that make movies were actually found—so I talked to biographer Scott Eyman about the screenwriting process in old Hollywood. Eyman has been writing biographies of people such as Cary Grant, Mary Pickford, Louis B.

Mayer, Charlie Chaplin, John Wayne, and countless others since the mid-1980s. He explained to me that "the major studios all had story editors based in New York City whose job entailed finding likely stories and novels before they were published, so that the movie rights could be snapped up, hopefully at a reasonable price. Some books that were successful but weren't regarded as such before publication also got bought, of course."

In almost every old movie I've watched, it will say "based on a short story by _____" or "originally a novel by _____." I had always wondered why they didn't simply start with ideas for stories and then write the screenplays, but it makes sense to base movies on good books.

After the stories were found, Eyman says that "writers were hired from journalism, theater, and novels. Hollywood money was generally more than the other disciplines paid, and California was usually a better place to work. Most writers who had the opportunity gave the movies a shot at least once, but not all of them stayed. Novelists and playwrights are not used to being rewritten, but screenwriters have to be."

This is still true of today's screenwriters: they have to be open to changes in their script because that's just how the business works. If something is a good story but not marketable, the system will change it to make it so. This was different before sound came into the picture, Eyman says: "In silent pictures, hiring writers was much more casual because the scripts didn't involve dialogue so much as they involved describing the action."

Hollywood's screenwriters, according to Eyman, were paid $200 a week at the very least. This is equal to around $3,000–$5,000 a week today. The screenwriters moved at around the same pace as they did today: one script could take months or longer, but some wrote quickly. "[The difference between back then and today is] most screenwriters today haven't written novels or successful plays. They can come right out of college or TV," Scott Eyman says.

I wonder what elicited this change—perhaps the merging of television and movies or a change of focus to a great story instead of an experienced writer. Either way, it is clear the screenwriting process has exponentially changed since the Golden Age.

Directors are the hardest positions in the film industry to define. There's a director of cinematography, but isn't that a director? Does the director hold the camera or not? How much say does the director have in editing the film? I can't answer those questions, because I'm not a director (yet), so instead, I will do what I always do: research random

A Tour of the Old Hollywood Studio System

people from the past and find out weird stories. Get your glasses on! Or not, because we're probably doing it on a computer.

Frank Capra was the first director that came to mind. He directed some of the biggest, most influential films of the 1930s and 1940s including *It Happened One Night, Mr. Smith Goes to Washington,* and *It's a Wonderful Life*. Apparently, Capra was working selling books for a philosopher when he saw a newspaper ad for a new movie studio opening. He called and told them he wanted the job and that he had prior film experience. Which was a lie. He had never worked in film before.[14]

Arguably the most famous Hollywood director ever was Alfred Hitchcock, and although he allegedly did many questionable things, he didn't lie his way into a job. Hitchcock trained as a copywriter but then entered the film industry as a title card designer in 1919—he designed the cards that would display the title and the credits. Just like Capra, he found his job from a newspaper.[15] From there, Hitchcock began his career as a director of silent films. He wouldn't reach his peak creativity until 30 years later. His prime era included 1958's *Vertigo*, 1959's *North by Northwest*, and 1960's *Psycho*.

Based on these two stories, it seems (I didn't know this because I didn't exist before computers) that people found jobs through newspapers—even high-profile jobs such as directors. Many aspiring directors would get jobs working in the film industry as copywriters, secretaries or re-writers and work their way up.

I also asked Scott Eyman how directors in the film industry were found: "In the early silent days, the director could be the cameraman, an actor in the film, an actor newly recruited from the stage like D.W. Griffith, or an actual director. Later on, as the studio system formed, it became more rational. Younger directors who had made an interesting low-budget film could be promoted to major pictures, directors could be recruited from the stage or even radio, as with Orson Welles, who did both stage and radio."

It seems that old Hollywood put less thought into who they hired and more thought into what that person made and what they could make.

Directors were paid a lot, according to Eyman: "In the '30's and '40s, about $300 a week on the low end of Poverty Row—which sometimes just paid a higher flat fee for rushed shooting schedules of a week or so—to $4–5,000 a week or so on the high end."

There was a big difference between high and low directors and movies. If an unknown director was directing a B picture for a small studio, they might not have as much say. But if Billy Wilder or Alfred Hitchcock was directing a major film at a major studio, they had enough time and resources to change the script and make it their own.

Ultimately, despite all the suffering and discrimination enforced by the studio system, it created an environment for mass creativity and production, where films and stories were worked on a short timeline yet were still of high quality. I admire just how organized and ready the studios were to build stars, stories, and legacies out of nothing but sheer creativity and hard work (and plenty of money, but that's obvious).

Why is the old Hollywood studio system relevant today? Through my research I have realized that classic Hollywood's system is more present in today's pop culture than we notice. For example, Disney's star making system reminds me of classic Hollywood. In the 2000s, we saw a rise in Disney stars from their own TV shows on the Disney Channel, which Disney used to launch music careers, merchandise lines, tours, and movies using every single marketing tool possible. Starting with Disney stars such as Justin Timberlake, Christina Aguilera, Hilary Duff, and Britney Spears, this star-making system continues further into the decade with stars such as Miley Cyrus, the Jonas Brothers, Selena Gomez, and Demi Lovato.

These celebrities were carefully curated, according to their public comments after leaving the Disney machine. Their images were made not based on who they were as a person or what they wanted to achieve but on what Disney needed at the time. Disney relied on a very calculated media approach for its young stars, and due to the young audience of Disney's material, it had to be extremely careful with image curation. This was because many parents would go after the young stars for "not being good role models" to their nine-year-olds. This era of young stars is reminiscent of the studio system—especially the way that Disney carefully created public images.

But even outside of the Disney machine, classic Hollywood's system still has a huge impact on culture more broadly. The studio system was the foundation for today's system—and there are traces of it in everything today, from the PR relationships present in the modern day to the protection of celebrities' images.

Should Ladies Behave?
Pre-Code Women Say No

Should Ladies Behave?, a 1933 MGM Pre-Code comedy, centers on a woman who goes for a much older man whom she does not know is her aunt's new boyfriend. The film isn't a well-known Pre-Code, but I think it establishes what women did in the Pre-Code era, which was "misbehaving," even within today's societal standards. Before we discuss what these women attempted to do in these movies, let's talk about what a "Pre-Code" film actually is.

"The Pre-Codes are always really popular. I don't think you'll be able to get in," my friend and mentor Lara Gabrielle told me when we were in line for a movie at the TCM film festival. "The young people love them." Every year, I head down to Los Angeles to socialize with the classic film community, watch movies, and occasionally catch a midnight screening of *Xanadu* or *Jailhouse Rock*. I was surprised that there even were young people at the festival at all and even more surprised by the fact that they liked Pre-Codes more than any other genre—Pre-Codes are the earliest "classic" films you can watch.

I saw *The Wiser Sex*, a 1932 Pre-Code filled with women in dark lipstick and leopard coats talking about their men. Claudette Colbert sports a blonde wig for half the film. "That was *really* old," my 80-year-old grandma commented as we left the theater. Hopefully, that sentence tells you just how old these films are.

The first Pre-Code films are almost 100 years old—so why would the young people love them so much? What even are Pre-Codes? One blog that features Pre-Codes is called "cinematically insane," which should describe the era well for you (visit https://willmckinley.wordpress.com/). The Pre-Code era was a time in film that spanned from roughly 1929 through 1934.

Sound films were just beginning to get their footing in modern culture, and Hollywood couldn't handle what that meant. The Pre-Code era ended in 1934, when William Hays reinforced the code across all of Hollywood, forcing actors, screenwriters, and directors to take a less raunchy, less violent, and debatably less entertaining route to make their films. There was a code for movies before 1934, but that year the code was strengthened and applied to movies more strictly.

In the 1920s, Hollywood was seen as a vile, disgusting place full of alcohol and sex and was frowned upon. This was because of the Fatty Arbuckle sexual assault scandal (explained in "Looking at Old Hollywood Through the Lens of the 'Me Too' Movement") and the William Desmond Taylor murder. The movie business didn't have the same moral stance it can have today. However, audiences wanted to see these things in films, so Hollywood couldn't exactly prove them wrong if sex and drinking was what sold. There's something about Pre-Code films that *screams* today's problems. When I hear women talk in most of these movies, it sounds like exactly what Mindy Kaling would script for a show.

For example, one of the first Pre-Codes I watched was the little-known *Young Man of Manhattan* from 1930, starring Claudette Colbert and Ginger Rogers. In the film, Claudette's character talks about how she still wants to work after being married, saying how much she loves her job in the newspaper business. The movie centers on a couple, Claudette Colbert and Norman Foster, and the conflicts in their relationship: his alcohol addiction, her higher earnings, and both of them being pursued by other people. This is just one example of a Pre-Code and how it seems so modern. Once the Hays code took over, films seldom touched on alcohol addiction, infidelity, and women working jobs and making a lot of money—and even with those topics, specific things couldn't be said.

"Between 1929 and 1934, women in American cinema were modern! They took lovers, had babies out of wedlock, got rid of cheating husbands, enjoyed their sexuality, led unapologetic careers, and in general, acted the way many think women acted only after 1968," Mick LaSalle says in his book *Complicated Women: Sex and Power in Pre-Code Hollywood*.[1]

This quote perfectly encapsulates what is so interesting about this time for women in Hollywood. There seems to be some historical erasure about just how free and crazy these five years were for women in film. They were able to do just about everything—until they got limited by a man (William Hays). Women were what brought in the big bucks. Men went to the films for the women, and women went to films for the women. Think about how many more people would line up to see a Jean Harlow movie today as compared with a male star like William Powell or Spencer Tracy. Speaking of this, the height of Pre-Code female empowerment was the blockbuster Jean Harlow smash *Red Headed Woman*.

Do you know how most female pop stars have eras of reinvention where they change their look and their style of music and clothing? I think that started way before modern pop music—it started when actresses would change their look when they were doing a drastically different movie than they or anybody else had done before. Jean Harlow did this with *Red Headed Woman*. Harlow dyed her hair red for the part, and in doing that, shed her blonde bombshell image and stepped into a little bit more respect from audiences with the new color change. "So, gentlemen prefer blondes, do they?" Jean Harlow says, lying down after dying her hair red. "Yes, they do." She's ironic, she's sarcastic, she's everything. This quote references Anita Loos's novel *Gentlemen Prefer Blondes*, a peak–flapper era classic.

Red Headed Woman is about Lillian, a "gold digger" who comes between her boss and his wife. She uses her sex appeal to lure men in

Jean Harlow as Lillian Andrews in *Red Headed Woman*, 1932 (MGM) (Wikimedia Commons).

and then discards them when she gets what she wants from them. She seduces, blackmails, lies, and sins her way into the highest financial and social circles while still looking incredible in costumes designed by Adrian, along with perfect makeup and styling.

Red Headed Woman and *Baby Face*, both released in the Pre-Code era, have lots of similarities, so if you enjoy *Red Headed Woman*, you'd probably enjoy Barbara Stanwyck in *Baby Face*. It's truly a remarkable Stanwyck role. As she says in the movie: "Use men to get what you want."

Pre-Code Hollywood was absolutely obsessed with these gold-digging and seductive women and often put them in lead roles. Unlike the later years of Hollywood, early 1930s Hollywood often depicted them as strong heroines instead of man-hating whores—at least in the beginning of these Pre-Codes. Toward the end, the woman often finds a man to stick with.

Lillian is somehow portrayed as both psychotic and likable at the exact same time. Jean Harlow plays the role masterfully, with enough wit, magnetism and charm to justify her decisions. I certainly didn't feel bad for Lillian, but I also didn't feel bad for Bill, her boss, whom she continuously forces into being romantic with her. He should be able to control himself ... he's a grown man! But no—this movie has the underlying belief that men cannot, in any circumstances, control themselves. According to Lillian, men are animals, and all you have to do to get what you want from them is to tap into that.

This film solidified Jean Harlow as a force in Hollywood. There was the war epic *Hell's Angels* that propelled her into the spotlight, but *Red Headed Woman* made it clear that she was there to stay. She is neither a victim nor an assailant. She is simply an indifferent, sometimes unlikable, sometimes admirable character, like all the other characters. The movie doesn't judge Lillian or other characters from an ethical standpoint. Even the wife who gets cheated on doesn't seem like a saint—she's mildly annoying.

Danny Reid of the Pre-Code.com blog said of this: "All of the women contained are either shallow, stupid, or so manipulative, while all the men are helpless bores. And while there's a lot to be said for nobility, where the Pre-Code films shine is in the arena of tantalizing and vivacious debauchery, usually with a nice tidy moral to send the audience home with."

Now's the fun part. Let's talk about what makes this film such a textbook Pre-Code.

There's a ridiculous amount of drinking, firstly, a staple in any Pre-Code. At least Lillian's best friend warns her: "Hey, don't drink that! It's poison!" But that doesn't help much. Lillian still takes the shot. Alcohol is used as a way of coping with anything and everything in Pre-Code films, which is interesting considering how close the movie was to Prohibition time.

And then there's the showcase of Harlow's body. In almost every single scene, she's wearing a revealing piece of clothing, or changing, or just hanging out in her underwear. You'll notice this as a recurring theme. It's interesting that there are countless scenes of women in their underwear in Pre-Codes, but only one of a man (Clark Gable in *It Happened One Night*) that I can think of. I'd be interested to know why that is, besides the obvious sexism and objectification. Perhaps more men were watching movies? Or maybe the fact that Hollywood has targeted so many movies at men?

This is also a completely modern thing. Films marketed to men (including more risqué content appealing to some of them) usually don't draw in a female audience, even if the film was made with women in mind. For example, the promotion of the 2009 feminist film *Jennifer's Body* has been noted as wrong for what the film actually was. It was less about women's bodies and more about their independence.

Speaking of movies with female friendships, my favorite scenes in this movie are with Una Merkel and Jean Harlow. People often don't talk about platonic chemistry, but they work really well on-screen as best friends.

Pre-Codes tackle more important issues facing women, aside from *Red Headed Woman*'s "issue" being that some of us want to seduce men for our own good. For instance, *Only Yesterday* is a Pre-Code film that tackles pregnancy out of wedlock, female empowerment and independence, and it even has some prominent queer characters. Doesn't that sound like a modern movie? Once again, the power of the Pre-Code.

Only Yesterday is the most 21st-century Pre-Code I've heard of. The movie is about Mary Lane, a woman who becomes pregnant before her boyfriend goes off to fight in World War I.

Unlike other films where mother and child do not have a father in the picture because of death or tragedy, this situation seems almost liberating. As Richard Brody wrote in the *New York Times*, "The shift that comes off as the most powerful is the change in gender roles resulting from the movement for women's rights. Julia, a suffragette (whose own marriage is a model of high-spirited equality), delivers a speech, soon after Mary's arrival in New York, announcing that women 'are not dependents any longer' and declaring that Mary's pregnancy out of wedlock 'is no longer a tragedy—it isn't even good melodrama.' In fact, Mary raises her child with much love, little fuss, and no expectation of Jim's [the father's] involvement."[2]

As for the queer representation, the UCLA Film Department said this of the gay characters in the film: "While 1933 had seen a flurry of flagrantly gay characters, *Only Yesterday* is the only Hollywood film (of its time) to present a gay couple as a matter of fact. Franklin Pangborn is an interior designer who brings his handsome partner (Barry Norton) to a penthouse party. While these characters are supposed to show the decadence of the twenties, they are sympathetically presented." In 1933, characters on screen could not be completely "out" in a film, so it would have to be disguised in some way. This, however, is the least thinly veiled example I could find in a Pre-Code movie.

Gold Diggers of 1933 is about a group of showgirls who live together: Polly, Fay, Carol, and Trixie. The Depression threatens to kill their jobs and Broadway. Their neighbor, Brad, a rich songwriter whom one of the showgirls is in love with, funds a new musical about the Depression for the girls to star in. Brad's wealthy family threatens to disown him when they discover he is in show business, so the showgirls and Brad create a scheme to trick the millionaires.

Gold Diggers of 1933 has every single cliché that Pre-Codes discuss: women's bodies, drinking, gold diggers, portly men in three-piece suits, dance numbers that exist to show off legs, women hanging out in their underwear half the time, and—my favorite—women tricking men to get money and status. The movie is basically about how women should take advantage of men as much as possible to get what they want. It's satisfying for me as a classic movie lover to see women get ahead using their brains by the only means possible at that time—manipulation of men—which just goes to show what women had to resort to. While so many movies are about men taking advantage of women, it feels, within that time frame, almost liberating to see these stories play out.

This is what I mean when I say that women are the stars of the Pre-Codes. What would *Gold Diggers of 1933* be without the gold diggers? They are downright hilarious: on champagne, Ginger Rogers's character Fay says, "My doctor recommends it."

I love Ginger Rogers in this movie. She's my favorite actress, and I think she is so underrated outside of the Astaire and Rogers movies. She is hilarious, and this movie would be perfect even if she were the

Should Ladies Behave?

only one in it, but she isn't. There are many more hilarious women in this movie: Joan Blondell, Ruby Keeler, and Aline McMahon. They're the perfect ensemble cast.

In *Gold Diggers*, men are secondary to the women's relationships with each other and their careers. When Polly and Brad (the main characters) get married, she doesn't immediately plan to "settle down" or quit her career. Instead, it seems to be a supportive and loving partnership where both parties nurture each other's careers.

This film would even be progressive without the insane risqué songs, dance numbers, clothing, and storylines. The costuming in *Gold Diggers* was revolutionary. Some of the bodysuits and performance wear that the showgirls wear on and off stage seem incredibly modern. For example, the opening number "We're in the Money," the first satirical dance number about the Depression, features bralettes and bottoms made out of coins. Ginger Rogers sings with the other showgirls:

> We're in the money
> Come on, my honey
> Let's spend it, lend it,
> Send it rolling around!

Later in the movie, the musical that the characters are making becomes the film, and we see a lot more modern costuming: shiny bodysuits, low hemlines.

This movie isn't entirely modern. In one of Dick Powell's piano numbers ("I Could Sing a Torch Song"), he croons: "I couldn't sing a gay song, it wouldn't be sincere." That was enough to make my sister and me laugh for minutes.

More Pre-Codes: *Female* is a 1933 film about an executive, Alison Drake (played by Ruth Chatterton), who is a womanizer but for men. Odd that word doesn't exist. Actually ... it does. I just can't say it here. Ha. She falls for one of her engineers, Jim Thone, the only man who doesn't want her back.

For a modern example of who Alison is, you can turn to Meryl Streep's character in *The Devil Wears Prada*, a precise and hard-working woman who can come off as cold. Alison is much less extreme than Miranda Priestly, though. One thing that made me draw this comparison was the famous line that Miranda says when she wants someone to leave: "That's all." Alison says it in the very beginning, to a man who she invites over to her house for dinner (and more?).

Female is very much about Alison's power in the corporate world

Ruth Chatterton in *Female*, 1933 (Warner Bros.) (Wikimedia Commons).

(she owns a car company), and as compared to *Gold Diggers*, it shows just how wide the scope was for women in film in the early 1930s. The key difference is, in the beginning of Alison's character arc in *Female*, she truly doesn't care what other people think. She tells a cab driver after he supposedly insulted her behind her back: "Now, listen. Things people say about me don't bother me. Thanks just the same." Alison's unusual attitudes don't end with the way she approaches mean comments. When asked whether she is going to marry, she says, "No, thanks, not me." Did the history books teach you that women were even allowed to say that in a film in the early 1930s?

However, *Female*, being a Pre-Code film starring a woman, has the usual themes. There's a scene that doesn't serve much purpose where Alison is lying on a table getting massaged in only a towel. This presents similar predicament to the revealing beach party films 30 years later: liberation or objectification?

Female has many similarities to another Pre-Code from 1932, *Man Wanted*, which is about a woman with a male secretary. It stars Kay Francis and Una Merkel, two Pre-Code darlings. It is a play on the usual role of a woman as a secretary and a man as the executive. *Female* is in the same territory.

In films post–1934, I rarely see dialogue like this, where women don't have men as their number one priority. I can name tons of films that are like this before 1934 but only a couple from after the Hays code. And it's not just some scenes. It's almost every single scene where we get a perfect line about how Alison doesn't have time to commit to a man. Here are some of them:

"I'm a busy woman. I can't be annoyed with jealous or moody men all day."

Someone talking about Alison: "She's never met a man yet who's worthy of her. And she never will!"

"You're a very *cool* young man. Uh, have some vodka."

This film also showcases a simpler time: Alison can go out in a casual outfit and get a hamburger and immediately start socializing and find a guy she likes. That would probably never happen today, sadly. When I go out for a hamburger nobody talks to me. That's probably for the best, though.

The first 30 minutes of *Female* is comedic gold. After that, Alison meets an engineer named Jim Thorne and falls in love with him. Like with other men, Alison tricks him into coming over to her house to talk about work, when she really just wants to be with them. This time, though, you can tell that Alison is truly interested. It reminds me of a modern-day office rom-com set-up, where one of the people starts talking about work because they think the other one is not interested. It seems remarkably modern—except in the second half of the movie, Alison changes herself to make Jim like her, which leads to a very disappointing ending. This film deserves a modern remake where it ends better.

My favorite Pre-Code I've seen (so far) is *Call Her Savage.* I saw the film in Griffith Park at the Autry Museum while visiting L.A. Adam Piron, who leads Sundance Institute's Indigenous Program, introduced the movie brilliantly.

If you want to watch this film, go watch it before you read this section. There will be spoilers. If you're reading on because you don't want to watch the movie, this is your last warning. I don't know why I felt that was necessary. Maybe because I want every single person in the world to watch *Call Her Savage.*

The movie is about Nasa Springer, a vivacious and rambunctious young woman who lives on a ranch. She loves riding horses and spending time with her friend Moonglow, a native man. Her dad is not a fan of her bold behavior and ships her off to Chicago. Naturally, she is happy, because she gets to leave him. But what follows is a lesson on the often cruel nature of capitalism, sexual harassment, motherhood, and the suffering of modern life in the 1930s. She marries a drunken, horrible man, and she has a baby who dies, but she realizes that the ranch was where she belonged the entire time—and she comes to the conclusion, after her mother dies, that her dad was not her dad: she's half Native American, just like Moonglow. She ends up with him.

The movie is an enlightened drama about what it really meant to be a woman in the early 1930s—yet it still has Pre-Code sentiment all over it, from the 20-second shots of Clara Bow getting dressed, to the excess drinking, unsubmissive woman, and sexually abusive men. Even for a Pre-Code, *Call Her Savage* is strikingly modern. The movie has a relatively left-leaning approach (for the time) to the Native Americans and treats them for the most part like normal people, not historical tragedies stuck in the past, removed from the modern world. In many scenes, Moonglow is in cities, speaks fluent English (despite what many believed at the time), and is a normal human being (unlike the perception of the time).

This film's approach to men is revolutionary. Men are not fairytale dream princes waiting to sweep Nasa up and support her monetarily so she can have nine children (unlike in *Female*). Men oftentimes are cruel and condescending and do not understand what Nasa has gone through. They are waiting to leave her at the drop of a hat when she erratically slaps someone or shows her feelings.

This movie also has a scene in an openly gay bar. Two men are wearing makeup and acting "un-masculine," and the whole bar cheers. It seems that these two men may be in a relationship, though it is unclear. However, if you watch the scene, you will see how clear-cut it is that the scene takes place in a gay bar. It's mind-blowing when you think about it. More than 80 years before gay marriage was legalized in the United States, there was a scene with two gay men in a movie. This is why I love Pre-Codes so much. You get to immerse yourself in a completely new dimension that seems so modern yet so removed from modern society at the same time.

As we talked about in the last chapter, Hollywood was much less heterosexual than everybody believes these days. Many huge stars were gay or bisexual and had secret relationships. This even played out on camera in 1928's *Wings*, which showed the first gay kiss on screen.

Should Ladies Behave?

Call Her Savage makes me sad that there are so few Clara Bow sound films. Many thought her Brooklyn accent was "ugly," but I didn't even notice it in this movie.[3] I hate how critical they were of her. After Bow had a mental breakdown in the first years of the 1930s, she resurrected her career one last time with *Call Her Savage* and *Hoopla*.

If you've watched this movie, there's no way you can say that Bow wasn't the best actress of her time, or at least of the 1920s. There's a way she conveys emotions that is so relatable, and she is a beauty icon. I'll talk about Clara Bow's story extensively in the next chapter.

When the lights turned back on after *Call Her Savage*, I heard a 40-year-old man behind me say, "That was actually so good." My whole point in writing this book is not that you should only watch classic films—not even that you have to watch them all the time—but just that you shouldn't write them off because of how old they are. Try them every once and a while, and learn something new. I watch modern TV, modern movies, and YouTube, and I also sneak a 1930s film in there. I think it is so interesting to see how people acted in the early 1930s. Especially women.

You don't have to change anything to be a classic movie person. You just have to watch them when you want to and be interested in a part of the past. You can find any area of history in old movies. I want to learn about mental health in the 1940s? I turn on *The Snake Pit*. I want to learn about journalistic ethics and anti–Semitism? *Gentleman's Agreement*. I want to learn about 1930s ice skating? *Ice Follies of 1939* or *Sun Valley Serenade*.

Movies don't have to be good to be fun. You can watch 2000s rom-com chick flicks and know they're not the best films of all time. But they're *so fun*! Not everyone has the same taste as me, but you get what I mean.

The point of why I wanted to talk so much about Pre-Codes, and specifically Pre-Code women, is to show you that old films are way more contemporary and relevant than you think. Many films nowadays don't empower women as much as early Pre-Codes do. Today's blockbuster Hollywood movies are filled with unattainable beauty standards, bad jokes, and overused storylines. And yes, there's the occasional gem, but I much prefer digging into the archives for *my* sleepover nights. Just turn on a Pre-Code. You might be pleasantly surprised by how good it is.

A Cultural History of the "It Girl"

It was the 1910s, the era of gut-crunching corsets and women's suffrage protests, a fairly boring decade in the grand scheme of Hollywood as we see it today—not many people can name a movie from the 1910s. Short silent film actors like Bebe Daniels and Mary Pickford were making 15- to 20-minute productions that didn't exactly dominate headlines.

That was until women gained suffrage in the United States. After almost 40 years of campaigning, women in the United States finally gained the right to vote when the 19th amendment was ratified on August 18, 1920, giving the decade a memorable beginning.

The movement allowed women to go out dancing without corsets and engage in more scandalous behavior than ever before. Flappers wore makeup, and shorter, rectilinear dresses, and they did whatever they pleased. This was the point in time that American culture started to separate from the waltz, strictly-ruled European culture of the previous several centuries (think Marie Antoinette).

The flapper is a ubiquitous figure. She marked a new era of liberation for women, just after women got the vote; with a strong economy, women could afford to be confident and independent. In my opinion, flapper fashion is some of the best (so classy), and it seemed like the showgirls, dancers, and actresses were having so much fun in this era. Most actresses claim that their flapper showgirl days on Broadway were the best times of their lives. Now, of course, I'm always for vintage style but not "vintage values." I'm cautious because I know this era is romanticized, but I think fashion deserves romanticization!

In 1927, the flapper era was at its peak. Sound on film was just starting to gain traction, and the first "talkie" (i.e., films where people talked), *The Jazz Singer*, had just been released in October. The film that started the common phrase the "it girl" was the film *It* from 1927, starring the irreplaceable Clara Bow.

A Cultural History of the "It Girl"

Clara Bow was born on July 29, 1905,[1] to Sarah and Robert Bow in Brooklyn, New York. Bow had an incredibly traumatic childhood because her mother and father abused her,[2] and her mother also had mental health issues.[3] Bow escaped by losing herself in cinema. She loved to study actresses on the screen, and at age 16, she decided she wanted to be a movie star. In 1921, Bow entered the "Fame and Fortune Contest,"[4] a contest sponsored by movie magazine *Movie Picture Classic* to find stars, and she won![5] The contest promised a film career to her—and her first film was a small part in *Beyond the Rainbow* from 1922.[6] However, her small scenes had been removed, and when she went to see the movies with her friends, she was mortified.[7]

Sarah Bow's schizophrenia landed her in a hospital,[8] and a year later, she died.[9] This was complicated and traumatic for Clara because her mother abused her emotionally.

Clara Bow worked extremely hard in the early 1920s, serving grueling hours on movie after movie after movie.[10] This eventually would take a toll on her mental health but not until she had reached her peak popularity. By the mid–1920s, she had become a household name because of her movies but also because of the way she applied her lipstick in a "bow" shape, which is still referred to by her apt name.

Bow starred in *The Plastic Age* with a young Clark Gable (a big money-maker), then returned in 1926, with *Mantrap* and *Dancing Mothers*. In 1926, Bow signed a five-year contract with Paramount, where she would make her signature films.

Around this time, Bow developed a sexualized reputation (which happened with several "it girls" and happens even now), with one rumor stating she had sex with an entire baseball team, which was blatantly incorrect.[11]

Bow's big hit in 1927 was *It*, the origin of the "it girl." The movie is about Betty Lou, played by Bow, who seduces her boss, but when he hears an untrue rumor about her, must prove it wrong by ramping up her sex appeal and "it" factor. Bow also starred in *Wings*, a blockbuster movie: the first Best Picture winner.

By this point, Bow was at a tough spot in her life. She had always struggled with her mental health, and the overworking was not helping. But as if that wasn't enough, this was around the time of the advent of sound films. Bow was scared and hated making sound films because, at the time, sound required actors to stay in one place and not move and express as much, which was hard, because a big part of her charm came from expressive acting in silence. However, Bow made the transition, unlike a lot of other actors, and she starred in *The Saturday Night Kid* and *Dangerous Curves* among others in 1929.

By the 1930s, Bow was at the end of the amount of work she could handle. The press was wildly exaggerating and most times simply fabricating lies about Bow's sexual behavior, leading to the downfall of her reputation. It wasn't huge, but she was no longer at her peak stardom anymore. "They make it seem like I talk out of the side of my mouth," she said to *Photoplay* in 1931. That same year, Bow was admitted to a hospital for her mental health struggles where she met Rex Bell, a "cowboy actor." They married and Bell was a calming influence on her, and she returned to Hollywood for two more movies, *Call Her Savage* and *Hoopla*, which are among her best (as you heard me say earlier). "I'm anxious to throw off the old personality, even on the screen," she told *Photoplay* in 1931. "I'm going to be grown up and discreet. I'm going to play more dramatic stories, a more dignified type of role. I'm going to make pictures which give me something to do. I'm going to work hard."[12] I find this quote disheartening because Bow worked so hard during the 1920s, and it was clear she was at the end of her star power.

By the 1930s, Bow wasn't the skinniest flapper anymore, but she had changed to the more curvy 1930s figure. I'm not sure if this was a natural change or Bow trying to fit in with industry standards that were now in Jean Harlow territory.

Bow retired at age 28 and had two boys with her husband in the 1940s. She admitted herself to a mental hospital again in the 1940s and was diagnosed with schizophrenia. Bow died at age 60 of a heart attack.[13]

Bow had a pretty sad life, but considering her mental health challenges, I find it inspiring that she accomplished so much. It seems like she was so different from her reputation, and I believe her crowning as the ultimate old Hollywood "it girl" is deserved. As you'll see, a traumatic life and hatred of fame is a pattern for most "it girls" in Hollywood.

As I'll talk about later in this chapter, it's important to know what beauty standards were like back then to give us an accurate "roadmap" of why we are where we are now. Plus, Clara Bow movies are so much fun. If you want to get an idea of her persona, there are many films to watch. If you like talkies, I would say *Hoopla* (1933) or *The Saturday Night Kid* (1929), and if you like dramas, *Call Her Savage*. If you're interested in silents, try *It* (1927) and *Wings* (1927), but honestly, any of her films will show why she's still such an enduring figure.

The next "it girl" was Jean Harlow. The first blonde bombshell. The inspiration for the ubiquitous icon Marilyn Monroe. You could argue on that—there are certainly 1930s actresses I like more. I mean ... Ginger Rogers is the best actress of all time. Claudette Colbert is incredible. Katharine Hepburn is the reason we can wear pants. But I wouldn't say that anyone but Jean Harlow defined this decade in beauty standards. Let's go back to the beginning.

I was first introduced to Harlow through the entertaining but wildly inaccurate Carol Baker– starring biopic *Harlow*. Then I watched *Wife vs. Secretary* and I couldn't quite get why Harlow was such a big star back then. I think it's because at the time she was a star, she was the first huge "dumb blonde" actress and the first major actress to have platinum blonde hair which was followed by a wave of popularity for dying one's hair blonde, which is still going on today—75 percent of American women dye their hair.[14] If you look at any picture of Harlow, you'll first notice her eyebrows. Or, more likely, her lack of them. Believe it or not, this was a huge trend in the 1930s, with actresses like Lucille Ball saying her eyebrows "never grew back."[15] Jean Harlow popularized the curvy, feminine figure like the 1910s had. It seems that decades switch off in terms of style. For example, brighter 1960s-esque styles were more popular in the 1980s and more subdued 1990s makeup styles mirrored the 1970s. This includes the 1950s when the main "it girls" were repopularizing the more curvy look from the 1930s. This is known as the "20-year trend cycle."

Jean Harlow was born Harlean Harlow Carpenter to Montclair Carpenter, a dentist, and Jean Harlow Carpenter, who had dreams of becoming an actress.[16]

Mama Jean[17] divorced Montclair in 1922[18] and moved to Hollywood[19] but then to Illinois[20] where Harlean went to high school. Harlean married a guy named Charles McGrew,[21] but they quickly divorced after living together for two years.[22]

Harlean tried out for acting roles with her mom's name and it didn't take long before she landed a role in *The Saturday Night Kid*.[23] I think of this film as how Bow passed the "it girl" torch to Harlow. This was the exact time when Bow's career was on the decline and Harlow's was just beginning. However, her big break was Howard Hughes's *Hell's Angels* from 1930.[24] She became a national phenomenon and women all over started dyeing their hair platinum blonde in the exact shade.[25] If there's one signifier of an "it girl," it's that all women want to look like her, which can be incredibly damaging, even more so in the present day.

Another big factor in this is that the 1930s was the middle of the Great Depression, which was one of the worst points in American history, and everyone was looking for a way to escape through films. This is not very different today—it's just we are escaping through a different medium, social media. I think Jean Harlow's films are a big window into what women aimed to be at the time. I aspire to be more of a Ginger Rogers, or a Katharine Hepburn, but that's just me. Reading about the women of the 1930s, I'm surprised by how few differences there are between current-day women's reactions to beauty standards vs. back then. We still dye our hair, we still feel self-conscious about our bodies, and we still wear makeup and are shamed for getting older.

Continuing with Harlow's story: she gained even further stardom in 1931, starring in her first movie with Clark Gable and another Hughes movie, *The Public Enemy*. In 1932, while Harlow was filming *Red Dust* with Clark Gable, she suffered a personal tragedy and became a widow (she had been married to Paul Bern for one year).[26]

I bring this scandal up because it was her dignified response and calm actions that gained her even more respect from moviegoers before one of her biggest movies, *Red Dust*, was released. The period of 1933 to 1936 was Harlow's most successful period. She was a movie machine during this time, cranking out hit after hit: *Dinner at Eight* from 1933 continues to be one of her most well-known films, and *Red Headed Woman* from 1932 is a Pre-Code classic, along with all the movies she made with Clark Gable, *Hold Your Man* (1933), *China Seas* (1935), and *Wife vs. Secretary* (1936).

In the mid–1930s, William Powell and Jean Harlow fell in love.[27] However, their relationship was not able to go on because Harlow got very sick with influenza (eventually determined to be kidney failure).[28] She was filming *Saratoga* when the cast and crew recognized her frail condition.[29] She was brought home under her mother's care and then was transferred to a hospital. Despite every effort the hospital made to keep her alive, she died at age 26 in 1937.

When I visited the Hollywood Museum in L.A., I saw the newspaper that was three-quarters covered with the biggest headline I have ever seen: "Harlow Dead." I can tell how big of a shock that was to everyone who knew her. *Saratoga* was more than 80 percent finished, and MGM struggled with if they were going to release it but ultimately decided it would be a good tribute to Harlow, so they finished it using a floppy hat and an extra[30] and it was the highest grossing film of the year, which just shows how beloved she was to the world. Until the 1990s when private medical records were uncovered, it was a huge mystery as to why Harlow died. But now it has been proven that she died of kidney failure, and it was inevitable because she had scarlet fever as a child, and medical knowledge in the 1930s would not have been able to save her.

Harlow's movies have never been my favorites. I love some of them, but her short filmography got in the way aside from the fact that I didn't see anything different about her. I completely admire who she was as a person, with her mental health struggles and her writing skills (she wrote novels and short stories).

Jean Harlow is such an important figure in the beauty standards today, especially considering that she was one of the first super-famous blondes (and not talking about the thin eyebrows— those are outdated). If Harlow had lived today, she would still fit the beauty standards. That's a fascinating thought experiment. Imagine what Harlow's Instagram would look like!

The standards didn't change much with the next "it girl" of the 1940s, Rita Hayworth.

Rita Hayworth's story involves racial discrimination, abuse, and mistreatment, and you can find it anywhere. I researched her life for any remotely happy facts and couldn't find any. And I looked for a long time. If you're interested in her story, I recommend *If This Was Happiness* by Barbara Leaming.

One thing that I realized when I watched *The Strawberry Blonde*, one of Hayworth's first films, is that all the "it girls" have a similar mystery, wanted by a lot of guys and a stupid persona where they don't have anything interesting to say and are mostly just there for their looks. All the women (except for Audrey Hepburn who had an intelligent persona) have a similar persona, and it's still a standard today. Think Megan Fox in some movies, Regina George in *Mean Girls*, or even Elle Woods in *Legally Blonde*.

Hayworth's most famous role is in the film noir *Gilda*, and Hayworth famously said that men would fall in love with Gilda and "wake up with Rita." In *Gilda*, she plays the classic femme fatale, and I would say that this is the classic femme fatale movie maybe alongside *Double Indemnity*.

A femme fatale is a seductive woman who causes trouble by luring in men and using them. I think the femme fatale is so interesting because she's a cross between smart and dumb at the same time. The thing that's different about the 1930s girls vs. the 1940s girls is the war, which added a huge amount of women to the workforce. Hayworth plays mostly dumb characters, like in *The Strawberry Blonde* (1941) and *You Were Never Lovelier* (1942), but in the former, Hayworth does a classic thing where she is both dumb and smart at the same time. It's cool to watch her switch between them in her role in *The Strawberry Blonde*. She knows how to take advantage of men by telling them to meet her "three weeks from Wednesday" as a way to trash them. But then she gets herself in a sucky relationship and she's stuck with him. Do you see what I mean by dumb/not dumb at the same time? Hayworth was incredibly versatile and could play any role—whether it was a serious working girl, a ditzy girl next door, a femme fatale, or anything a casting agent wanted her to be. The typecasting wasn't so much Hayworth as it was the system.

Hayworth became a classic pin-up girl during the war, which meant photos of her with less clothes were everywhere. Betty Grable was also a famous pin-up.

Rita Hayworth made some popular movies, including the cold noir *Gilda*, the war escape Technicolor musical about nothing, *Cover Girl*, *Pal Joey* with Frank Sinatra, and *Down to Earth*, the dazzling Technicolor musical, and her two musicals with Fred Astaire, *You'll Never Get Rich* and *You Were Never Lovelier*.

Hayworth's career started to fade by the late 1940s, and she only made a couple more hits in the 1950s. But by the late 1940s, two women who were working actresses and models would soon be the two women everyone thinks about when they think of the 1950s: Marilyn Monroe and Audrey Hepburn.

We've covered their stories on our podcast, but here's a review in case you are unfamiliar with them. First, Monroe. Norma Jean Baker was born in 1926.[31] On her birth certificate, she was Mortensen, but she was always called Baker. Her childhood was spent in foster homes[32] due to her mother's mental illness, and this affected Norma Jean for the rest of her life. As a child, Norma looked up to Jean Harlow.[33] She became a model, and from there, her first film role was as a high-school girl in a movie from 1947 titled *Scuda Hoo! Scudda Hay!* but her part was cut (see the theme here?). To make her well-known persona, she bleached her hair and changed her name to Marilyn Monroe. She worked up to her more famous early roles in the Marx Brothers' *Love Happy*, *Asphalt Jungle*, and *All About Eve*.

She started to gain more popularity with 1952's *Monkey Business* and *We're Not Married*. However, she only became the icon she is now with the treasured *Gentlemen Prefer Blondes* and *Niagara*. With the success trailing off of those, Monroe was able to secure more leading roles through the 1950s: *How to Marry a Millionaire*, *There's No Business Like Show Business*, and the signature *The Seven Year Itch*, to name a few. However, her later career in the mid to late '50s and early '60s was warped by psychological problems and drug use, topics that are still highly controversial.

Seeking more serious and dramatic roles, Monroe studied acting with Lee Strasberg in 1956.[34] She learned the technique of method acting, where an actor studies and identifies a character's true emotions and motivation. Marlon Brando famously used this technique in *A Streetcar Named Desire*.

Going into the new decade, Monroe did *Some Like It Hot* (1959), which is regarded as one of her best roles. From there, she only had a few more roles, in *Let's Make Love* in 1960 and *The Misfits* the next year, and then the unfinished *Something's Got to Give*. Following being fired from *Something's Got to Give*, she died of a drug overdose. You or your subconscious probably know about it because it's been plastered on the covers of magazines for the last 60 years.

Now for Audrey Hepburn. If you know who she is, there's one image that you know: Holly Golightly from *Breakfast at Tiffany's*.

Audrey Hepburn was born in Ixelles, Belgium, on May 4, 1929.[35] She was originally named Audrey Kathleen Ruston. Her mother was a baroness[36] (what even is that?). Hepburn's father left her family when she was young, which she struggled with for a lifetime. Hepburn was also a dancer before, during, and after World War II. There are many stories about this in the book *Dutch Girl* by Robert Matzen. Hepburn's family faced hardships during the war—she and her mother didn't have a lot of food to eat, and their house burned down. After the war, Hepburn started taking small parts in movies so she could make money. From there, she got a role on Broadway in *Gigi*. Hepburn's understudy during the production for *Gigi* was my cousin Jill Kraft which is a little factoid I adore sharing.

She gave a wonderful performance and was spotted by William Wyler, a big Hollywood director, who cast her in *Roman Holiday* opposite Gregory Peck (a famous leading man in old Hollywood).

Gregory Peck was a very established actor (he starred as the non–Jewish reporter in *Gentleman's Agreement*) but he liked Hepburn so much and saw her talent that he made sure she was top billing. I love *Roman Holiday* and her performance was so good that she won an Oscar in the first movie she starred in. Her career skyrocketed from there, and she made other classical films like *Sabrina, Funny Face, Charade, War and Peace*, and many more. A lot of people associate her with the film she did in 1961, *Breakfast at Tiffany's*.

For Monroe, she took the torch from Jean Harlow, being the classic "dumb" attractive girl with a curvy figure. And Hepburn was a new

"Wate-On" ad from the 1950s shows the changing beauty standard (Wikimedia Commons).

force in Hollywood because she didn't have a 1950s "classically attractive" figure. She called herself gamine, which means boyish. So with these two opposing images of beauty, the 1950s were a very different decade in beauty standards. One aspect of this was the food surplus.

The 1950s post-war food surplus made the popular figure a curvy one. What is so interesting for me about this decade was that there were even ads popularizing things to do to gain weight! Here's an example. I just find it mind-blowing that we have gone in such a different direction now that there are pills to get skinnier, when 70 years ago it was the exact opposite.

Another example of the body trend being completely different is the old cartoon *Hilda*.

When I saw this cartoon I marveled at how much trends have changed and how film has helped me see that story and better understand how society tricks us into feeling bad about ourselves.

There's so much fat shaming and body comparison these days that it makes me sick to even look at that stuff online. The way that women are scrutinized endlessly for their size and men get to do whatever they want is more sexist than most things I see in 1930s movies, honestly. I feel that watching these old movies can teach us to not be ashamed and to understand diet culture and how no one fits it perfectly or ever will. I struggle with this stuff daily, but just knowing that diet culture is an illusion and has always changed helps me more than anything.

Anna May Wong
Typecasting and Asians in Hollywood

In March 2022, *Everything Everywhere All at Once* was released in theaters. The film is about a Chinese immigrant named Evelyn, played by Michelle Yeoh. An interdimensional change transforms the universe and Evelyn must navigate her newfound powers and her journey through philosophical thoughts and realms. The film swept the 2023 Oscars—a completely unexpected turn. The Asian representation the film symbolizes has been a long time coming.

The first movie to have a primarily Asian cast was the 1961 musical comedy *Flower Drum Song*. The film was a modest success and did not score any major hits, but nowadays it is looked upon as an innovative film for its diversity, although many find its stereotyping offensive, as with most films starring Asians at the time. The trend of all–Asian cast films did not become a consistent trend until very recently, with the release of *Crazy Rich Asians* in 2018. Robert Ito wrote in the *New York Times* of the film, "For Asian and Asian-American viewers, the film, which opens on Aug. 15, is important not just as something of a cinematic Halley's comet—before 'Joy Luck Club,' there was 'Flower Drum Song' in 1961, and then, what? There's also an eager hope that if this movie succeeds, it just might stave off another quarter-century drought."[1] *Crazy Rich Asians*, according to Anna May Wong biographer Katie Gee Salisbury, "proved films with all Asian casts can be commercially successful." Salisbury wrote the astounding book *Not Your China Doll*, a biography of Anna May Wong. I interviewed Salisbury over the phone a few months ago.

Before *Crazy Rich Asians*' release, a movement called #StarringJohnCho went viral. The movement edited John Cho, a Korean American actor, into films with white male leads: *The Martian, Avengers*, and more.[2] The movement also pointed out how rarely Asian Americans appeared in the movies. Many white actors were playing Asian roles, as in *Aloha*, where Emma Stone plays a part–Asian and Hawaiian character. Stone told *The Guardian* in 2015: "The character was not supposed to look like her background which was a quarter Hawaiian and a quarter Chinese. I've learned on a macro level about the insane history of whitewashing in Hollywood and how prevalent the problem truly is. It's ignited a conversation that's very important."[3]

Casting white actors as Asian characters has a long and disturbing history in Hollywood, one that Anna May Wong played a part in dismantling as the first Asian American movie star. She was born Wong Liu Tsong in 1905 to second-generation Chinese Americans, and her childhood was very American. Her family's neighborhood was a popular spot for filming movies. Anna loved to watch the famous movie stars in grease paint and costumes as they performed for the camera, directors eagerly shouting.

By age 11, she decided she wanted to be a movie actress and made her acting name her English name, Anna May Wong. Eventually, a film recruiter picked her out for a film called *The Red Lantern*, but her role as an extra was so small that when she saw the film, she couldn't even tell which one was her! Her first large-enough role was in *Bits of Life*, Hollywood's first anthology film, which told four separate stories. But her real break was in *Toll of the Sea*, a silent from 1922. It was the first Technicolor film to be widely released in theaters! The story was about an interracial relationship, and at the end she throws herself off a cliff, which was a very demanding role, especially for a 17-year-old. "In the 1920s it was very popular for the Asian characters, especially women, to die at the end of the film," Katie Gee Salisbury says.

Anna May Wong in the 1930s (*Photoplay Magazine*. Wikimedia Commons).

Unfortunately, Hollywood restricted the roles

Anna was allowed to have, due to anti-miscegenation laws. About this, Anna said: "No film lovers can ever marry me [on screen]. If they got an American actress to slant her eyes and eyebrows and wear a stiff black wig and dress in Chinese culture, it would be alright. But me? I really am Chinese. So I must always die in the movies so that the white girl with the yellow hair may get the man."[4] What Wong described is the exact plot of *The Toll of the Sea*.

Sadly, most if not all of Anna's roles are exoticized with oriental caricatures (which was a harmful characterization in which all Eastern cultures were blended into one stereotype). Katie Gee Salisbury said that these caricatures were often either a vamp (essentially a femme fatale) or a china doll (a submissive and feminine Asian woman).

Looking at them today, the stereotypes in early film roles for Asians and African Americans seem so out of line—it's hard to imagine these portrayals were ever okay with people. She spent years working in stereotyped roles in Hollywood, often as ethnicities that were not hers: a Native American in *Peter Pan* and an Inuit in *The Alaskan*.

By 1928, she was fed up with the industry and moved to Europe, following in the footsteps of Josephine Baker who also moved to Europe to try to escape the racism of America at the time. "Why is it that the screen Chinese are nearly always the villain of the piece, and so cruel, a murderous, treacherous snake in the grass? We are not like that. We have our own virtues. Why do they never show these on screen?" she said. "I got so weary of it all."[5]

Wong spent two years in Europe doing European movies, but she was homesick for America, so she decided to move back to Hollywood in 1930. Since nothing had changed, she continued in her "oriental" typecast roles—for which she received half the pay of her male co-stars.

A good role came in 1932 with *Shanghai Express*, co-starring Marlene Dietrich, which was hailed by American critics but not so much the Chinese ones, who felt it was not an accurate depiction, which Anna knew was true. She always felt she was too Chinese for Hollywood but too American for China. "In the industry, people often assumed she was from China, even though she was a third-generation American," Salisbury says.

A big moment for Wong was when she lost out on the lead role in *The Good Earth* to German actress Luise Rainer, who got an Oscar for her role, played in yellowface. It was incredibly uncomfortable for her to watch a white actress win an Oscar for a role she could've played.

Anna would have one more significant film: *Daughter of Shanghai*.

This was the first film to have two Asian romantic leads, which is interesting because it was made in 1937, more than 20 years after films became popular. It took Hollywood so long to even have a tiny amount of diversity.

By the late '30s, Wong's career started to fade out slowly over the following decades. She died in 1961. Her career was half in silent film, and this book is not going to cover that (there's just too much to talk about), but luckily, she was in many films with sound from the 1930s—most famously *Shanghai Express*, a 1932 adventure rom-com about Magdalen (Marlene Dietrich) who meets her old flame Donald Harvey (Clive Brook) in Peking during a civil war. Donald learns that Magdalen has become a prostitute called Shanghai Lily. They travel together by train, unaware that spy and army leader Henry Chang is on board.

A train is the perfect motif for a story because it keeps moving and at the same time stays grounded with the same characters. Some of the best mysteries in history include the train motif: from *The Great Train Robbery*, a silent film from 1903, to books like *Strangers on a Train* and *Murder on the Orient Express*.

Shanghai Express effectively uses the plot device of a train to keep together characters who otherwise would have parted. The only real problem is that there's not enough of Anna May Wong. She's in a few short scenes, and she does them well. But her other films have far more of her in them.

Many people agree that Wong's later filmography is weaker. To strengthen that hypothesis, there's *When Were You Born*, the 1937 cult-ish astrology movie with Anna May Wong. Yep, that's right—this was a B movie (the not-as-famous, not-as-financially-successful old movies with less-famous actors) in which you'll find the weirdest movies with the weirdest plotlines. "B-films during the studio era often resonate decades later because they explore issues and themes not found in higher-budget pictures," an anonymous essay from the Library of Congress says.[6] B movies were a place to explore things that couldn't be explored in the movies everybody went to go see.

When Were You Born is about an astrologer (Anna May Wong) who helps the police solve a murder. This movie is so cosmically weird that they actually delayed filming it until "Mercury, Venus, and Jupiter wheeled into conjunction with the sun."[7] The movie starts with a sleazy guy who explains what each astrological sign means. He also wrote the film and he really creeps me out. He says that some astrological predictions say that one day "women will cut their hair and wear trousers."

If there's anything about *When You Were Born* that's remotely good, it's Anna May Wong's performance. Near the end of her stardom, she always gave a fantastic performance where you can't stop watching her onscreen. A notable film in Wong's later filmography that I mentioned earlier is *Daughter of Shanghai*, the first major Hollywood film to have Asian romantic leads. The movie is about ... well, it's kind of complicated.

There are smugglers, and Anna May Wong is a detective who tries to catch them, and she gets help from her Asian male lead, Philip Ahn. As I said, B movies are crazy. They're not made to be classics; they're made to be weird. Before Wong made *Daughter of Shanghai*, she visited China (she filmed her journey, documented in archival footage on YouTube nowadays) which gave her a deeper connection to her roots.

She came back to Hollywood with the intent of playing more sympathetic Chinese roles—and she made *Daughter of Shanghai*. As the daughter of an anthropologist, I think everyone making a film about another culture should have to do field work to understand that culture more fully.

Overall, the movie is incredibly revolutionary for its time. I think that Anna May Wong's chemistry with Philip Ahn is striking. Ahn gets to play a sympathetic role: not the villain but the hero of the story. Ahn and Wong work together in the story, both getting their individual moments to shine. Wong plays a tough and brave character, because she had it rewritten to make her less of a passive character and more of a brave heroine. The movie had the working title *The Anna May Wong Story* because the character resembled her so much.[8]

The late film critic Brian Taves noted something interesting about Wong, particularly around the late 1930s: "The frequency with which portraits and articles about Wong appeared in magazines demonstrated her incredible popularity with the mainstream Caucasian audience. The evidence of press coverage strongly suggests that moviegoers had more progressive inclinations than the conservative studio chiefs and producers who made the casting decisions."[9]

Nineteen-thirties audiences may not have picked up on the other political and racial undertones of *Daughter of Shanghai*. All of the villains are white, and all of the smugglers take advantage of the refugees and immigrants who want to make it to America to have better lives by making money off of them for cheap labor and work.

Anna May Wong's character is also the only non-white dancer at the club where she works, and the white women discriminate against her for no apparent reason. The only positive white character in *Daughter of Shanghai* is an Irish man, and given America's history with the Irish, it seems that the film was more than just a B picture: it was a message to the people of the 1930s. The actor and film critic Bob Calloway mentioned this undercurrent in the final scene of the film: "The last sequence of the film has three characters from nationalities that have traditionally been oppressed in America rebelling against these wealthy wasps who are trying to exploit them."[10]

If you take away the smugglers, crime and aliens, you get a story that would be ahead of its time today: all oppressed people teaming up to dismantle the systems that keep them unhappy.

Given that it took *forever* to have more films with Asian romantic leads again, it seems that it takes the longest for the movies to be affected by progressive ideas—Hollywood is terrified of misstepping in any way with films because box office failures happen often.

It's incredibly interesting watching this film today, with our current mindsets, and seeing how much it satirizes cultural ignorance: in one scene, Phillip Ahn pretends to speak Russian to the ship's captain, when he actually just says "Alpha Beta Gamma Delta Epsilon." The white shipmates completely trust him, because they assume since he's Asian, he'd be too dumb to rat them out. The head of the ship even asks if Kim Lee (Ahn's character) wants to be his interpreter.

Wong's character Lan Ying Lin also gets exoticized, just like Wong in real life. However, in the movie, she uses it to her advantage. No one suspects her, so she can't easily get caught. "The movie itself never exoticizes Lan Ying, and the only time it does, is when she's performing onstage to fool everyone. In the *Thief of Baghdad*, this image was used to show her as the villain. In *Daughter of Shanghai*, it's a heroic act," Calloway elaborated on Wong's image in the late 1930s.

Wong and other Asian American stars' impact on Hollywood isn't talked about enough today. She was the first Asian American movie star, but she was also a fashion icon and a phenomenal actress, and she isn't getting enough credit for that.

Wong's onscreen fashion is phenomenal. She was known for her chic, feminine style and her use of pearls and necklaces. Asian symbols like dragons often made appearances in her clothing. Fashion designers often put her in beautiful Chinese-style dresses and paper fans.

"I love American clothes," she said to *Picture Play* in 1927, "but I realize that I look better if my gowns have a suggestion of China about them. And it's good business, too!"[11] Wong was even listed as the best dressed woman of 1935 by Mayfair Mannequin Academy.

In 2015, the Met Gala theme was "China: Through the Looking Glass," and *Vogue* wrote an article about Wong's fashion being the inspiration. "Wong's character Shosho is then brought out front where she delivers a riveting dance performance, and all while clad in a scanty, armor-like costume that Barbarella and the robot double of *Metropolis* would fight over. Others might steal an element—the towering chandelier-esque topper, the breastplates, or the metallic hot pants, say—for it is doubtful that any mere mortal would dare imitate her *entire* look; but then again, Beyoncé or Lady Gaga just might."

I love this quote because this is exactly what I thought of when I saw the Viking-esque costume Wong wears in *Piccadilly*. It totally looks like a modern pop star costume! I will never stop saying that 1920s and 1930s costuming is so ahead of its time.

I cannot wait for a recreation of the costume in the upcoming anime movie *Anime Wong*. (I made that up).

Following her career in the 1930s, Wong had trouble landing roles in the 1940s before finally getting her own TV show in the 1950s. Wong thought she would make her return to Hollywood with *Flower Drum Song*, but she died of a heart attack in her sleep in 1961.

Wong has left a legacy of perseverance and strength. Imagine the courage it takes to handle being cast as the woman who was "exotic" and who only served as a plot device for the white woman to get her man. It must've been exhausting! And yet, she did it. And people remember her today for it.

People today understand why representation is so important, but people in the 1920s and 1930s didn't. The horrific representation in early Hollywood shows that not all representation is good representation. Diversity matters when the characters represented are dynamic and different in their own ways: it's the best way to show that people are people and anyone you might have bias against may actually be just like you—with the same problems and the same interests. Wong inspires me because of how hard she pushed for what she believed in.

In Hollywood going forward, this will only become more clear as we pave the way for more and more diverse casting and stories. Anna May Wong was the first to do what she did. What truly stands out about Wong is that she didn't stop working when she realized she faced a huge obstacle (how people perceived her). She instead chose to do the work and prove people wrong. She never lost the faith that she could and would do better, which is the best aspect of a young mindset not tinted by negativity.

Looking at Old Hollywood Through the Lens of the "Me Too" Movement

In 2017, one of the widest-reaching social movements of the 21st century started a wildfire online. It came to public consciousness due to many events happening at the same time: Harvey Weinstein, Bill Cosby, and James Toback's sexual abuse allegations (among many, many others), tweets from sexually harassed and assaulted women, public lawsuits against abusers, and an army of women telling the world what had happened to them. #MeToo became the hot topic that the news, the blogs, the lawsuits, Twitter, and even pop stars (Ke$ha and Taylor Swift) were talking about. The movement was a direct result of social media and the internet—every single person on this planet with a computer or phone has a voice.

While sudden and intense at the time, the movement was a long time coming, so long that classic Hollywood has a plethora of examples of this horrific abuse happening—even in the films it produced. During the watershed #MeToo movement of the late 2010s, a documentary from 10 years before resurfaced. *Girl 27* is a documentary from the late 2000s centered on the rape and assault of movie extra Patricia Douglas at a 1937 MGM sales convention. The film became relevant 10 years later because it was long-standing evidence of sexual assault, which the movement needed at the time. One article in *Time* magazine brought this to light: "How Classic Hollywood's Party Culture Turned Women into Prey." The article, written by Erin Blakemore, discusses how female extras working in classic Hollywood were not protected by their studios and became "entertainment" for men at Hollywood parties—and how this led to the 1937 assault.

Apparently, Loretta Young was watching *Larry King Live* with her biographer Ed Funk and her daughter-in-law Linda Lewis back in 1998 when the subject of date rape came up. Lewis tried her best to make the "proper" lady understand the new terminology. "[It's] basically when you're with someone that you trust, or literally on a date with them, and you're not compliant, or you're saying no, and they're not listening. It doesn't have to be violent, it doesn't have to be rip-your-clothes-off. It's when your no isn't no."

Young responded to Lewis's explanation: "that's what happened between me and Clark."[1]

The three adults discussed what happened together, and the story seemed to take shape. Gable and Young were on an overnight train coming back from production. The two were in separate sleeping compartments, and Gable joined her. Young was unable to say no to Gable's advances. She never told anyone, not even her daughter, who allegedly was the result of the encounter, for decades. Shortly following the train ride, Young found out she was pregnant. A *Buzzfeed News* article by Anne Helen Petersen in 2015 exposed this story after Petersen talked extensively with Young's daughter-in-law, son, and biographer to reveal the full story to the public.[2]

This article also discusses the then-recent allegations against Bill Cosby and serves as an important precursor to the #MeToo movement two years later. Petersen states: "This is a story about the past, of course, but one with chilling echoes in the present: in the ever-accumulating allegations against Bill Cosby, or this week's revelations about the rape of a 16-year-old member of *The Runaways* in 1976. It's easy to look at Young's elaborate cover-up and label it ridiculous. It's harder to see what happened to her as indicative of larger structures of power—patriarchy, of course, but also Hollywood—that continue to make it so difficult for these stories to be told."

The past is more connected to the present than we realize—and we can learn more from it than we might think.

The quote above talks about Young's "elaborate cover-up." Young was a Catholic, which made the idea of abortion a sin. This left her no choice but to have the baby. Clark Gable was also married at the time and was known in the press as a notorious womanizer—Young didn't want to burden either of their public images with a child. At the time, it was hard enough for women to explain what had happened to them: of course, the word "rape" existed, but that was far too rough-sounding for many of these women's experiences. And they would probably not be believed, even if they dared to speak out.

Young told her family, who understood the dire consequences of a baby conceived out of wedlock—for any young woman, not even considering the weight of the public eye. They devised a plan. Often if a young actress told their studio they were pregnant, they would plan a quick abortion to avoid ruining the public images of the young stars.

Young shot two movies, made public appearances before her pregnancy was noticeable, and then fed fake stories to the press: she was having whirlwind weekends in Manhattan, and then the next second she was sick and had lost considerable weight.

Loretta Young's mother continued to tell stories to the press about her, which seemed to stop any conspiracies that she was pregnant. Many speculated about what her undiagnosed illness was, and the Young family invited a reporter into their house. Young lay in bed, with pillows placed strategically to hide her obvious pregnancy.

Despite the huge possible scandal, Young managed to avoid the press knowing about her child, Judy, by saying she had adopted a child. By January 1936, Loretta Young was back at work. It's unbelievable how little respect the industry pays to mothers. Young got only two months off before she had to be back at work, with shifts lasting longer than 12 hours. It was an incredibly elaborate lie that was detangled decades and decades later—and proves just how demoralizing the industry was on young women and still is today. The craziest fact is that Judy Young (Gable and Young's daughter) had Gable's ears and had to go through a procedure to pin them back—not for aesthetic reasons but purely because they would give it away.

These stories didn't begin in 1930s Hollywood—they have been a part of film culture for as long as it has existed.

The first Hollywood scandal is widely believed to be the Fatty Arbuckle case. Before that, there were minor scandals, but none took the world's attention like this one. Hollywood was only at its very beginnings in the early 1920s and still in the silent film era. It would be six years before the first film with sound.

In 1921, Fatty (Roscoe) Arbuckle starred in 18 silents for Paramount Pictures. He was paid an unprecedented amount of money for any star to make at the time: $3 million, which is around $50 million today. His comedy *Crazy to Marry* had just come out at the time, and his friend Fred Fischbach planned a party to celebrate. The party was held at the St. Francis Hotel in San Francisco.

Apparently, Arbuckle was having his car repaired when he sat down on an acid-soaked rag. According to *Smithsonian* magazine, "the acid burned through his pants to his buttocks, causing second-degree burns."³ He did not want to attend the party due to his burns, but his friend had planned such an elaborate party that there was no way he could cancel it. If only Arbuckle had not gone to the party.

Virginia Rappe, a 25-year-old model and actress, arrived at the hotel for a Labor Day party. When Arbuckle woke up at the hotel, he realized many uninvited guests were at the gathering. He was scared that the number of people would cause the police to find the party, which could be detrimental to his reputation because of Prohibition.

In the story told by a witness, Maude Delmont, Arbuckle allegedly, after several drinks, raped Virginia Rappe. She was taken to another room and doctors were called. She continued to stay at the hotel but was taken to the hospital and died on September 9, 1921, of a ruptured bladder.

This scandal started wild rumors in the newspapers about Arbuckle and destroyed his reputation. His new film was taken out of theaters immediately following the news. There was only one question, though: did he do it? Medical evidence and witnesses were examined, and Arbuckle was acquitted of all charges.

Following the case, Will Hays (recognize him from "Should Ladies Behave? Pre-Code Women Say No"?) banned Roscoe Arbuckle from ever appearing on screen—and even though he was later allowed to come back, his career was already dead. He changed his name to William B. Goodrich (Will B. Good) and tried to make a living directing films for his friends, but he failed and died 12 years later, in 1933.[4]

This case had a massive impact on pop culture, but in hindsight, it must have scared many men. One sexual assault accusation could completely sabotage a career, as evidenced by Arbuckle. Despite Arbuckle being innocent, this shows that when women's stories are told and believed, they have power. The public believed the women in this case—and I think this forced abusers to be even more secretive about their wrongdoings. Assault was taken seriously, and it was a big deal in the public consciousness. Even in 1921.

Speaking of secretive—in old Hollywood, sexual assault within a working relationship was very common. Executives used their power and influence on young stars' careers to get away with assault. Even women outside of old Hollywood had to deal with this behavior frequently. Working women were often treated horribly and were expected to do everything men wanted them to in exchange for jobs—now referred to as "casting couch culture." One example of this is Louis B. Mayer's alleged treatment of Judy Garland.

An article in from 2017 talks about how Mayer was Garland's "own Harvey Weinstein": "Although the epidemic of rampant sexual assault and harassment in Hollywood has only begun to make impactful headlines in the past month, it's an issue that's plagued the industry for decades." The article quotes Judy Garland, who wrote in her unpublished autobiography: "It's amazing how these big men, who had been around so many sophisticated women all their lives, could act like idiots."[5] According to Garland, Mayer would ask her to sit on his lap regularly during business meetings and touched her inappropriately in front of people. This happened many times, but when Garland grew up, she told him to stop: "Mr. Mayer, don't you ever, ever do that again. I just will not stand for it." One MGM executive remembered Garland telling them that if she did not do what Mayer wanted, he would say, "I'll ruin you and I can do it. I'll break you if it's the last thing I do."

After the heyday of MGM, Mayer has been accused of assaulting 60 women. Many of these stories have come out very recently, and that's the case with the Tippi Hedren story.

Tippi Hedren was initially a fashion model, gracing the covers of *Glamour* and *Life* magazines. Hitchcock wanted to cast her in a project. He put her through extensive screen tests and advised her on many things: clothing (which he had personally designed by Edith Head), filmmaking, acting, wine, and food.[6] And worse: how she should eat, act, and live.[7] Hedren was then cast in *The Birds*, a classic Hitchcock suspense film.

The filming of the movie was initially a good experience for Hedren,[8] but later in the filming, Hitchcock had his crew throw real birds at her, when he had assured her they would be mechanical birds.[9] After Hedren started crying after a week of this treatment, her doctor asked: "Are you trying to kill her?"[10] Hedren believes he did this because she refused his sexual advances.[11]

According to biographer Donald Spoto, Hitchcock hired two crew members to follow Hedren around; he wanted to know where she went after she left the set and how she spent her free time. Over the filming of the two movies they did together, *The Birds* and *Marnie*, Hitchcock demanded to have a glass of wine with her every night.[12]

Hitchcock also attempted to grab and violently kiss Hedren in the back of the car on the way to the set.[13] Hedren thinks that the plot about rape in *Marnie* was actually Hitchcock's fantasy that he made up to subtly spite her and make her uncomfortable while he had her under contract.[14] In Donald Spoto's 2008 book *Spellbound by Beauty*, he quotes Hedren as saying: "He stared at me and simply said, as if it was the most natural thing in the world, that from this time on, he expected me to make myself sexually available and accessible to him—however and whenever and wherever he wanted."

This happened despite Hitchcock having been married for more than 30 years—and Hedren had a daughter, Melanie Griffith, who would become a huge actress, who he refused to let on the set of his films. "I wasn't even allowed to visit my mom at the studio," she said.[15] Melanie's daughter and Hedren's granddaughter is Dakota Johnson, a famous actress who you might know from *The Five-Year Engagement* or *Fifty Shades of Grey*.

Even Tippi Hedren's hairdresser, Virginia Darcy, tried to tell Hitchcock not to be so obsessively possessive with Hedren. "Tippi felt rightly that she was not his property, but he'd say, 'You are, I have a contract,'" Darcy recalled.[16] After their two films together, Hedren told Hitchcock it would be her last film with him.

It seems like Hitchcock was stuck in a 1950s state of mind about women: you're my property—whereas Hedren was more in the new wave 1960s mindset about women. Hedren allegedly called Hitchcock a "fat pig" after his advances.

Hedren told the *Financial Times* in 2012: "I said I wanted to get out of my contract. He said: 'You can't. You have your daughter to support, and your parents are getting older.' I said: 'Nobody would want me to be in this situation, I want to get out.' And he said: 'I'll ruin your career.' I said: 'Do what you have to do.' And he did ruin my career. He kept me under contract, paid me to do nothing for close on two years."

It's odd to me how Hitchcock's films center on obsession and infatuation most of the time—and he also dealt with this in his real life, with actresses such as Grace Kelly and Tippi Hedren. Tippi Hedren's claims seem to be backed up by other sources, including her hairdresser, her daughter, and co-star Diane Baker.[17] However, the claims were refuted by Joan Fontaine and others who worked with Hitchcock, making it hard to know what actually did happen.

The Birds and *Marnie* were Hitchcock's last "classic" films—he had several flop films after that. I guess it caught up to him.

In 2012, a TV movie was made out of this story, titled *The Girl*. *The Girl* follows the exact narrative arc I just told you about, and it's essentially from Hedren's perspective. Hitchcock never fully spoke on the matter, but his other "blondes" spoke about their positive relationships with him, including Eva Marie Saint, Kim Novak, and Doris Day, who was still alive at the time.

The director of *Hitchcock*, the biopic of Alfred Hitchcock from 2013, said of *The Girl* that it "seems a rare one-note portrayal of a man who was a little more complex than that. A lot of people, who were there, do not recognise this portrayal of him as this monster." Many felt that Hitchcock was unfairly represented.

No matter what happened, at least Hedren doesn't have any spite remaining: "I've been able to separate the two. The man who was the artist. I mean, what he gave to the motion picture industry can never be taken away from him and I certainly wouldn't want to try. But on the other side, there is that dark side that was really awful."

Whether or not the claims are true, this incident reflects how Hollywood treated its stars at the time: Hedren would've reported it, but in the early 1960s, terms like sexual harassment didn't exist. This is similar to Loretta Young, who, earlier in the chapter, didn't know the terminology to describe "what happened between me and Clark."

It also reflects how the public treated sexual assault before the #MeToo movement: many were reluctant to believe the women. When asked why she spoke out, Tippi Hedren said: "I did it because this is legion all over the world. There's nothing unique about it. Women complain all the time about somebody trying to make a pass at them or have a relationship in which they are not interested. I don't put up with that kind of thing. I wanted to let women, especially young women, know never to allow that kind of approach and to be forceful in telling people you're not interested in having that kind of a relationship. It's not a bad thing to say no."[18]

The more I research this, the more I learn about how much old Hollywood really did contribute to the #MeToo movement. Practically every single story I've told you has been talked about shortly before or during the movement. It goes to show the importance of old stories on modern culture.

You might be wondering why I'm not talking about sexual assault happening in the actual old movies, or you might know that, for the most part, there was none. Nobody talked about sexual assault in film—or at least very rarely. Three examples I can think of are *Diary of a Lost Girl*, the little-known Louise Brooks movie from 1929, *Marnie*, which we talked about, and *Repulsion*, a Catherine Deneuve film about a woman who is scared of men and gradually recedes into delusion. I'm not the #1 expert on 1970s Hollywood, but I know that Hollywood loosened up enough to showcase a scene of this kind of mistreatment toward the end of the 1970s and the early 1980s, showcased by Irene Cara's horrifying audition scene toward the end of the movie *Fame*.

Old Hollywood Through the Lens of the "Me Too" Movement

I thought that, for a book about old Hollywood, it would be tough not to mention the harsh mistreatment of women in this way—I believe that it can help victims to hear other people's experiences. In my experience, struggling with mental health every day, it has always helped me to hear how other people who are struggling made it through.

The fact that people can be used as objects without their permission is so obviously wrong that I can't even believe it is questioned. More thought should go into the fact that women have been struggling with sexual abuse and assault for an excruciatingly long time—it's not just the last 50 years that women have been in the workplace. It has been way longer than most people realize.

Why Were There "No Female Directors" in Old Hollywood? The Secret History of Women During Hollywood's Inception

In 2023, the world practically shut down because of one movie. *Barbie* brought every woman (and sometimes man) into the theater from pure curiosity over how the film would present the controversial doll everyone remembers from their childhood—whether it was the little girls dreaming of a better life in the 1950s or a modern girl buying a Barbie at Toys "R" Us (wait, does that still exist?).

To me, aside from the film being incredible, the most amazing thing about the landmark achievement *Barbie* is that Greta Gerwig is the first female director ever to make a film that grossed $1 billion at the box office. I know, at first mention, it might not seem so crazy, but there are only 53 movies in cinema history that have grossed a billion dollars, and only one of them was directed by a woman. The fact that it took until 2023 to do this is a testament to how hard it has been in the last hundred years for female directors in the film industry.

But you'll notice that I said one hundred years. Because female directors were *huge* in old Hollywood before that.

Just like we talked about with Jews, women found a new path, aside from the path already paved for them: a life of housekeeping, cooking, and taking care of children. And since film was a new industry, they could invent it and create it themselves.

The first female filmmaker, Alice Guy Blaché, was one of the first filmmakers ever. She created the first film to tell a story. It was called *The Cabbage Fairy*, and it was made in 1896. Blaché became the first woman to operate and create her own studio. She opened Solax Studios in New Jersey. Before Hollywood, New Jersey was the center of movies.

Why Were There "No Female Directors" in Old Hollywood?

Blaché told *The Moving Picture World* in 1914: "There is nothing connected with the staging of a motion picture that a woman cannot do as easily as a man, and there is no reason she cannot master every technicality of the art.... In the arts of acting, painting, music, and literature women have long held their place among the most successful workers, and when it is considered how vitally these arts enter into the production of motion pictures one wonders why the names of scores of women are not found among the most successful creators of photodrama offerings."

That was more than 110 years ago, and we are still battling this stereotype of women in film. This quote articulates perfectly why Blaché was the perfect "first female director." Her personality was brave and perfect for such a trailblazing career. And the craziest thing is that Blaché had a daughter named Simone.[1] We were probably switched at birth, and I was really born in the 1910s. It would make total sense.

Before Blaché's story film *The Cabbage Fairy*, movies were mostly just short films of crazy things going on onscreen: magicians, disappearing acts, dancing. "Before very long, every moving picture house in the country was turning out stories instead of spectacles and plots instead of panoramas," Blaché told the *New York Tribune* in November 1912.[2]

Blaché made many silent movies during this period, including the high-budget film *The Life of Christ*, a weird movie sort of based on the New Testament. She also made a "comedy" film that was very ahead of its time: *The Consequences of Feminism*. The film was a farce of society where women and men swapped roles. Men made themselves "pretty" for women, talked, sewed, cooked, and took care of children while the women drank their coffee, read their books, and fought about men. Another Guy film that was ahead of its time was *Algie the Miner*, one of the first movies to showcase a gay character.

Alice Blaché's career ended sadly. Solax couldn't compete with the major Hollywood studios, so it shut down. She moved to France, and when she came back, she couldn't find a single print of any of her films. This was very common during the silent era. Nobody thought that films would be impactful or important at all, and so they were destroyed.

Films would be destroyed especially when printed on nitrate film, an unstable, flammable type of film stock that could explode if not managed in the right conditions. Luckily, film stock and technology changed in the 1930s and pretty much all films made after that can be found (unless they aired on TV).

This wasn't Blaché's only tragedy in her film career. "Léon Gaumont published a history of the Gaumont Film Company, which didn't mention anything before 1907. He omitted all of Alice Guy Blaché's work as a director. Consequently, nobody knew for a long time how significant a role she played in setting up his very successful studios and in the birth of film itself," Alicia Malone wrote of Blaché in her book *Backwards & In Heels*.[3] After her death, she has been re-acknowledged for just how important she was in the history of film.

Lois Weber was Blaché's female-director peer and ultimately became more successful. What set Weber apart was her passion for portraying social issues in film. The movie that made her popular was 1916's *Where Are My Children?*, a silent drama film about abortion and birth control. The film centers on a district attorney who is prosecuting a doctor after the death of his client following an abortion. Meanwhile, he also discovers that his wife has been having frequent abortions so as not to inconvenience herself as a figure in high society. While the film takes a strong stance against abortion, Weber wrote the film in a time when illegal and indecent abortions by sketchy doctors were affecting women's future ability to have children.

Weber addressed many other controversial topics in her career: following *Where Are My Children?*, she tackled the legalization of birth control pills again in *The Hand That Rocks the Cradle*. She addressed poverty in *The Blot* and *Shoes*, capital punishment in *The People vs. John Doe*, and drug abuse in *Hop, the Devil's Brew*.

In addition to pushing the boundaries of controversy and politics, Weber also pushed boundaries in film and visual storytelling. Her landmark short film, 1913's *Suspense*, has some of the earliest examples of split-screen storytelling and car-chase scenes. And along with that, Weber starred in and wrote the film herself!

By the middle of the 1920s, women were working less and less as directors. "As the 1920s rolled on and the Great Depression came, women directors started to be phased out. And a lot of that has to do with money, because movies all of a sudden had to make a profit, banks came in to finance movies, Hollywood started to be run as a business, and executives were put in charge. Women at the time weren't thought of as being executive-minded or able to run a business or able to cope with large amounts of money," Malone stated later in her TED talk.

However, there were still plenty of women writing films—mostly because women's films were so popular. This is exemplified by Frances Marion, a screenwriter who first wrote for Mary Pickford. Marion wrote

Why Were There "No Female Directors" in Old Hollywood?

many classic films: *Dinner at Eight, The Red Mill, Blondie of the Follies, Poor Little Rich Girl, Camille,* and *Anna Christie*. Marion was mentored by Lois Weber, the innovative, boundary-pushing director. Marion also wrote films for Greta Garbo, Shirley Temple, and Marion Davies, and she wrote more than 130 films in the classic era and won two Academy Awards.

Marion became well known in the industry for writing (and sometimes directing) films with strong female leads, and early in her career, she became the highest paid screenwriter in Hollywood for decades.[4]

"Women had always found sanctuary in writing; it was accomplished in private and provided a creative vent when little was expected or accepted of a woman other than to be a good wife and mother. For Frances [Marion] and her friends, a virtue was derived from oppression; with so little expected of them, they were free to accomplish much," Cari Beauchamp wrote in her biography of Frances Marion. It seems that writing could be the way out of stressful daily life for many women, even women who weren't screenwriters.

Many powerful women became screenwriters in the 1920s and 1930s: Anita Loos, June Mathis, even Ginger Rogers's mom, Lela Rogers. By the 1930s, female directors, unlike female writers, had disappeared almost completely.

There was only one feature length female director (who made more than one movie) in the 1930s: Dorothy Arzner. According to Criterion, Arzner "broke into the Hollywood boys club."[5] Arzner directed 20 movies, and her impact on Hollywood is unparalleled. Her most famous work is *Dance, Girl, Dance,* a 1940s feminist film about a burlesque star played by Lucille Ball and a ballerina played by Maureen O'Hara. Arzner allegedly initiated a big change in the script, making the mentor/ballet dancer of the two girls a woman. This makes the movie even more about female relationships.

The movie was a flop on immediate release, but looking back, critics have named it a landmark feminist film because of the scene where O'Hara's character talks to the audience at the burlesque show: "What's it for? So you can go home when the show's over, strut before your wives and sweethearts and play at being the stronger sex for a minute? I'm sure they see through you. I'm sure they see through you just like we do!"

Strong female perspectives in 1940s films weren't just rare, they were nonexistent. Nobody was talking about how the *women* feel in all the burlesque club scenes, à la *Gilda* starring Rita Hayworth (1947). Does anybody ask them how they feel? This is the only movie of the era to address the perspective of women, and that's also what made Arzner such an outstanding director.

In *Dance, Girl, Dance*, the mentor for the two women, a former Russian ballerina, dies in a tragic accident, and the two are left to fend for themselves and deal with their careers, each in different ways. Maureen O'Hara's character, Judy, struggles to find jobs in ballet, and Bubbles (whose stage name is Tiger Lily) succeeds at performing for men every night as a "burlesque queen."

One of the most innovative things about the film is its focus on female friendship over romantic relationships. The movie is all about the two women who star in the film and way less about the men ... they're unimportant in the plot's development and structure.

"She was a star spotter," film critic B. Ruby Rich said of Arzner; "she had an amazing sense of who had 'it': Clara Bow, Katharine Hepburn, Lucille Ball, Joan Crawford ... over and over, she is shaping a persona that these actors then build on to make very successful careers after they leave her filmmaking." These comments appeared on the Criterion Channel in 2019, when the channel created a series with many of Arzner's best films.

Merrily We Go to Hell, a stark drama about alcoholism, proved that Arzner followed in Lois Weber's footsteps by tackling a dark and controversial topic, as Weber had done in 1916 with *Hop, the Devil's Brew*. The movie stars the wonderful Sylvia Sidney. She plays an heiress who rescues an alcoholic Fredric March and inspires him to write a play, but he relapses and returns to old habits. "*Merrily* is a damning portrait of the stakes of marriage, in which the woman takes on the burden of loving a man who is too narcissistic and oblivious to pay attention to her. The humor and banter of the film mask the underlying emotional turmoil," Judith Mayne wrote in an essay for Criterion.[6]

What made the film so unmistakably Arzner was challenging marriage as the ultimate "happy ending" for a woman. March's character Jerry has an almost split personality, not unlike the previous year's *Dr. Jekyll and Mr. Hyde*, an adaptation of the Robert Louis Stevenson novella which was in itself a metaphor for mental illness. The last scene, according to Pamela Hutchinson of *The Independent*, "makes a mockery of the idea of a happy ending."[7] When Joan (Sylvia Sydney) suspects that Jerry is unhappy in their marriage, she proposes an open marriage, a shocking prospect even now, much less in 1932! Joan then goes on a date with Cary Grant. Sylvia Sidney and Cary Grant should've made more movies together. The movie ends up being a statement not just

Why Were There "No Female Directors" in Old Hollywood?

on non-monogamy and alcoholism but also on marriage and the constraints it puts on female freedom.

Since Arzner didn't make many films, most of her movies weren't huge hits—but they were funny and genius in hindsight. *Honor Among Lovers* wasn't one of them. It seems shallow and conservative through today's lens. I do love when Ginger Rogers says, "I want to know what is caviar. It looks like rubber. Smells like fish!" and then the guy she's having lunch with says, "It's a fish when they're very young," at which point she says, "I don't believe it. They're round. And I never heard of a round fish." Seeing 19-year-old Ginger nail these lines is the best part of *Honor Among Lovers*, an otherwise stiff comedy-drama about a man who falls for his secretary. It doesn't seem very Arzner.

Regardless, her genius didn't end with film: Arzner invented the boom mic on the set of Clara Bow's *The Wild Party*, Bow's first talkie. For their voices to be amplified, actors usually had to wear or hold a poorly disguised microphone, which could be awkward (depicted perfectly in the scenes in *Singin' in the Rain* where Lina tries to talk for the microphone). When Bow was having a nervous breakdown, forgetting where the mic was placed, Arzner attached the mic to a fishing rod. Boom—the boom mic was invented and audio capture was forever transformed. Everyone uses a boom mic now so that visible mics don't have to appear in any shot. Another innovation that Arzner popularized was the mobile camera, which she used in *Merrily We Go to Hell* and which allows the audience to move with Jerry (Fredric March) as he sways, tipsy on booze.

The only other female working director in the 1930s was Wanda Tuchock, who co-directed the 1934 teenage rebellion movie *Finishing School*. She only directed one movie, so I don't think she truly counts as a huge director like Arzner was. *Finishing School* was a classic Pre-Code—elements of female friendship, explicit relationships, and underage drinking and lots of partying. The uniqueness of *Finishing School* comes from the fact that it shuns none of these things, and treats it as if it is routine for teenagers to be involved in such endeavors, which was unusual in the industry at the time. In the Pre-Code era, these behaviors usually concerned adults, not teens. Maybe this was Tuchock's unique perspective she brought to the film.

Sadly, Dorothy Arzner retired from directing for reasons unknown in 1943. Many speculate it was because of the homophobia and sexism in the industry at the time—Arzner was a lesbian. At least there were strong women onscreen to make up for the lack of off-screen diversity.

"The studios knew that audiences had become predominantly female, and these films often centered around love and domesticity—but they gave glimpses into what women's independence could look like outside of the home (even if they frequently ended with wedding bells). Though they were typically written and directed by men, they were vehicles for the riveting female stars of the era: Bette Davis, Lauren Bacall, Katharine Hepburn, Ginger Rogers, Ingrid Bergman, Joan Crawford, Rita Hayworth," Michael Schulman, the *New Yorker* arts and film writer, told me in an email last spring. "These women brought a wit and maturity to the screen; they weren't just objects of desire but strong personalities whose characters sliced through the world with agency."

The next female director was Ida Lupino, who made her directorial debut in 1949 with *Never Fear*. Lupino had been an actress for Warner Brothers, and when she rejected a role with Ronald Reagan in *Kings Row*, Jack Warner suspended her. While on suspension, Lupino had plenty of time to learn the art of directing and editing processes. Collier Young, her husband at the time, formed an independent company called The Filmmakers Inc., where she would direct her first films. The most notable was the 1953 noir film *The Hitchhiker*, which became the first noir directed by a woman.

The Filmmakers Inc. went out of business in 1955, and Lupino turned to the new medium of television for her newfound directing passion. She directed episodes of *The Twilight Zone, The Lucy & Desi Comedy Hour, Gilligan's Island, Batman, Columbo,* and *Bonanza*. One of my relatives, Bernie Hoffman, actually appeared on *Bonanza* as the bartender!

Following Lupino and Arzner's careers, female directors were still few and far between until the late 20th century. In the 1980s, many women became studio heads or executives, including Sherry Lansing, who became chairman and CEO of Paramount. However, even today, there are still comparatively few female directors. In fact, there were far more in the 1910s and 1920s than there are now!

TCM host Alicia Malone, in her 2017 TED talk, spoke about female directors: "People say to me, 'It's Hollywood. It's a boy's club. It always has been, it always will be.' And that's when I like to show them images of the very first filmmakers in Hollywood, which helps to change their idea of what a director looks like. In the late 1890s at the start of cinema, right up to the 1920s, there were more female filmmakers than there are today. So that means, before women could even vote, they had better positions in Hollywood."

Why Were There "No Female Directors" in Old Hollywood?

Lack of female directors in the entertainment industry is a bigger problem than it seems. It's not because women are inherently "bad directors"—neither sex is inherently bad at anything. It seems that it's the studios and male executives holding these women back, even today. A *Buzzfeed* article by Ariane Lange explains the "vicious cycle" that women endure in Hollywood and other professions: "It happens in both television and film: A 2017 study from the University of Southern California's Media, Diversity & Social Change Initiative found that female directors who made one film were significantly less likely to direct a second film than their male peers in a 10-year span. Supporting those numbers are stories from hotshot directors like Karyn Kusama and Catherine Hardwicke, who reaffirm that, even with critical buzz and box office chops, women face more obstacles than men in getting to—and staying in—the director's chair."[8]

It looks like there's nothing we can do except keep pushing and creating more stories, in hopes that someday, women will have equal power over the way the world sees everything—not just Hollywood.

A Public Service Announcement on Colorized Films

Do. Not. Watch. Colorized Films. I repeat: Do not watch colorized films. This is the one rule about classic movies. With the mention of a colorized film, the entire classic film community goes silent and tells you they hate them. Ask any classic movie fan. Any of them will say so.

Bill Powell sat on a couch—his skin an unnatural shade of peach, with an aura around his body. I shivered because he looked like a ghost. The first colorized film I watched was *My Man Godfrey*, a screwball comedy with William Powell and Carole Lombard. It was incredibly interesting for two reasons: it is a great film, and the colorizing was done so horribly that every second I watched it, I hyper-focused on the way the characters looked as if they were supernatural beings floating in a preschooler's coloring pages stained with Skittle juice. Call me crazy, but when you watch colorized *Casablanca*, you'll agree.

Colorized films are films that were originally shot in black and white that have been colored to "add to the experience" of watching them. This process became popular in the 1980s, when color TV was finally the standard, and companies wanted to make money off of the newly invented video tape player, where you could play any movie at home if you rented it at the video store. They attempted to breathe new life into the Golden Age of Hollywood by modernizing old movies with colorization.

In 1983, pop culture was far from the films of the 1930s when portly men in three-piece suits called women with fur coats "gold diggers." Instead, kids and adults put on their shoulder pads and electric blue eyeshadow and rolled their eyes at the films of the past. Hal Roach Studios, an American motion picture and television studio, marketed these classic films to new audiences—both to old people who hadn't seen these films since their childhood and to kids who may have been more keen on color films than black and white. They used new computer technology to put color onto these seemingly "lifeless" films.

A Public Service Announcement on Colorized Films

I asked Michael Schulman, staff writer at the *New Yorker*, what those of you who are scared off by the idea of black and white films should do: "I'd encourage anyone who's squeamish about sitting through black-and-white movies to give them a chance. Once you train your eye to sit with monochrome, you'll get a much better feel for the beauty of classic movies. Savor the interplay of light and shadow, the smoke-filled alleyways of film noir, the glamor and otherworldliness of the screen gods and goddesses. Plus, colorized films tend to look garish."

See? There are only a couple of things that classic movie fans agree on. This is the main one.

The first film to receive colorization and release was *Topper*, the 1937 Constance Bennett and Cary Grant vehicle. There were two sides to the argument in favor of colorized films: some argued that colorization would create a new audience, and some argued that the lighting in black and white films was not adequate for colorization.

In 1987, the Senate called a hearing on colorized films, in part due to so many Golden Age stars speaking out against them. Ginger Rogers called colorized films "embarrassing and insulting." Director Sydney Pollack called them "morally unacceptable" and Woody Allen called them "cheesy artificial symbols of one society's greed."[9] All three testified before the Senate in May 1987.

In the hearing, the 76-year-old Rogers talked about watching a colorized version of *42nd Street*, a film he starred in with Ruby Keeler and other 1930s stars. "I'm glad that Busby Berkeley [the film's choreographer] isn't here to see what they are doing to his art. It would break his heart to see those brilliant dance numbers done-in by flat, lifeless computer color."[10]

Rogers then read a letter from Jimmy Stewart (who spoke further about this on *The Tonight Show* in 1987) about the colorization of his film *It's a Wonderful Life*: "The artificial color was detrimental to the story, to the whole atmosphere and artistry of the film. When I think of Frank Capra's fine cameraman, Joe Walker, and the time he spent on the delicate lighting and built-in shadow of 'It's a Wonderful Life' and to have that work wiped out by computerized color, which destroys the delicate shadows and depths of each scene, it makes me mad."

Before the hearing, film critics Gene Siskel and Roger Elbert did a special episode of their show, with Siskel claiming that computer colorization was vandalism: "They arrest people who spray subway cars, they lock up people who attack paintings and sculptures in museums, and adding color to black and white films, even if it's only to the tape shown on TV or sold in stores, is vandalism nonetheless." Ebert also spoke: "What was so wrong about black and white movies in the first place? By filming in black and white, movies can sometimes be more dreamlike, elegantly stylized, and mysterious. They can add a whole additional dimension to reality, while color sometimes just supplies additional unnecessary information."[11]

This brings us to something film-goers often refuse to acknowledge that I mentioned at the very beginning: film *is* art. Would you go into a museum and paint a black-and-white photo with color? No, because it seems wrong to change artists' artistic choices for financial gain. There are reasons these films were shot in black and white (aside from color film costing more). Black and white adds a classic vintage 1950s old-timey car kind of feel. While at times black and white can be boring, it can also add to the humor, sentiment, and plot of these films.

As a teenager, I've seen my peers get scared off by black-and-white films, preferring old classics like *The Wizard of Oz*, a (partially) color film, over any black-and-white films from the same era. It seems boring to wash all of the color out of film, especially after an entire life of seeing vivid color in every film and TV show you've watched. But there's an inherent value to seeing what people watched back then. One thing I find to be interesting about black and white film is that, in its time, most people dreamed in black and white. This makes me associate dreams with film—which is what they are. From the Great Depression until the early 1960s, black and white dreams were the norm, and color dreams were a rare thing, dubbed "Technicolor dreams" by experts.[12]

This reinforces the fact that film has a deep effect on human consciousness. If viewing films determines the colors in our dreams, imagine what else it influences in our lives. This is why I believe that coloring films is detrimental to the viewing experience: it feels like changing history and erasing the past. We should re-release these films into theaters, regardless of colorization, and watch them in every classroom. Film is an effective method of teaching young people about the past in a more entertaining way than a history textbook's stale pages filled with dates and names. Don't pretend like these films were in color the whole time!

Following the hearing, the National Film Preservation Act became law. This act changed many things, but for colorization, it made each colorized film exhibit a statement before the film played: "This is a colorized version of a film originally marketed and distributed to the public in black and white. It has been altered without the participation of the principal director, screenwriter, and other creators of the original film."

A Public Service Announcement on Colorized Films

For more than one reason, colorization ended up becoming a short fad. Computer technology has advanced and made colorization much easier, but it does not have the same popularity it used to.[13]

This debacle reminds me of the current entertainment industry, which makes big bucks from capitalizing on old media—whether biopics, remakes, or remixes and interpolations of old songs. In the same way that 1980s Hollywood attempted to make money off of old stories and media, this has been repeated in today's landscape on a much wider scale. When will we learn that nothing can replace fresh and exciting stories?

I think the reason that Hollywood currently reaches for these endless remakes of the past instead of creating new media is the lack of a monoculture. This word usually refers to farming, but it also describes a common culture that everyone who lived through that time experienced. For example, in the 1960s, the Beatles were ubiquitous. Every single boomer I talk to lights up when I mention the Beatles. Every one of them remembers finding out about the JFK assassination. In the 1980s, a certain popular artist's video could drop and the entire world would be talking about it.

Today, this seems to have changed because of the internet and the streaming of movies and music. People want to access old movies (in this case, any movie that isn't brand new), old music, indie artists, new releases, or whatever they want. This has created a lack of common ground. When we talk about the 2010s and the 2020s twenty years from now, will we have the same references? Will there be touchstone popular moments everybody knows? Personally, I doubt it. "As an era, the '90s does feel distinct and tangible and whole, with its own semi-unified fashion sense and sound and cultural ethos; these specifics radically differ, of course, from person to person, but I'm guessing the 2000s or the 2010s don't conjure up quite as vivid a mental picture for you," Rob Harvilla wrote in his book *60 Songs That Explain the '90s*.

Nostalgia has become our culture: most popular media points back to another reference, because studios don't think they can pull in viewers without "nostalgia bait." This is relevant with classic movies because no one remembers most of these eras enough to have nostalgia for them anymore, so we can essentially view them with new eyes.

This 21st-century era is also vastly different from the 20th because we now have the power to consume whatever media we like: whether that is old, unknown, or new material. Classic films have taught me a new universe I'd never seen before. It wasn't the world of a Netflix TV show my family watches five episodes of every night; it was the world my grandparents lived in, the world that my great-grandparents lived in.

We don't have to resort to changing the past to market it to new viewers—for instance, with colorization, we can see it as it was, learn how to create completely new stories, and take that knowledge into every aspect of life.

Epilogue

Finishing this book took many, many hours just sitting at my computer, eyes burning in front of the screen, researching film movements, actors, genres, directors, and everything you can think of related to classic Hollywood. Near the end of that process in spring of 2024, I interrupted my solitary writing for a couple of hours to go to an event at my local library. My mom told me it was an event where I'd "get to talk to a bunch of old ladies."

When I arrived, I anxiously looked at the yellow Safeway cookies lined up on the table. What was I doing here? I'd have been better off just staying home, finishing my book. *Play it safe, Simone*, I thought to myself. But then as I looked at the old women sitting down, waiting to talk to me, I thought I'd give it a try. The library's teen program supervisor gave me some questions printed out on colorful construction paper to ask them.

I struck up a conversation with many of them, discussing their lives and stories. I found it very calming. There's something about people over 60—I feel like I don't have to hide my true self around them, whereas if I were with a group of teens, I'd anxiously try and figure out the best thing to say to not alienate my peers.

I love how when people get to be a certain age, they lose most of their uptightness and just let go. I talked to one woman, Nancy, who told me she didn't have enough time to write a book. "I would love to write a book," she said and sighed. "Why don't you?" I asked.

She looked me in the eye. "Well, I'm 87. I only have so much time left. I want to spend it with my eight grandkids and my five great-grandkids. I don't want to spend it in front of a screen writing."

"I guess I can understand that. I just don't think of my time that way," I said.

"And how old are you?"

"Almost 15."

Epilogue

We both burst out laughing at the absurdity of our age difference, and I realized that my fear of everything not working out the way I wanted it to was stupid. I saw myself in this woman; I could see myself (maybe) being happy getting older. And I could see why I've loved the subtle wisdom of old films: because they tell me, even if I don't realize it, that life goes on.

In April 2010, when I was a six-month-old baby, my grandmother died after a long battle with multiple sclerosis. I've felt her absence in my life since I can remember, and I know that my mom feels this way too. My only other connection to my mother line disappeared in a split second. In some way, I think that talking with old women is comforting to me because of this.

I talked to Sheryl next, who assured me that my book project was valuable. When she asked me what advice I'd have for the older generation, I told her that I think many older people don't realize that my generation is going to change the world, or at least we're going to try. Most of us know the pain going on in the world, and we want to try to help. We're better than the clichéd, screen-obsessed teenager. Sheryl replied: "We're all barraged with so much more information on everything than we were. I mean, we [Boomers] read the paper maybe once a day, and the news would come on at 6:00, and we'd have some idea of what was going on. But we didn't really care. And unfortunately, I think we didn't care enough. Because my generation could have, and I believe should have, done a lot better than we did. And for anyone who is not valuing the potential in our youth, I feel really sorry for you—because the youth have a completely new attitude that they're seemingly not picking up on."

It was refreshing to see somebody truly valuing our youth, and her words restored my faith in this project, especially after what almost happened last year.

On June 20, 2023, news broke that the entire leadership team working at Turner Classic Movies, even executives with decades of experience, were all laid off, due to Warner Brothers completely cutting TCM's budget.[1] This news was devastating to the Golden Age movie community because TCM is the only thing that holds us all together year after year. It's the only lifeline connecting those movies to us in the current moment.

The entire classic film community (including me) rallied to save the past of Hollywood. We were all so worried, fretting about what it could be like without our intelligent and deeply ridiculous tight-knit

Epilogue

community we've built around TCM. But worrying about anything means you care. People care about these movies deeply, because we all have our separate experiences with each of them: maybe it was entering a movie theater with your grandmother in the 1960s, holding her hand as you watched Audrey Hepburn dance around a French nightclub. Maybe it was when you saw *The Wizard of Oz* for the first time in your first grade classroom. The fact that the classic film community came together to save our fate gives me hope that we can save the things that are going wrong simply by banding together, by sharing that we're not okay—we're mad! After the news broke about the lay-offs, Steven Spielberg and other notable Hollywood figures met with TCM and devised a plan to essentially save it.

In mid–April 2024, I went to my second Turner Classic Movies Festival. I was astounded that every single person I talked to shared similar excitement about the book coming out, about the festival itself and all of the movies. Every single one of them cheered me on as if I'd known them my whole life, when in actuality I'd just met them. For a relatively small niche community, I think that's incredible. I feel so supported by each and every one of you. The biggest moment was when I got to meet the people who run TCM, including Alicia Malone, one of my role models.

At the closing night party, I had some revelations. I felt like I had found my people. Every single person in the room was laughing, talking about movies, and bonding over shared experiences. I felt like I knew every single one of them. In that moment, I realized just how important stories are in our lives.

Stories are what make us human. Without them, we're merely people of our own experience. Without them, we don't know anything besides our existence. We don't know anything aside from what we've already done. Imagine your existence without that book you read that changed your life. Without that movie that completely altered your outlook on living. Without that story your grandfather used to tell you over and over again (doesn't he know he already told you?).

As I continue on this path I've paved for myself, I think about the millions that have paved this path for me: the ones who did it all so that I could be where I am today. The fact that I get to watch the last 100 years go by simply by pressing play on a new movie.

I feel nothing but gratitude for who I've become and where I am. Because it's truly incredible that I am right here, right now, doing my best with what I have.

Epilogue

While it seems that the world is plunging further into a nosedive every single day, with every single news headline, there's always hope. And the hope starts with the young. The biggest American rights movement in history were led by the young. The biggest fashion movements usually start with the innovative teens who haven't lived enough, so they question everything. The most popular actors and musicians have always embodied youthful, teenage energy: the Beatles, Taylor Swift, the youth music movements of the 1980s including Madonna, all the late 2000s Disney stars, and an endless array of entertainers—and even outside of that with people like Greta Thunberg.

Being a teenager means being hopeful, being cynical, being ambitious, and being risky. The teenage perspective can change the world, because it hasn't been tainted with the negativities and responsibilities of adult life yet. It's completely open-minded. That's exactly what we need right now.

Whether it was the young girls pioneering the flapper movement, the working women in the 1940s or the young people who spearheaded the Civil Rights movement, we know that teenagers and young people can change everything about society.

I've been trying to avoid this the entire book, but every time I see a new movie, I become more and more disappointed in current Hollywood. Is there *one* movie these days without bad computer-generated imagery? Without a franchise involved? Without cringey dialogue and a horrible screenplay? I'm upset with where movies have gone outside of a very few. To think that the world is in a crisis, and one of the biggest and most influential industries is spewing crap movies out all the time, and that's supposed to inspire hope?

Yet despite all of this, I have an overwhelming amount of hope for Hollywood, because of three movies. I recently watched *Turtles All the Way Down*, a film about a young teenager with OCD—and it completely changed my outlook on my experience and the way I think about movies. Now, movies aren't just vehicles to help us learn. Movies are expressions that we are not alone and we never have been. Movies show us that we don't have to be afraid.

I also watched the smash *Barbie* last year, and realized that even today, movies can change people's minds about social issues. They can change everything about how people think, just because of the different perspectives some people have never even thought about before. Movies can still be fun, they can still change culture, and they can still have huge pop culture touchstone moments. It's just more rare these days.

Epilogue

Movies help us make fun of culture, help us contextualize issues: from *American Fiction* to *Barbie* to *Imitation of Life*, from *Citizen Kane* to *Meet Me in Saint Louis*. It doesn't matter the year or time period. Pain and basic human emotions have no age.

Old movies have taught me that stories and movies have no expiration date: movies are timeless, built on basic human emotion that can't be pinpointed to any one time period. Happiness, struggle, and humor have been relevant since the beginning of time—and they always will be. I'm only 15. But I've lived so many lives because of stories. Stories are the universal language. Forget everything else. If anything, we're here to tell our stories to each other, because there is nothing better than sharing funny and touching excerpts of our lives. Before I first started watching classics, I didn't realize that they would enrich my life the way they have. I never knew that the photos and people I looked at in my history classes had once been real, living beings, just like me.

Film humanizes everyone. For different moments in the last few years, I have *been* a working girl in the 1940s. I have *felt* the pain of the housewives in the 1950s, unable to achieve their dreams and break the glass ceiling they longed to touch. I've watched the struggles of minorities on screen and felt like I was right there with them. I've been immersed in the worlds, the time periods. And because of that, I've learned more than I ever would have without the small amount of boredom and discomfort I felt at the beginning.

In *Turtles All the Way Down*, I saw my experience with my OCD, my experience with my best friend, my experience with grief and loss, and my entire life played before me. And I immediately realized that the key to making this happen is to tell real people's stories. No, I no longer want to see movies about the most rich, the 1 percent. This is why so many classic movies have deeply resonated with me. It's because a lot of the time, they tell real stories. About real pain, real hardships. Isn't that kind of all we can ask for?

This is what I want to do. These are the kinds of stories we need to create. It doesn't matter the format. This is what I'm supposed to do. And that's why I was drawn to this entire journey in the first place. It comes down to helping others feel less alone. And movies make me and everyone feel less alone.

My Favorite Films

Call Her Savage (1932)
42nd Street (1933)
Torch Singer (1933)
Imitation of Life (1934)
Thirty Day Princess (1934)
The Gilded Lily (1935)
Follow the Fleet (1936)
Shall We Dance (1937)
Bringing Up Baby (1938)
Carefree (1938)
The Women (1939)
Bachelor Mother (1939)
Kitty Foyle (1940)
The Major and the Minor (1942)
My Sister Eileen (1942)
Ball of Fire (1942)
Meet Me in St. Louis (1944)
Dark Passage (1947)
Adam's Rib (1949)
Roman Holiday (1953)
It Should Happen to You! (1954)
Rear Window (1954)
The Man Who Knew Too Much (1955)
North by Northwest (1959)
Charade (1963)
How to Steal a Million (1966)
Bonnie & Clyde (1967)
The Graduate (1967)

Where Do You Go from Here?

These are great books, podcasts, and videos that will give you way more about classic films then I was able to touch on here. I hope you enjoy them; I did, and I drew on these for lots of inspiration.

Podcasts
Teenage Golden Age (Eliana's and my podcast)
Let's Talk to Lucy
The Screwball Story
You Must Remember This
Talking Pictures
The Plot Thickens

YouTube Channels with Good Videos on Classic Hollywood
Be Kind Rewind
Mina Le
Cinema Cities
TCM
Criterion Channel
The Hollywood Collection

Books (not even scratching the surface—these are the ones I've read and liked)
Hollywood: The Oral History by Sam Wasson and Jeanine Basinger
Oscar Wars by Michael Schulman
The Movie Musical! by Jeanine Basinger
Clara Bow: Runnin' Wild by David Stenn
Bombshell: The Life and Death of Jean Harlow by David Stenn
Captain of Her Soul: The Life of Marion Davies by Lara Gabrielle
The Genius of the System by Thomas Schatz
The Star Machine by Jeanine Basinger
High Society: The Life of Grace Kelly by Donald Spoto
Enchantment: The Life of Audrey Hepburn by Donald Spoto
Ginger: My Story by Ginger Rogers

Old Films, Young Eyes

Not Your China Doll: The Wild and Shimmering Life of Anna May Wong by Katie Gee Salisbury
By Myself and Then Some by Lauren Bacall
This Was Hollywood: Forgotten Stars & Stories by Carla Valderrama
Harlow in Hollywood by Darrell Rooney and Mark A. Vieira
Cary Grant: A Brilliant Disguise by Scott Eyman
Ava Gardner: The Secret Conversations by William Hope and Peter Evans
Natalie Wood: The Complete Biography by Suzanne Finstad
Edith Head: The Fifty-Year Career of Hollywood's Greatest Costume Designer by Jay Jorgensen
Love, Lucy by Lucille Ball
Do Tell by Lindsay Lynch
Eleanor Powell: Born to Dance by Lisa Royère and Paula Broussard
Elizabeth Taylor: The Grit and Glamour of an Icon by Kate Anderson Brower
Preston Sturges: Crooked but Never Common by Stuart Klawans

Chapter Notes

Preface

1. Stephanie Rivas-Lara, Becca Pham, and Yalda Uhls, "What Stories Do Teens Want to See in Movies and TV?" Greater Good, November 28, 2022. https://greatergood.berkeley.edu/article/item/what_stories_do_teens_want_to_see_in_movies_and_t.

How Classic Films Are Reflected in Today's Pop Culture

1. Elise Taylor, "Met Gala Themes Over the Years: A Look Back at Many First Mondays in May," *Vogue*, November 8, 2023.
2. Emily Kirkpatrick, "Designer Bob Mackie Says Letting Kim Kardashian Wear Marilyn Monroe's Dress Was 'a Big Mistake,'" *Vanity Fair*, May 17, 2022. https://www.vanityfair.com/style/2022/05/bob-mackie-kim-kardashian-marilyn-monroe-2022-met-gala-dress-big-mistake.
3. Maureen Lee Lenker, "Bob Mackie Says Kim Kardashian Wearing Marilyn Monroe's Gown Was a 'Big Mistake.'" EW.com, May 16, 2022. https://ew.com/celebrity/bob-mackie-kim-kardashian-wearing-marilyn-monroe-dress-big-mistake/.
4. Alys Davies, Tiffany Wertheimer and Guy Lambert, "Kim Kardashian: Marilyn Monroe's Gown Not Damaged, Ripley's Claims," BBC, June 16, 2022. https://www.bbc.com/news/entertainment-arts-61801906.
5. Christopher G. Feldman, *The Billboard Book of # 2 Singles* (New York: Billboard Books, 2000).
6. Randy J. Taraborrelli, *Madonna: An Intimate Biography* (New York: Simon & Schuster 2002).
7. Abel Green, "Film Reviews: A Star Is Born," *Variety*, September 29, 1954.
8. Taylor Swift Style, the Original Taylor Swift Fashion Blog. https://taylorswiftstyle.com/post/20002176026.
9. Divya Venkatamaran, "In 2023, Old Hollywood Glamour Is Well and Truly Back," *Vogue Australia*, March 27, 2023. https://www.vogue.com.au/fashion/news/old-hollywood-style/news-story/8a6be64b2fc9c9fd6b7ed6248a48578c.
10. *Ibid.*
11. Stephanie McNeal, "1940s Fashion Is the Hottest Trend for Fall Thanks to This TikToker and Her Grandma," *Glamour*, August 15, 2023. https://www.glamour.com/story/1940s-fashion-inspiration.
12. Drew Taylor, "Greta Gerwig Reveals 32 Films That Inspired 'Barbie' World, from 'All That Jazz' to 'Wizard of Oz' (Video)," *The Wrap*, July 18, 2023, https://www.thewrap.com/greta-gerwig-barbie-movie-inspiration-letterboxd/.

Beach Party!

1. A phrase I learned from my father, which he heard stated by an art history teacher, Dr. Kleinz.
2. "Hans Elias," Wikipedia. https://de.wikipedia.org/wiki/Hans_Elias#-Italien-Schweiz-Italien_1934%E2%80%931935.
3. Colter T. Bolton, ed., *Surf Culture: The Art History of Surfing* (Laguna Beach:

Laguna Art Museum in association with Gingko Press, 2002).
4. Stephen J. McParland, *It's Party Time! A Musical Exploration of the Beach Party Genre* (Winston-Salem, NC: John Blair, 1992), p. 44.
5. Samuel Z. Arkoff, *Flying Through Hollywood by the Seat of My Pants: From the Man Who Brought You* I Was a Teenage Werewolf *and* Muscle Beach Party (New York: Birch Lane Press, 1992), 38–39.
6. McParland, 121.
7. *Ibid.*
8. Alan Betock, *The I Was a Teenage Juvenile Delinquent Rock'N'Roll Horror Beach Party Movie Book: A Complete Guide to the Teen Exploitation Film, 1954–1969* (New York: St. Martin's Press, 1986), p. 102.
9. McParland, 101.
10. Tom Lisanti, *Hollywood Surf and Beach Movies: The First Wave, 1959–1969* (Jefferson, NC: McFarland, 2005), 282–294.
11. McParland, 102.

Guess Who's Coming to Dinner?

1. Sidney Poitier, *The Measure of a Man: A Spiritual Autobiography* (San Francisco: HarperSanFrancisco, 2000), 121.

What's So Bad About Feeling Good?

1. Simone O. Elias, "Zoom Boom in the Classroom—the Lowdown on 'Distance Learning," *Brentwood News*, August 28, 2020. https://brentwoodnewsla.com/zoom-boom-in-the-classroom-the-lowdown-on-distance-learning.
2. Julian E. Barnes, "Lab Leak Most Likely Caused Pandemic, Energy Dept. Says," *The New York Times*, February 26, 2023. https://www.nytimes.com/2023/02/26/us/politics/china-lab-leak-coronavirus-pandemic.html.
3. "Putting the Ease in Disease," *This American Life*, September 2020.

New Hollywood

1. Kristin Marguerite, Doidge, "The Pop Innovations of a 50-Year-Old Soundtrack," *The Atlantic*, January 16, 2018. https://www.theatlantic.com/entertainment/archive/2018/01/the-pop-innovations-of-a-50-year-old-soundtrack/550244/.
2. Alec Scott, "When 'The Graduate' Opened 50 Years Ago, It Changed Hollywood (and America) Forever," *Smithsonian Magazine*, December 2017, https://www.smithsonianmag.com/arts-culture/graduate-opened-50-years-ago-changed-hollywood-forever-180967222/#:~:text=In%20casting%20the%20leading%20man,%2Dyear%2Dold%20Dustin%20Hoffman.
3. Linette Lopez, "How Baby Boomers Became the Most Selfish Generation," *Business Insider*, November 30, 2016. https://www.businessinsider.com/how-baby-boomers-became-the-most-selfish-generation-2016-11.

The Effect of TV on the Movies

1. Tim Purtell, "1946: The Year for Movie-Going," *Entertainment Weekly*, April 29, 1994.

The Jews Run Hollywood?

1. Tabby Refael, "Jews and Hollywood: It's Complicated," *Jewish Journal*, June 29, 2023. https://jewishjournal.com/cover_story/360158/jews-and-hollywood-its-complicated/.
2. Andrew Lappin, "The Origins of Dave Chappelle's Antisemitic 'Jews Control Hollywood' Trope," *Times of Israel*, November 17, 2022. https://www.timesofisrael.com/the-origins-of-dave-chappelles-antisemitic-jews-control-hollywood-trope/.
3. *Ibid.*

Chapter Notes

4. Avishay Artsy, "How Jewish Émigrés Impacted the Birth of Film Noir," KQED, October 17, 2014. https://www.kqed.org/arts/10144066/how-jewish-emigres-impacted-the-birth-of-film-noir.

5. Ibid.

6. A.O. Scott, "Steven Spielberg Gets Personal," *The New York Times*, November 9, 2022. https://www.nytimes.com/2022/11/09/movies/steven-spielberg-the-fabelmans.html.

7. Robert Kraft, *Memory Perceived: Recalling the Holocaust* (Psychological Dimensions to War and Peace) (London: Bloomsbury Academic, 2004), 125–126.

8. Joyce Antler, *Talking Back: Images of Jewish Women in American Popular Culture* (Hanover: University Press of New England, 1998), 10, 77, 172.

9. Mark Horowitz, "Why Are Jews Funny?" *The New York Times*, December 1, 2017. https://www.nytimes.com/2017/12/01/books/review/jewish-comedy-serious-history-jeremy-dauber.html.

10. Sharon Rosen Leib, "A Museum Snubbed Hollywood's Jewish Founders. Its Next Exhibit Hopes to Make Amends," *The Forward*, September 7, 2023. https://forward.com/culture/559820/academy-museum-of-motion-pictures-jewish-hollywood/.

What Musicals Say About 1950s Subculture

1. Raymond Strait, *Here They Are: Jayne Mansfield* (New York: S.P.I. Books, 1992), 116.

2. Kelcie Mattson, "The Beatles Probably Wouldn't Exist Without This Movie," *Collider*, February 20, 2024. https://collider.com/beatles-movie-the-girl-cant-help-it/.

3. Philip Norman, *John Lennon: The Life* (New York: Harper Collins, 2008), 98.

The 1940s Working Girl

1. Christina Cheddar Berk, "Heels Head Lower, Is the Economy Heading Higher?" CNBC, November 17, 2011.

"No law says you've got to be happy"

1. "Film Noir," *American Cinema*, Annenberg Learner. Archived from the original April 18, 2021. Retrieved April 18, 2021.

2. "Hans Elias," Wikipedia. https://de.wikipedia.org/wiki/Hans_Elias#-Italien-Schweiz-Italien_1934%E2%80%931935.

3. Donald Marshman, "Mister 'See'-Odd-Mack,'" *Life*, August 25, 1947, 100–01.

4. "They Live by Night (1948)." https://www.classicfilmnoir.com/2022/11/they-live-by-night-1948.html. Accessed March 23, 2024.

5. "The Live by Night (1948)," *Film Noir*, https://www.classicfilmnoir.com/2022/11/they-live-by-night-1948.html.

The Snake Pit

1. Robert Kraft, "What's It Like to Be a Teen Living with OCD?" *Psychology Today*, March 7, 2023.

2. Anna Swanson, "'The Snake Pit' 70 Years Later: Cinema's Relationship to Mental Institutions," *Film School Rejects*, March 14, 2021. https://filmschoolrejects.com/the-snake-pit-70-years-later-cinemas-relationship-to-mental-institutions/.

3. Keira Boyle, "Hysterical Victorian Women," Historic UK, December 1, 2023. https://www.historic-uk.com/CultureUK/Hysterical-Victorian-Women/#:~:text=Hysteria%20was%20the%20most%20well,reaching%20for%20her%20smelling%20salts.

4. Dorian Bowen, "Depictions of Mental Illness in the Classic Film Era (1930–1965)," Video Librarian, May 4, 2023. https://videolibrarian.com/articles/lists/mental-illness-classic-films/.

Chapter Notes

The Romantic Comedy and How Modern Rom-Com Tropes All Draw Inspiration from One

1. "The shirt off his back." Archived September 28, 2019, at the Wayback Machine. snopes.com, May 10, 2014. Retrieved December 7, 2009.
2. "Claudette Colbert Salutes Frank Capra at the AFI Life Achievement Award," American Film Institute. https://www.youtube.com/watch?v=TI8XetlS-uU
3. Ted Sennett, *Lunatics and Lovers: A Tribute to the Giddy and Glittering Era of the Screen's "Screwball" and Romantic Comedies* (New York: Limelight Editions, 1985), 1.
4. George Axelrod, *Will Success Spoil Rock Hunter? A New Comedy in Three Acts* (New York : S. French, 1957), 40.

A Tour of the Old Hollywood Studio System

1. Jeanine Basinger, *The Star Machine* (New York: Alfred A. Knopf, 2007), 12.
2. Ibid., 38.
3. Ibid., 47, 51.
4. Ibid., 47.
5. Ibid., 46.
6. Ibid., 41.
7. Ibid., 41–42.
8. Ibid., 38.
9. Ibid., 44.
10. Rob Nixon, "Some Like It Hot," Turner Classic Movies. https://web.archive.org/web/20180125020049/http://www.tcm.com/this-month/article/71636%7C0/Some-Like-It-Hot.html. Accessed March 26, 2024.
11. David Chierichetti, *Edith Head: The Life and Times of Hollywood's Celebrated Costume Designer* (New York: HarperCollins, 2003), 15.
12. Theresa Avila, "Debbie Reynolds Fought to Preserve Hollywood's Most Iconic Costumes," *The Cut*, December 29, 2016. https://www.thecut.com/2016/12/debbie-reynolds-helped-preserve-hollywoods-iconic-costumes.html
13. Ibid.
14. John Wakeman, ed., *World Film Directors: Volume One, 1890–1945* (New York: H.W. Wilson Co., 1987), 96.
15. Francois Truffaut, *Hitchcock* (Paris: Gallimard, 1983), 27.

Should Ladies Behave?

1. Mick LaSalle, *Complicated Women: Sex and Power in Pre-Code Hollywood* (New York: Griffin, 2002), 1.
2. Richard Brody, "The Spirit of the Women's-Rights Movement in a 1933 Film," *The New Yorker*, December 22, 2017. https://www.newyorker.com/magazine/2018/01/01/the-spirit-of-the-womens-rights-movement-in-a-1933-film.
3. Pamela Hutchinson, "Clara Bow: The Hard-Partying Jazz-Baby Airbrushed from Hollywood History," *The Guardian*, June 21, 2016. https://www.theguardian.com/film/filmblog/2016/jun/21/clara-bow-wild-child-hollywood-history-silent-film.

A Cultural History of the "It Girl"

1. David Stenn, *Clara Bow: Runnin' Wild* (New York: Cooper Square Press, 1988), 9
2. Ibid., 265.
3. Joe Morella and Edward Z. Epstein, *The "It" Girl, The Incredible Story of Clara Bow* (New York: Harper & Row, 1976), 11.
4. Stenn, *Clara Bow*, 16.
5. Ibid., 19.
6. Ibid., 21.
7. Ibid., 22.
8. Ibid., 23.
9. Ibid., 45.
10. Ibid., 98.
11. Steve Harvey, "No One Was Out of Bounds," *Los Angeles Times*, April 22, 1993.
12. Paul Jervis, "Quit Pickin' on Me, Says Clara Bow!" *Photoplay*, January 1931.

Chapter Notes

13. Stenn, *Clara Bow*, 280.
14. "75% of Women Now Color Their Hair Compared to 7% In 1950," South Florida Reporter, October 1, 2017. https://southfloridareporter.com/75-women-now-color-hair-compared-7-950/#google_vignette.
15. Lucille Ball, *Love, Lucy* (New York: Berkley, 1996), 76.
16. David Stenn, *Bombshell: The Life and Death of Jean Harlow* (New York: Doubleday, 1993), 7–9.
17. From now on, I will refer to her mom as "Mama Jean" because that is what she was called back then; otherwise, it is confusing.
18. Stenn, *Bombshell*, 14.
19. Ibid.
20. Ibid., 21.
21. Ibid., 26.
22. Ibid., 33.
23. Ibid., 35.
24. Ibid., 47.
25. Ibid., 66.
26. Katie Dowd, "The tangled tale of Jean Harlow, her dead husband, and a woman found drowned in Sacramento," *SF Gate*, July 16, 2021.
27. Stenn, *Bombshell*, 199.
28. "Jean Harlow Dies, 1937," History.com.
29. Stenn, *Bombshell*, 220.
30. Stenn, *Bombshell*, 241.
31. Donald Spoto, *Marilyn Monroe: The Biography* (Kindle Edition) (N.p.: Dansker Press, 2007), 48.
32. Ibid., 50.
33. Ibid., 74.
34. Ibid., 664/
35. Donald Spoto, *Enchantment: The Life of Audrey Hepburn* (New York: Three Rivers Press, 2006), 9–10.
36. Ibid., 5.

Anna May Wong

1. Robert Ito, "'Crazy Rich Asians': Why Did It Take So Long to See a Cast Like This?" *The New York Times*, August 8, 2018. https://www.nytimes.com/2018/08/08/movies/crazy-rich-asians-cast.html.
2. Ibid.
3. Nigel M. Smith, "Emma Stone Says Aloha Casting Taught Her About Whitewashing in Hollywood," *The Guardian*, July 17, 2015. https://www.theguardian.com/film/2015/jul/17/emma-stone-admits-her-casting-in-aloha-was-misguided.
4. LaSalle, *Complicated Women*, 61.
5. Alicia Malone, *Backwards & in Heels: The Past, Present and Future of Women Working in Film* (Coral Gables: Mango, 2018).
6. Office of Communications, "Librarian of Congress Adds Home Movie, Silent Films and Hollywood Classics to Film Preservation List," Library of Congress, December 27, 2006. https://www.loc.gov/item/prn-06-234/films-added-to-national-film-registry-for-2006/2006-12-27/.
7. *The Richmond News Leader*, February 28, 1938. https://www.newspapers.com/article/the-richmond-news-leader/132118609/.
8. Cynthia W. Liu, "When Dragon Ladies Die, Do They Come Back as Butterflies? Re-Imagining Anna May Wong," in Darrel Hamamoto and Sandra Liu, eds., *Countervisions: Asian American Film Criticism* (Philadelphia: Temple University Press, 2000), 23–39.
9. Brian Taves, "Daughter of Shanghai," Library of Congress. https://www.loc.gov/static/programs/national-film-preservation-board/documents/daughter_shanghai.pdf. Accessed March 27, 2024.
10. "Unseen Classics—Daughter of Shanghai," YouTube, May 24, 2019. https://www.youtube.com/watch?v=1fx4XmRHbzo.
11. Quote from Katie Gee Salisbury, Anna May Wong expert.

Looking at Old Hollywood Through the Lens of the "Me Too" Movement

1. Debbi Baker, "Did date rape lead to daughter for Loretta Young, Clark Gable?" *The San Diego Union-Tribune*, July 13, 2015.

Chapter Notes

2. Anne Helen Petersen, "Clark Gable Accused of Raping Co-Star," *Buzzfeed News*, July 12, 2015.
3. Gilbert King, "The Skinny on the Fatty Arbuckle Trial," *Smithsonian Magazine*, November 8, 2011.
4. Ibid.
5. Ahsan Sadaf, "'I'll Break You': Judy Garland Faced Her Own Harvey Weinstein in MGM Head Louis B. Mayer," *National Post*, November 14, 2017. https://nationalpost.com/entertainment/celebrity/ill-break-you-judy-garland-faced-her-own-harvey-weinstein-in-mgm-head-louis-b-mayer.
6. Donald Spoto, *Spellbound by Beauty: Alfred Hitchcock and His Leading Ladies* (London: Cornerstone Digital, 2009), 170.
7. Donald Spoto, *The Dark Side of Genius: The Life of Alfred Hitchcock* (New York: Ballantine Books, 1983), p. 456.
8. "Tippi Hedren: Alfred Hitchcock tried to destroy my career," *The Times*, September 11, 2008. Retrieved July 24, 2013, HitchcockWiki.com.
9. Ruben V. Nepales, "Tippi Hedren reveals real horror of working with Hitchcock," *Philippine Daily Inquirer*, August 11, 2012. Retrieved July 23, 2013.
10. Nepales, Ruben V. (August 11, 2012). "Tippi Hedren reveals real horror of working with Hitchcock". *Inquirer Entertainment*. Retrieved July 23, 2013. https://entertainment.inquirer.net/53591/tippi-hedren-reveals-real-horror-of-working-with-hitchcock.
11. Alan Evans, "Tippi Hedren: Alfred Hitchcock Sexually Assaulted Me," *The Guardian*, October 31, 2016. https://www.theguardian.com/film/2016/oct/31/tippi-hedren-alfred-hitchcock-sexually-assaulted-me.
12. Spoto, *Spellbound by Beauty*, 183.
13. Ibid., 174–75.
14. Evans, "Tippi Hedren."
15. Spoto, *Spellbound by Beauty*, 173.
16. Tony Lee Moral, *Hitchcock and the Making of Marnie*, rev. ed. (Lanham, MD: Scarecrow Press, 2013), 340.
17. Spoto, *Spellbound by Beauty*, 182.
18. Thelma Adams, "Casting-Couch Tactics Plagued Hollywood Long Before Harvey Weinstein," *Variety*, October 17, 2017. https://variety.com/2017/film/features/casting-couch-hollywood-sexual-harassment-harvey-weinstein-1202589895/.

Why Were There "No Female Directors" in Old Hollywood?

1. Alison McMahan, "Key Events and Dates: Alice Guy Blaché," in Joan Simon, ed., *Alice Guy Blaché: Cinema Pioneer* (New Haven and New York: Yale University Press and Whitney Museum of American Art, 2009), 126.
2. "How a Woman Makes a Fortune out of 'Movies': Part V: Drama and Fashion," *New York Tribune*, November 24, 1912.
3. Malone, *Backwards & in Heels*, 26.
4. Cari Beauchamp, *Without Lying Down: Frances Marion and the Powerful Women of Early Hollywood* (Berkeley: University of California Press, 1997), 9.
5. "The Pioneering Female Director Who Broke into the Hollywood Boy's Club," On the Channel. https://www.criterion.com/current/posts/6420-the-pioneering-female-director-who-broke-into-the-hollywood-boys-club. Accessed March 26, 2024.
6. Judith Mayne, "Merrily We Go to Hell: Gingerbread, Cake, and Crème de Menthe," The Criterion Collection. https://www.criterion.com/current/posts/7384-merrily-we-go-to-hell-gingerbread-cake-and-creme-de-menthe. Accessed March 26, 2024.
7. Pamela Hutchinson, "Merrily We Go to Hell: How Dorothy Arzner Skewered Hollywood's Happy Ending for Women in the 1930s," *The Independent*, June 14, 2021. https://www.independent.co.uk/arts-entertainment/films/features/dorothy-arzner-merrily-we-go-to-hell-b1863258.html.
8. Ariane Lange, "The Vicious Cycle Holding Female Directors Back," *BuzzFeed*, April 2, 2017. https://www.buzzfeed.com/arianelange/the-lost-generation-of-female-directors.

Chapter Notes

9. Penny Pagano, "Colorization Gets a Senate Hearing," *Los Angeles Times*, May 13, 1987.

10. Stephanie Jacobson, "It's a Colorful Life: Colorizing Black and White Movies," *Hein Online Blog*, December 22, 2023.

11. "Colorizing, Hollywood's New Vandalism (1986)." Archived December 20, 2016, at the Wayback Machine, Siskel & Ebert, Buena Vista Television, 1986; air date unknown

12. Eva Murzyn, "Do we only dream in colour? A comparison of reported dream colour in younger and older adults with different experiences of black and white media," *Science Direct*, December 2008.

13. Jacobson, "It's a Colorful Life."

Epilogue

1. Maureen Lee Lenker, "What's going on at TCM? Insiders detail the fight to protect the network—and why it matters," *Entertainment Weekly*, August 7, 2023. https://ew.com/tv/tcm-insiders-detail-fight-to-protect-turner-classic-movies-network/

Index

The Academy Museum 53
Adam's Rib (film) 74
African Americans 24, 27, 135
Ahn, Philip 137–138
Allen, Woody 11, 53
American International Pictures 20–21, 24
Annie Hall (film) 96
Anyone But You (film) 97
Arbuckle, Roscoe "Fatty" 114, 142–143
Arkoff, Samuel 20–21
Arzner, Dorothy 151–154
Asian Americans 133–138
Astaire, Fred 5, 11
Athena (film) 56–57
Attack of the 50-Foot Woman (film) 14
Avalon, Frankie 21–22

baby boomers 25, 41–42, 162, 172
Bacall, Lauren 12, 16, 77–78, 103, 154, 170
Ball, Lucille 64–65
Barbie (film) 16, 20, 73, 148, 164–165,
Beach Blanket Bingo (film) 22, 24
Beach Party (film) 23, 25
The Beatles 55
Beatty, Warren 37
beauty standards 123, 126, 127–129, 132
Bergman, Ingrid 16, 105, 154
The Birds (film) 122, 125–126
Blaché, Alice Guy 148–150
Black musical artists 55
Bluebeard's Eighth Wife (film) 97
Bly, Nellie 86
Bogart, Humphrey 5, 17, 77–78
Bonnie & Clyde 24, 36–39, 45, 167
Born Yesterday (film) 16, 75
Bow, Clara 15, 106, 122–125, 126, 152–153
Breakfast at Tiffany's (film) 15

Breen, Joseph 48
Bringing Up Baby (film) 73, 93, 167
burlesque 151–152

The Cabbage Fairy (film) 148–149
Call Her Savage (film) 121–123, 126
Capra, Frank 111
Casablanca 7, 11
Chaplin, Charlie 50, 51, 106, 110
Chappelle, Dave 46
Charade (film) 6, 88, 99, 131, 167
Charisse, Cyd 58
Chatterton, Ruth 119–120
The Children's Hour (film) 28
The City Without Jews (film) 28
Civil Rights Movement 7, 24, 30, 53, 164
Clooney, George 17, 96
Colbert, Claudette 61, 89, 90–91, 93–94, 97, 99, 114, 127
colorized films, colorization 156–159, 160
Columbia Pictures 19
Cooper, Bradley 13
costuming 107, 108, 119, 139
Crawford, Joan 106, 152, 154
crop top 19–20
Crossfire (film) 52

Dark Passage (film) 77–78
Davis, Bette 12, 105–106, 108, 154
Day, Doris 13, 61- 63, 145
Dee, Sandra 20
de Havilland, Olivia 84
Del Rey, Lana 14
Disney 21, 25, 112, 164
Dr. Jekyll & Mr Hyde (film) 79, 87, 152
The Doctor Takes a Wife (film) 100
Double Indemnity (film) 81–82
Duck Soup (film) 11
Dunaway, Faye 37

179

Index

Elias, Hans (author's grandfather) 17, 80
Everything Everywhere All at Once (film) 133

fashion (1940s) 3
Female (film) 119–121
female directors 148–149, 151, 154
The Feminine Mystique 61
film 68–69
Finishing School (film) 153
Flower Drum Song (film) 133, 139
Frank, Anne 51–52
Friedan, Betty 61
Funicello, Annette 21-22
Funny Face 5
Funny Girl (Broadway musical) 13, 52

Gable, Clark 63, 89–91, 103, 117, 125, 128, 141–142
Gabrielle, Lara 91–92, 113
Garland, Judy 13
Gaslight (film) 16
gay (actors, characters) 104, 118, 119, 122, 149
Gaynor, Janet 13
Gen Z 5
Gentleman's Agreement (film) 28, 49, 50
Gentlemen Prefer Blondes (film) 6, 12, 54, 107, 115, 130
German expressionism 79
The Ghost in the Invisible Bikini (film) 24
Gidget (film) 18–21, 25, 80
Gigi (play) 131
The Gilded Lily (film) 99
The Girl (film) 145
The Girl Can't Help It (film) 55
Gold Diggers of 1933 (film) 118–119
Gosling, Ryan 11
The Graduate (film) 24, 36, 39–42, 53, 79, 167
Grant, Cary 17, 95, 98, 102–104, 109, 152, 157, 170
Great Depression 2, 79, 94–95, 127, 150, 158
Guess Who's Coming to Dinner (film) 28–30, 73

Harlow, Jean 12, 16, 94, 115–117, 126–129, 131
Hays, William 114, 143
Hays Code 21, 39, 41, 48, 87, 92, 114, 121, 143

Hayworth, Rita 12, 73, 104–105, 108, 129, 130, 151, 154
Head, Edith 91, 107–108
Hedren, Tippie 144–146
Hepburn, Audrey 5, 15, 16, 28, 91, 98–99, 102–103, 108, 129–131, 163
Hepburn, Katharine 12, 16, 29, 66, 73–76, 98
Hilda cartoon 132
Hired Wife (film) 100
His Girl Friday (film) 70
Hitchcock, Alfred 13, 114, 140, 143–144
Hitler, Adolf 49–50, 79
Hoffman, Dustin 41
Holden, William 5
Holliday, Judy 16, 75
The Hollywood blacklist 46
Hollywood, the Oral History 11
Honor Among Lovers (film) 153
Hudson, Rock 104

I Love Lucy 63–65
Imitation of Life (film) 28
Industry plants 56
"It" girl 61, 124–127, 129, 131
It Happened One Night 1, 89–91, 93–94, 97–101
Italian neo-realism 80
It's a Wonderful Life (film) 7, 157
It's Always Fair Weather (film) 58

Jennifer's Body (film) 117
Jeter, Mildred 29
Jews 28, 46–53

Kaling, Mindy 65, 114
Kamakawiwoiole, Israel 13
Kardashian, Kim 9
Kelly, Gene 12, 58
Kelly, Grace 12, 17, 103, 108, 145
Kennedy, John F. 9, 10, 29
Kiriakou, Olympia 92
Kiss Them for Me (film) 54
Kitty Foyle 8, 71, 72, 167
Kohner, Frederick 18, 19
Kraft, Hy 46, 88
Kraft, Jill 131
Kraft, Robert 51

La La Land (film) 11
lavender marriages 104
Legally Blonde (film) 7, 8, 16, 23, 89, 129
Lennon, John 55

Index

Lizzie (film) 87–88
The Lost Weekend (film) 87
Loving, Richard 29
Loving v. Virginia 29, 30
Loy, Myrna 24, 27, 32, 34, 55, 64–65

Mackie, Bob 11
MacMurray, Fred 81, 99
Madonna 12
makeup 27, 64, 66, 91, 102, 105–106, 116, 122, 124, 127–128
Malone, Alicia 11, 150, 154, 163
Man Wanted (film) 120
Mansfield, Jayne 54–55
March, Fredric 13, 152–153
Marnie (film) 144–146
Mary Poppins 5
Mason, James 13
Material Girl (song) 12
Max Factor 106
Mayer, Louis B. 50, 53
McCartney, Paul 55
McDaniel, Hattie 28
#MeToo movement 140–141, 146
Mean Girls (film) 89, 129
meet cute 97
mental institutions 84–85
Merrily We Go to Hell 152
Met Gala 2010 15
Met Gala 2015 139
Met Gala 2022 9
MGM (Metro Goldwyn Mayer) 14, 20, 63, 74, 75–76, 102–103, 109, 113, 115, 128, 140, 144
Mickey Mouse Club (show) 21
The Mindy Project (TV show) 65, 101
Monroe, Marilyn 9, 10, 11, 12, 34, 44, 61, 99, 102, 103, 107, 127, 130
The More the Merrier (film) 68–70
My Favorite Wife (film) 93, 95–96
My Man Godfrey (film) 93–95, 156
My Sister Eileen 72, 167

National Film Preservation Act of 1987 158
Netflix 1, 43, 98, 159
Nicholson, Jim 20–21
nitrate film 149

Only Yesterday (film) 117–118

Paramount Pictures 24, 50, 81, 99, 102, 108, 125, 154

The Parent Trap (film) 96
The Patsy (film) 91
Peck, Gregory 131
The Philadelphia Story (play) 73
Please Don't Eat the Daisies (film) 62–63
Poitier, Sidney 28, 29
Powell, Jane 57
Powell, William (Bill) 128, 156
Pre-Code films 6, 39, 113–118, 120–123, 128, 143, 153, 174
Presley, Elvis 55–56

Rebel Without a Cause (film) 80
Red Dust (film) 128
Red-Headed Woman (film) 115, 116
Reynolds, Debbie 57
RKO 102
Roberts, Julia 96
Rogers, Ginger 11, 12, 14, 15, 63, 71–72, 81, 100, 103–104, 108, 114, 118, 119, 128, 151, 153–154, 157, 169
Roman Holiday (film) 6, 98, 103, 108, 131, 167
romantic comedy 74, 89, 90–93, 95–97, 99, 101
Rosie the Riveter poster 60, 68, 69
Russell, Rosalind 72, 100

Sabrina (film) 5, 16
Saladino, Andrew 20, 23
Salisbury, Katie Gee 133–134
Schulman, Michael 154, 157
screwball comedy 74, 91–95, 97, 100, 102
Selznick, David O. 28
Senate hearing on colorized films 1987 157
The Seven Year Itch (film) 44
The Seventh Veil (film) 87
sexual assault 114, 140, 143, 144
Shall We Dance 14, 100, 167
Shanghai Express (film) 135–136
Should Ladies Behave (film) 113
Simon & Garfunkel 40
Singer, Eliana ??
Singin' in the Rain (film) 6, 45, 55, 57, 58, 153
Sleeper (film) 11
The Snake Pit (film) 83–87
Solax Studios 148–149
Some Like It Hot (film) 98, 106, 131
Stanwyck, Barbara 80, 108, 116
A Star Is Born (film) 13, 105

Index

A Star Is Born (1953 remake film) 105
star system 105
Stewart, Jimmy 13, 17, 103–104, 157
Stone, Emma 11, 134
Strasdin, Kate 11
Streisand, Barbra 13, 52
Sturges, Preston 59
Sullivan, John 59
Sullivan's Travels (film) 59
surfing 19
Swift, Taylor 7, 15, 105, 140, 164

Technicolor 13, 16, 130, 134, 158
teen noir 80
@teenagegoldenagebook 7
teenagers 6
Temple, Shirley 91
That's Entertainment (film) 12
They Live By Night (film) 80
Thirty Day Princess (film) 98
Three Faces of Eve (film) 87–88
Ticket to Paradise (film) 96
Tracy, Spencer 29, 73, 76
Turner Classic Movies 162–163
Turtles All the Way Down (film) 164
20th Century–Fox 54, 102

vegetarianism 57
"Vogue" (song) 12

Warhol, Andy 11
Warner Brothers 50, 53, 102, 154, 162
Wasson, Sam 11
Weber, Lois 150–152
When Were You Born (film) 136–137
Where Are My Children? (film) 150
White actors 27, 133–134
The Wild Party (film) 153
Wilder, Billy 49, 81, 97, 112
Will Success Spoil Rock Hunter? (play) 97
Wings (film) 122
The Wiser Sex (film) 113
The Wizard of Oz (film) 13, 16, 53, 158, 163
Woman of the Year (film) 73
Wong, Anna Mae 133–139
World War I 2, 117
World War II 16, 44, 51–52, 58, 60–61, 68–70, 73, 79–80, 87, 104, 131

Young, Loretta 100, 140, 142, 146
Young Man of Manhattan (film) 114

www.ingramcontent.com/pod-product-compliance
Ingram Content Group UK Ltd.
Pitfield, Milton Keynes, MK11 3LW, UK
UKHW042013140426
5217IPUK00015B/1153